SPINE OF THE ANTIQUARIAN

Agio
PUBLISHING HOUSE

PUBLISHING HOUSE

Gabriola, BC Canada V0R 1X4

Spine of the Antiquarian
ISBN 978-1-927755-97-6 (paperback)
ISBN 978-1-927755-98-3 (casebound)
ISBN 978-1-927755-99-0 (ebook)

Printed on acid-free paper that includes no fibre from
endangered forests. Agio Publishing House is a socially
responsible company, measuring success on a triple-
bottom-line basis.

10 9 8 7 6 5 4 3 2 1

DEDICATED TO JUDY

Noir Intelligence Series

The Black Hat
Spine of the Antiquarian

SPINE OF THE ANTIQUARIAN

BOOK TWO
of the
Noir Intelligence Series

A Novel

H.B. Dumont

A lexandra Belliveau was acutely aware that in the duplicitous world of espionage and intelligence, nothing exists in the absence of context. More importantly, intelligence and context are askew in the world of espionage where there are truths, partial truths and make-believe truths.

"Mount up, *mon colonel*," Alexandra called as she fastened the strap on her helmet. Her Harley-Davidson purred. "I'm really looking forward to a relaxing ride with no time constraints or work deadlines looming – especially not having to second-guess the menace of invisible shadows and having to stare at nothing while being wary of everything. Retirement is looking good."

This ride would also be a celebration of her divorce from André. For the first time in their relationship, he had agreed with her on all the terms she had proposed. Not only had he not contested the divorce, but he had directed his solicitor to speed up the proceedings. It was an acknowledgement that nothing had gone wrong with their marriage. She had not *failed*. It was wrong *before* they exchanged vows and remained disastrous throughout.

The divorce decree brought a mixture of freedom and fear – freedom to move on with her life unencumbered by a tether to long-ago partisan pledges, fear that had haunted her since childhood, flooding the void with the all-too-familiar feelings of abandonment and loneliness. Childhood was a time she wanted to forget.

She pined for a fulfilling personal relationship that had been beyond her grasp but not beyond her desire. She remained naïvely hopeful but astonished that she could still be lulled by those little girl fairy tales. She took a deep breath to stave off the palpitations as she reminded herself ruefully that this distortion had become the norm. But it was not normal.

She looked at Paul Bernard who wore an affectionate grin as he courteously bowed. His mere presence awakened the *joie de vivre* she had not experienced for a very long time. The yoke was hers to discard or retain.

"Absolutely! You can rest assured I will be completely focused on your profile from the rear perspective, AV," Paul replied as he secured the strap on his helmet and turned on his communication system. He had called her AV the first time they had met as young teenagers and experienced the emotions of puppy love in Montigny-lès-Metz. AV were the initials of the name she shared with her grandmother – Alexandra Vanessa. "I'll follow Alexandra the distinguished dragon slayer anywhere she wants to lead me," he declared into his microphone to test the system.

"Don't get distracted. I need your attention on the road," Alexandra breezily replied as she adjusted her microphone. Privately, she relished his compliment. Not once in her 25-year marriage to André had he ever flattered her in such a personal manner.

"Are you reading me, Paul?" she asked. How she looked forward to being able to speak with him for the entire trip. André disliked motorcycles with a passion, especially Harley-Davidsons which he said emitted the most disturbing, uncivilized noise. At one point in their marriage, he threatened to leave her if she didn't sell her bike. She lamented the fact that she never took him up on his offer. Instead, she parked her bike at her friend, Josephine's place.

"Loud and clear. We have communications, madame. Lead the way."

"Roger that. We'll stop around Trier for coffee and again closer to Mechernich. That should put us in Cologne in plenty of time for dinner."

They had planned to drive east out of Luxembourg City on the E44 and then cross into Germany before going north at Trier on Highway 60.

This road trip would be the first big ride since the fateful morning when the black Mercedes had rammed her Harley-Davidson in Garches south-west of Paris, and Thon had abducted her. Paul had rescued her while other Harley riders distracted her abductor.

"How are you feeling? Is your bike handling okay?" Paul enquired cautiously. Although her bike had been repaired, he remained concerned for her safety.

"I'm all right. No shaking or noticeable vibrations from Sophia. She's actually riding very smoothly for a 1972 classic that survived a round in the ring with a heavyweight." Perhaps there was some irony in the fact that the California Highway Patrol had originally owned her Harley. It had been sold to a CIA agent at a State asset disposal sale. He brought it with him when he was assigned to Western Europe.

As they rode, they debriefed the events of that calamitous day in Garches before engaging with their secondary purpose, which was to find out as much as they could about Kurt Welter, the World War II Luftwaffe fighter ace. His surname was the same as that of Michel Welter, the Luxembourgian medical doctor and politician whose name was on the street sign in Luxembourg City where she had lived as a child. Kurt Welter had been credited with shooting down 63 Allied aircraft on 93 missions. It seemed strange to Alexandra that Welter had survived all those air battles only to be killed in his car at a railway crossing after the war. She had pondered whether the politician and war hero were related or whether their last names were merely coincidence.

This question was one of the loose ends from Thon's murderous rampage. Perhaps it was nothing, just serendipitous, a false interlude. But maybe it was important. It needed to be checked out. Caution if not due diligence was in order.

Her mother's tenant in the house on 47, rue Michel Welter had been one of Thon's victims. Alexandra had been the last intended target as the daughter of a former member of the French underground resistance, the *Maquis*, during the war, and subsequently a French counterintelligence agent.

But as providence would have it, Alexandra survived and Thon died at the hands of one of his own Fourth Reich neo-Nazi soldiers. Thon, whose actual name was Ludwig Rudolf Heydrich, was from Trier. Neither she nor Paul had any intention of stopping at Trier to locate the farm where he grew up in order to honour his death. Instead, they would raise a middle finger in an appropriate biker salute as they rode by. The white-hatted good guys and gals had been victorious over the black-hatted bad guy.

They stopped for coffee just north of Trier as planned. The late morning fall air was still fresh with a soft haze. The rising sun brought welcome warmth but wispy clouds high overhead were mares' tails, the harbinger of a change in the forecast. It could be a great day for a ride if the clouds swung east. Their mantra, as newly minted retirees, was to take every opportunity to stop and smell the roses, so to speak.

As Alexandra swung off her bike and removed her helmet, she was greeted with a friendly "How are you, Alexandra?"

Looking in the direction of the familiar voice she recognized an associate dressed in biker leathers. They had never ridden together although they had exchange stories of some of their exciting biking destinations.

"Franz, I see you're still riding a Beamer." Her comment was in jest. He extolled the virtues of the BMW as a yuppie bike while she was an ardent Harley aficionado. "I'd like to introduce you to a colleague and friend, Paul Bernard."

"Nice to meet you, Paul. A colleague of Alexandra's is a friend of mine. Did you own your Harley-Davidson before you met Alexandra or has her mystical spell drawn you over to the dark side of the Harlistas?"

"Alas, I'm a willing victim of her incantations. She actually helped me select this Road King from the Place de la Bastille Harley-Davidson dealership in Paris. She also educated me about those Harley wannabes who jealously critique the Hog mystique."

"Oh, she has cast you under a spell with her renowned charismatic biker charm, her lifeforce," Franz countered with a grin.

"In Latin, lifeforce is referred to as *spiritus* and she does have that enigmatic spirit. I imagine you've experienced it too, Franz."

Ending the joust with a friendly smile, Paul put out his hand. "Very nice to meet you."

"So, Alexandra, are you still fighting crime as a forensic psychologist and teaching the techniques of the trade to up-and-coming academic protégés?" asked Franz.

"I've just retired and this is my inaugural ride as a retiree, well, semi-retired and quasi-employed biker. What about you?"

"I've recently cut back my hours to part-time. I wanted to get a few more rides in before packing the bike away for the winter. If the truth be known, I'm seeking refuge from the clamour of clients constantly requesting clinical counselling for psychological ailments of their own making. I can't talk now, as I have to be back in Bonn late this afternoon. I'd very much enjoy getting together to explore semi-retirement options. I'll send you an email. Are you back in Paris?"

"No, I bought a place in the old city of Luxembourg but I have the same email address. Look forward to renewing contact. Take care and ride safe, *mein freund*."

As Franz rode off, Paul commented, "Pleasant guy. I imagine he's a psychologist also."

"Yes, he's a clinical psychologist," Alexandra explained as they entered the café. "We met at a European Conference on Psychology and Behavioural Sciences in Geneva a few years ago."

"Geneva is a lovely location for a conference. We should put it on our list for destination rides."

"I agree. But let me tell you a bit about Franz. He has an interesting background. His family was and remains devotedly Christian. After Hitler became chancellor in 1933, Christians like his family who spoke out against Nazi doctrine were on the hit list for the concentration camps. So, his grandparents and their extended family moved to Switzerland. Although Switzerland was supposedly neutral, it was awash with spies of all stripes – German, Russian, British, French, Italian and every other nationality. After the war, his immediate family moved back to Germany, to Bonn. Many of his cousins are Swiss citizens, some of whom work in the Swiss banking system."

"Good. We can add Bonn to our riding schedule. I'd like to chat with Franz about his thoughts on Germanic culture."

"You would really enjoy hanging out with Franz and his wife. She is an addiction and trauma counsellor and an absolutely lovely lady. They are just salt-of-the-earth people, honest, hardworking, professional and unquestionably ethical in their personal and professional lives."

"I'll reiterate his words – a colleague of Alexandra's is a friend of mine. Hopefully, our paths will cross again soon." Paul had limited his social life to those in his own profession, rarely venturing into new social circles. After Suzette became pregnant with their first son, she declined to accompany him to office functions including the Christmas party.

Despite and perhaps because of the calamitous events in the weeks following their reunion at her mother's funeral, Paul had not had the opportunity to meet AV's friends with the exception of Josephine who preferred to be called Jo. She seemed to be AV's oldest and closest confident. Jo, he found out later, also rode a Harley-Davidson. When they first met, Jo alluded to some of the escapades that she and Alexandra had shared when they cruised the streets of the 5e arrondissement while students of the Université de Paris-Sorbonne. There was one more friend he needed to spend social time with to learn more about his puppy love. But that could wait.

⋈

"Bonjour, c'est Aulne" – *Hello, this is Aulne.*

"J'écoute" – *I'm listening.*

"Они едут в Линденталь" – *They are going to Lindenthal.*

"Да. Принято" – *Yes. Acknowledged.*

CHAPTER 2

As Paul picked up his coffee mug, Alexandra noticed that, for the first time, he wasn't wearing his wedding ring. Had he kept it on since Suzette's death perhaps out of loyalty to their marriage vows or was it a deeper duty to his Pope and Church? And why was he no longer wearing it?

"Do you remember when we were speaking with Roger d'Estaine, your mother's neighbour on rue Michel Welter and he said he thought I was your husband? I asked myself, what if?"

"Yes, I remember and I also thought, what if?" *How many times have I asked myself that question,* she pondered. She grieved and wept on long lonely nights too many to count since they first met as young teenagers in Montigny-lès-Metz, and were subsequently separated by events beyond their control.

She hesitated as a raft of emotions emerged that were more intangible than explicit. The moment seemed appropriate to bring clarity to their evolving relationship.

"We can't live in what-ifs from the past," she stated as if reflecting on a client's declaration, she now being her own psychologist. With a pause to catch her breath, she boldly qualified her response.

"But we can now plan for what-ifs in the future. So, what if we spend the rest of our days together not only as business partners in the game of sleuthing but also as soul mates?"

Paul reached across the table without hesitation, took her hands in his, stared into her hazel eyes and replied simply yet deliberately: "Yes, nothing would make me happier, Alexandra Vanessa."

He relished the sensation of her name rolling off his tongue as he had done an infinite number of times since they had first met as teenagers.

"I can't imagine a more fulfilling way to launch our retirement than to commit to a business and intimate partnership with you physically, mentally, spiritually, emotionally, and intellectually," he added.

Feeling his passion, she maintained his gaze and allowed silence to fill the void. Together, their hands held a multitude of undeclared pledges of endearment.

Paul continued, "The day you accompanied me to see my father that first time after your mother's funeral, he asked if you could excuse us as he had something personal to discuss with me."

"Yes, I remember," she acknowledged.

"After you left the room, he told me that in those few moments he saw us standing beside each other, he knew we were meant to be together. He knew it all those years ago when we first met in Montigny-lès-Metz. He said we were soul mates who had been torn apart due to extenuating circumstances. He gave me permission to leave Suzette. In fact, he told me to apply for a legal separation from Suzette so I would not end up on my deathbed wishing for a fulfilled life that I had never experienced with her but was within my grasp with you. He said the Pope wasn't always right and I should ultimately divorce Suzette. Fate pulled us apart when we were young teenagers and providence has brought us together. I struggled with the whole concept of the sanctity of the marriage vows but now I agree with my father that the Pope isn't always right."

Holding her hands more firmly, he looked at her in earnest, not seeking acceptance of his commitment but affirming his resolve. She reciprocated with the smile of a princess invited to dance by her Prince Charming at her debutant ball.

"To be perfectly honest, the first thought that went through my mind when I saw you at your mother's funeral reception was *foxy lady*. The second thought was, *candens es* which is Latin for you are hot. I fell in love with you when we first met in Montigny-lès-Metz all those years ago and have loved you ever since. It was *un coup de foudre* – love at first sight. You were in my mind every step as I ran all those marathons. My marathons were your marathons, my time to be with you exclusively. I could hardly constrain myself when I saw you at the funeral. So, there you have it, my hot foxy lady."

After what seemed to be an infinitely long pause, Alexandra professed the emotion of a lifetime of passion unfulfilled.

"You can't imagine how I have longed to hear those words, how many days and nights you have consumed my thoughts. Right now, you had better let go of my hands so we can mount up and ride. If you don't let go, I'm going to start crying and not stop forever, at least."

As she stood up, her cellphone buzzed with an incoming message.

"Some habits die hard, and technology has become most intrusive," she muttered with a tinge of frustration.

The incoming message was tagged "urgent" from Alder. She leaned over and whispered into Paul's ear. She allowed the intimacy of the moment to linger.

"Let me respond to a priority call from Tom Hunt before we mount up. Interesting that he is using his code name."

As she spoke with Tom, Paul watched a TV monitor in the café that was showing synagogues under attack in the United States.

The sub-script trailer read: *Terrorists attack synagogues in New York, Washington, Chicago, and possibly other unconfirmed locations*. Within seconds, the update visual tape at the bottom of the monitor read: *Police now confirm additional terrorist attacks in Seattle, San Francisco, Los Angeles, Dallas and Miami*.

A despondent library-like hush consumed the café as all patrons fixed their attention on the muted monitor. No one looked away, not even Paul whose focus jumped from the words at the bottom of the screen to the images of synagogues on fire, injured people laying on the ground and emergency vehicles arriving on mass.

Alexandra closed her cell phone and looked in astonishment at Paul, at the TV and then again at Paul. Her emotions ran the gamut from the freedom and exhilaration she knew from riding her Harley on the open highway to the satisfaction she knew from outwitting criminals as a forensic psychologist. Although she had never come so close to death as when she mentally duelled with Thon and his henchman while staring down the barrel of the pistol pointed at her head, she was aware that her lifestyle had taken a toll on her physical and emotional health. She was acutely aware that she needed a break that only time in the Harley saddle could provide. Yet she found herself awestruck as she stared at the images.

"Tom wants to meet us immediately," she whispered to Paul. There was no intimate pause. "There is some indication that these attacks were motivated by Thon's death. A neo-Nazi group with connections to Islamic terrorists is claiming responsibility in retaliation for a supposed US-led assassination of their leader. Tom is on his way to Luxembourg. He said he has been in communications with Sir James Pennington who advised that the radar is up at MI6 and Mossad. I confirmed we could meet him at my place. So much for our relaxed inaugural retirement ride."

Alexandra took a long deep breath. The memory of the gnawing pain from years of migraines and the faint scent of trepidation lingered. She became numb with the images from her past as they merged with the sights from the present. She and Paul were being drawn into a future marred with violence exponentially more devastating.

"Truths of those times are masked in the mists of the Moselle," her mother had faintly whispered under her breath when Alexandra had asked what her mother had done when she was younger. "Your roots are those of Charlemagne and your dynasty Merovingian. In them you will discover your strengths and unearth the truth."

Alexandra started to learn some of the details of what her mother had done at her mother's funeral. Only then did she come to realize just how prophetic and ominous her mother's words had been. The arcane world of espionage and intelligence was in her DNA, part of her destiny. Like arctic wolves, you can lock them up but you cannot silence their howls.

Tom's phone call reminded her that she and Paul would not be able to leave her mother's world behind. *But would working with Tom shed more light on her mother's warnings and would that increase or decrease the relentless headaches, the manifestation of her stressors?* she wondered.

CHAPTER 3

"I like your new digs, Alexandra," Tom commented. "I especially like the two Dutch paintings at the entrance."

"Thank you. Paul got them for me as a house-warming gift when we were in Amsterdam picking up my things from the apartment on Amstel and from my office at the university where I was teaching."

"I commend you, Paul. You are a connoisseur of the brush. Are you a collector of paintings or other forms of art yourself?"

"I have some. In my youth, I also collected coins, stamps and rare books but haven't pulled them out of storage for many years. That's one of the items on my to-do list now that I'm quasi-retired and supposedly have more time on my hands."

"Rare books? I'm intrigued. We should chat about an antiquarian collection that Major Mike Murphy left me. I've been slowly but selectively adding to it with signed first edition first prints. Collecting isn't so much a problem for me. Finding a safe place to store them is my challenge because I travel so much, spending days, weeks in hotel rooms."

"That's interesting. Sir James Pennington referred to his antiquarian collection," Paul replied. "In her Will, Alexandra's mother, Maria, left a box of antique books for her, some of which I recognize as being most collectable and valuable. One in particular is a very fine first edition, first print of the *Count of Monte Cristo* by Alexandre Dumas. Maria also left a fine first edition of *The Three Musketeers*." Paul raised his voice in order to get Alexandra's attention. "May I show Tom the Alexandre Dumas books your mother had?"

"Certainly," Alexandra replied from the kitchen. "They're still in the box in the hall closet. It's on my to-do list to sort through them." She popped her head around the corner and looked at Tom. "My mother left me a note in the box that explains something about an Antiquarian Book Collectors Club, which she belonged to with Sir James and Major Mike."

Paul delicately retrieved the novels, which were individually wrapped in tissue paper and enclosed in separate paper bags. Alexandra's mother, Maria, had taken great care to ensure that each was preserved in as pristine condition as possible. She had known quality when she saw it. Quality equated to value monetarily and from a collector's perspective.

"Oh, Alexandra," Tom exclaimed in admiration. "These are in excellent condition for their vintage. This *Count of Monte Cristo* and *The Three Musketeers* are indeed first editions both first published in 1844. Very nice!" he purred.

"I've recently come to appreciate that. Paul has agreed to educate me more about the world of antique book collecting. I've done some surfing on the web and am amazed at the value of select rare books. I just need to find the time."

"Most people I know who have retired say the same thing about time that seems to be elusive," Tom retorted. "Most commented that they seemed to have had more time when they worked."

Paul chimed in with a sigh. "I thought I would be able to throw out my calendar but that hasn't been the case thus far. Now that Alexandra and I are settling into the Luxembourg lifestyle, trips back to Paris to visit her daughter, Collette, and my son, Jean, in addition to riding time on the biker circuits, are the new reality. You realize, Tom, that your call to meet us cut short our inaugural retirement ride. That should tell you something about how seriously we interpret your invitation to a business relationship with a couple of recently retired pensioners."

"I'm very much aware of that, Paul, and appreciate you taking the time to meet me. I can assure you that you will not be bored on the one hand or having to live out of suitcases on the other hand. You will have time to ride, and to collect and organize your book collections."

"Coffee is served, gentlemen. Sorry about the absence of chocolate éclairs or croissants and Camembert but no time to shop. Let's talk business, especially the issue of the neo-Nazi attack on the synagogues and the allegation against the United States in retaliation for the so-called assassination of their leader, Thon, that sexually inept psychopathic pervert. What a disgusting joke he was."

Her anti-Nazi vitriol defined her position. While working, she had to be politically correct with some language she used when in public. In the privacy of her own home, she could be more exact with her adjectives and adverbs.

"Well," Tom chuckled, "this attack is an interesting twist of history."

"Elaborate, please," Paul asked. He had gained an appreciation of ancient history while travelling throughout the Mediterranean, specifically Greece. Defining historical events as twists would be subjective interpretation in what was supposedly an objective discipline.

Tom elaborated. "At the end of World War II, one of America's pledges to the free world was to de-Nazify Germany. But there were too many political and economic reasons not to follow through with that promise. A most prominent motivation not to comply was General Patton's decree that some senior ex-Nazis were to be employed as governing officials – *Bürgermeisters* – in German communities as a means of controlling the population. Others were employed as spies under the Purple Primer Program promoted by the United States and England. Only a few select U.S. politicians and semi-informed mandarins were aware of the rise of the Fourth Reich from the ashes of its predecessor, or at least were open to its possibility. This was part of the motivation for the Marshall Plan."

"Ah, now I understand your reference to the intrigue associated with the Fourth Reich movement. I sense there is more skullduggery than meets the eye," Paul commented. "Victors tend to write the history books."

"You're correct. So now the neo-Nazis of the Fourth Reich have struck in the heart of the American homeland supposedly in tandem with Islamic terrorists."

"And the strategic motivation is what?" Paul queried further.

"All along, we have suspected the Fourth Reich was financially backing some Middle Eastern terrorists with proceeds from wartime stolen Nazi gold to use against the West, particularly the United States. But we don't know why, and that has been worrying. So, isn't this a tempest in a teacup?"

"I see your point," Paul acknowledged. "From a strategic perspective, I understand the implications in the current and evolving global arena. But what's the connection with Thon?"

"No sane person would kill their golden goose. Does that suggest Thon wasn't the golden goose in the neo-Nazi vision of the Thousand-Year Reich? The alternative is that his murderer, a supposed loyal soldier of the Fourth Reich, was insane. We suspect there was a third option, an alternate political motive in his murder – to create a political maelstrom manifested in the attacks on the synagogues. History twisted, manipulated."

"How do we fit into your plans for a tentative partnership?" Alexandra queried. "Remember that Paul and I are quasi-retired and looking forward to putting in some serious Harley saddle time."

"Your reputations as recently retired professionals are your quintessential strengths because you are known for just that, and only that. Thus, you won't be suspected as recent members of the retirement community. You're local, known specialists in your own disciplines. As a result, you have your cover. You both have foundational and, in some respects, detailed knowledge of neo-Nazis. We will train you in the art and science of intelligence gathering. In addition, we will increase your knowledge of terrorism."

"Okay, but we aren't just a couple of carefree retirees," Alexandra qualified. "We have family. What we do will affect others. This reality certainly struck home with my mother's death. My and Paul's upbringings were warped by our parents' roles in espionage and policing. Paul and I became further entwined and, I surmise, remain entangled in Maman's world of French counterintelligence. My daughter, Collette, and Paul's son, Jean, through association, have been affected – Jean more so than anyone else, having been shot and nearly killed by Thon's Fourth Reich henchman at the warehouse in Versailles."

"Let me take you back to your mother's funeral," Tom responded. "I've been watching you two dancing in unison since the funeral reception."

Observing Paul and Alexandra subtly glance at each other with his revelation, Tom continued.

"Yes, I was there because we had a feeling Thon might show up and might strike again. We didn't have a positive ID of him but were hoping we could pick up on the unusual behaviour of any attendee. It wasn't until after the reception we realized that Thon had been present, disguised as a blonde female with bright red lipstick."

Again, Alexandra and Paul exchanged a quizzical expression.

"The head of security at the Hôtel Novotel in Luxembourg where you stayed and the waiter at the Café Kaempff-Kohler are also team members. They were planted to keep you under surveillance, as much for your protection as the tentative capture of Thon. We sensed you had become aware of their presence. Well done on your perceptiveness. The clerk in the jewellery store is also on the team. She had to introduce herself to you to initiate the relationship. She continues in that capacity as your neighbour, still watching over you."

"And Sir James?" Alexandra queried. "He retired from MI6 so was no longer on active service. He and my mother maintained contact more as friends than as colleagues, along with Major Mike Murphy."

"You can take the boy out of the country but you can't take the country out of the boy. Although formally retired from MI6, he remains an integral part of the intelligence team. As you know, Alexandra, your mother, Sir James and Major Mike Murphy worked together during the Cold War. Your mother had met Major Mike in 1943 when he was working with the military OSS – the USA's Office of Strategic Services. He later joined the CIA. Subsequently, Major Mike introduced me to Maria and Sir James as his protégé."

"Is that why Sir James was at the funeral?" Alexandra asked.

"Partially. He wanted to pay his last respects to a dear colleague. He was also another set of trained eyes watching over you. You need to know that although Thon is now dead, other threats continue. Hence, you need to remain cautious and cognizant of your surroundings at all times. Always remember what your mother repeatedly told you, Alexandra, to be ever so careful about what you say regarding those times when she was a member of the French Resistance, the *Maquis*, and later French counterintelligence. You are your mother's daughter and, as a result, you have been drawn into her duplicitous world of espionage. The Third Reich has morphed into the Fourth Reich and today's neo-Nazis are equally violent and deadly as the world has just witnessed with these nine attacks on the synagogues."

"And my daughter, Collette?" The worrisome tone of her question and the expression on her face were clear.

"We deduce the threat against your Collette has been minimized in one sense with Thon's death. But she too needs to maintain situational awareness. As you have asked her on numerous occasions, she needs to keep her radar up. By virtue of being your daughter and present at the scene when Thon was killed, she faces a threat regardless of what may surface from your association with me."

Alexandra paused and with a deep resigned sigh acknowledged her new world. She recalled how her mother would silently whisper under her breath when she asked about those times when her mother was younger.

"Truths of those times are masked in the mists of the Moselle," her mother would repeat.

It was now readily apparent she had been drawn deeply into her mother's vortex, her world of intelligence, of lethal intrigue, as had those around her. The singularity of black and white had been dwarfed by countless shades of grey. Retirement would be defined by this new reality.

"I don't think I need to remind you, Paul, of the requirement to be aware of your environment too," Tom continued. "Your own work gathering evidence at scenes of war crimes and presenting it as a witness at the International Criminal Court in The Hague is known. But your close association with Alexandra has left you in the thick of it."

"If I wasn't aware before, I certainly am now," Paul confirmed as he looked at Alexandra and reached over to take her hand.

"Where she goes, I go, and that's a given. We are business and committed life partners."

"I'm aware of that, Paul," Tom acknowledged.

"So, what's your assessment of the risk to my son, Jean? You know about his relationship with Alexandra's daughter, Collette."

"The risk to Jean is lower than for you and Alexandra but still significant because of his relationship with Collette. In addition, he has his own profession as a systems analyst with the Prefecture of Police in Paris recently seconded to the Police nationale. The two of them need to keep their respective and collective radar up. I would recommend the four of you meet in private to discuss the New World Order which continues to define us and others in our respective orbits."

"Hmmm," Paul murmured under his breath. "The New World Order, new relationships, new friendships, new professional affiliations. And I once thought the most significant decision in my retirement day would be whether I should play a round of golf or not. Why do I get the feeling life has only just begun?"

Tom smiled, confirming Paul's observation. "I'd like to invite you both to Langley, Virginia for an initial intelligence briefing at the CIA headquarters. Your function would be just to gather intelligence and report back. It's important to note that intelligence isn't necessarily evidence and vice versa. You can then think about what a working relationship might look like. We can chat thereafter and, if you are committed, we'll provide you with an advanced briefing on intelligence gathering and terrorism. Thereafter, we'll return to Paris and Luxembourg where we can work out details of the strategy and our relationship."

"Paul and I have talked about what a partnership with you might entail. We have tentatively agreed to explore a proposal that you might offer."

"I sensed that, Alexandra. In anticipation of your acceptance, I booked our flights and hotel reservations. Here are your tickets and confirmations. Just ensure your passports are up to date. We're living in the post–9/11 world of enhanced security."

"Might I conclude that Thomas A. Hunt, Deputy Chief of the Los Angeles Police Department, has at least one other persona?" Alexandra responded inquisitively.

"It's all about relationships," Tom conceded as he gave Alexandra a furtive smile. "I acknowledge that I'm in the presence of the master of professional affiliations and relationships. I wouldn't be surprised to hear you have already woven this topic into your university curricula, Alexandra."

"*Touché, mon ami,*" Alexandra chuckled as she returned his grin. "It forms the foundation of the art and science, and the sensing of forensic psychology."

"And that's why I need you on my team," Tom confided. "You're the best in your respective disciplines. You have a brilliant mind and an uncanny awareness of the senses, Alexandra, like your mother. With Paul's proven experience under fire and subsequent reputation with the International Criminal Court in The Hague, and as your sleuth partner, it doesn't get any better."

"One question, Tom," Paul asked, his eyebrows raised. "Since 9/11, I understand that U.S. Homeland Security has been on high alert and attuned to possible attacks on U.S. soil. How did this neo-Nazi attack on the synagogues go undetected?"

"These Aryans were on our radar but not highly profiled by U.S. Homeland Security folks because the FBI and other law enforcement agencies had been focused on Middle East Islamic terrorists. After the synagogue attacks, they taunted the FBI with a note stating that nine synagogues had been targeted because nine is symbol of the ceremonial menorah with its nine-stick candleholder lit during the celebration of Hanukkah. The note also warned that more synagogues would be attacked. Suffice it to say, the Aryans are now high on the watch list. This is where Alexandra's experience as a forensic profiler in the context of European cultures will add considerable value. As you are keenly aware, nothing exists in the absence of context. Your hands-on knowledge gathering evidence and intelligence will be vital."

Alexandra trusted her instinct, her *shrew*, but the stakes that Tom was offering were higher than she had experienced before as a forensic psychologist working for the Prefecture of Police in Paris and the Police nationale. She needed confirmation. Paul agreed.

"Okay, Tom, we're tentatively in. But before we go to Langley, I'd like to invite you to dinner to meet Collette and Jean. They need to know who we will be working with in order to gain confidence. They don't need to know who you work for, besides the LAPD, but they need to be able to put a face to a name, just in case."

"That's understandable," Tom replied. "When and where? I suggest we meet in private away from prying eyes and attuned ears."

"I'll call my friend Jo and set it up for her place if that fits, Tom. I'll send you an e-invitation to confirm the time and date."

"Someone's at the door, Alexandra," Paul called out.

"Can you answer it?

"Alexandra Belliveau?"

"Yes," she replied.

"We have a plant for delivery."

"I didn't order a plant."

"It's a gift from Josephine Desjardins."

"Okay. Put it by the window."

She opened the envelope that accompanied the plant. "Happy Homecoming," signed Josephine.

"Weird," she murmured.

Paul looked at her curiously.

"It's signed Josephine. She never uses that name with me. It's always been simply Jo. Just seems odd."

"I must get back to Paris," Tom announced as he climbed awkwardly out of his high-backed chair.

"Sore hip?" Alexandra observed sympathetically.

"An old KGB combat injury. One got away and I am left with a reminder of my mortality and a constant cue to be vigilant about a rematch. I don't need a meteorologist to tell me the weather is changing."

After Tom left, she re-examined the card that came with the plant.

"Strange that it says Josephine."

"Give her a call to thank her."

"I'll ask her at dinner, if I remember."

CHAPTER 4

D inner with Tom was described to Collette, Jean and Jo as just a social event to celebrate their new business and personal relationship, and possible new business partnership with Tom. Alexandra asked Jo and Collette to describe their impression of Tom. Paul asked Jean for his assessment too.

They were assembled at Jo's by the time Tom arrived.

"Tom, this is my daughter, Collette, and Paul's son, Jean," Alexandra announced.

"I'm pleased to meet you. Jean, I hope you're recovering from your wound. I've never been shot but understand that it can take a while to recover all your energy and endurance."

"I'm probably eighty percent back. Hopefully, I'll be close to one hundred percent recovery with continued physiotherapy. Most importantly, I'm able to ride my Ducati on very short outings now, just around the block."

"I understand you'll receive an award for your bravery in taking down the neo-Nazi at the Élysée Palace when your father was inducted as a Commandeur de la Légion d'Honneur, and for helping to save Alexandra's life at the warehouse in Versailles."

Jean acknowledged with a nod and a humbled smile. He was his father's son, not wanting to be publicly acknowledged for deeds of excellence.

"And, Collette, I understand that you'll be graduating this fall with a Master of Psychology degree."

"Yes, that's correct. I'm looking forward to working as a forensic psychologist like Maman. I'm currently completing my practicum with Frederik Jorgensen's psychology firm where Maman worked."

"Like mother, like daughter. I'm confident you'll be successful."

"Do you remember Josephine Desjardins, Tom?" Alexandra asked. "You briefly met Jo when you came over to become reacquainted with Sophia, my bike. Jo also rides a Harley."

"Yes, I do remember. May I personally thank you, Jo, for providing a safe haven for Alexandra and Collette during those threatening days when Thon was closing in for the kill."

"Life has always been interesting since our early days together when Alexandra and I attended classes at the Université de Paris-Sorbonne. It seems like only yesterday since we attended lectures in the Grand Amphitheatre and cruised the boulevards and back streets of the 5e and 6e arrondissement on our Harleys."

"So, Jean," Tom asked, "what's it like to be the sole Ducati rider in this extended family of Harley-Davidson enthusiasts?"

"It's a challenge leading them but soon I'll be joined by Collette. I'm teaching her to ride and she'll buy a Ducati too."

With the attention focused on Jean, Collette said, "We were holding back on this news until I had my licence. Now you all know that the competition is on. Jean and I will be flying the Ducati colours."

"Okay, but before the jousting gets too far along, let's sit down for dinner to celebrate Alexandra and Paul's business partnership," Jo announced.

"And another relationship," Paul quietly whispered in Alexandra's ear as he slid his hand down the small of her back, pulled out her chair and pushed it in behind her, before taking his seat close beside her.

Table conversation was relaxed and cordial as banter came easily. Tom's finesse in social dialogue accompanied by his warm and disarming smile eased his acceptance as just another member of the extended family, like a distant favourite uncle come to visit. Conversation seemed to center on where Alexandra and Paul planned to ride from the old city of Luxembourg, perhaps in the company of a couple of Ducati aficionados.

After dinner and after Tom had departed, Alexandra quietly confided in Jo and Collette, saying that she and Paul were seriously considering a business relationship with Tom to expand their police clientele to include the LAPD. It might also involve other major law enforcement agencies in the U.S. In addition, Tom could introduce them to some of his colleagues at Interpol.

Jo replied, "Yes, I get nothing but good vibes from Tom."

Collette took longer to respond and asked if she could think it over for a moment. She took a deep breath and closed her eyes, then opened them to finally confirm:

"I think so, Maman."

In quiet confidence, Alexandra asked Paul, "Thoughts, partner?"

Paul pondered Collette's reserved response and her mother's reflection. "So, what are you thinking?"

"Collette has inherited the *sensation of the mind* as my mother called the heightened intuitive awareness that I inherited from my father and mother. I trust Collette's feelings as much as I trust my own. Like mother, like daughter. There's just something out there that I'm stuck on." She paused for a brief moment before asking Paul, "What are your senses telling you?"

"I trust Tom. I would definitely want him on my team if I were asked to lead another foray to gather forensic evidence from another war crime scene anywhere in the world. I'm completely confident he would have my back if push came to shove. More notably, I would trust him with your life. Having said that, there is something mysterious about him. Perhaps that just comes with the territory, the arcane art of espionage and intelligence. I was exposed to a bit of it on those evidence-gathering missions working with interesting people in interesting places."

As they left Jo's, Alexandra asked, "You're confident about our relationship with Tom. Is that correct?"

"Yes, I'm confident," Paul confirmed. "My interpretation of my own intuition has increased considerably since being involved at the periphery of your mother's world of counterintelligence and Thon's murder, not to mention learning from you. If you're still uneasy, why don't you meet Collette and ask her why she said, 'I think so,' rather than an unequivocal yes? I can come with you if you wish."

"Good idea. I'll ask her now and set up a lunch. That will give her more time to reflect. And, yes, I want you there, mon colonel. I need your thoughts. If we enter into a formal contract with Tom, we need to be completely confident with each other as much as my mother, Sir James and Major Mike were. I'll also send off a coded message to Sir James mentioning that Alder has made contact and ask him for his endorsement of the proposed business relationship. I'll ask him if there is any indication of monkshood flowers as there was with Francine Myette."

"Although I didn't ask Jean for his assessment of Tom, I can now ask him about his sense of Tom's honesty. Jean isn't highly intuitive but he can certainly read people as possible opponents in life's game of chess. Since fine-tuning his psychological profiling software program for the Police nationale, he has developed a parallel program that examines future intent grounded in historical behaviour. I'll ask him to conduct a profile of Tom."

"Thanks. The more input we have, the better our ability to complete a comprehensive profile of a future business partner. This should be easier than completing the forensic psych profile of Thon. It'll also be less deadly if we make an error in judgement, although intelligence gathering will no doubt have its own perils."

❧ ❧

AT LUNCH, COLLETTE RECONFIRMED HER QUALIFIED ENDORSEMENT of Tom.

"He's a white-hatted good guy as you say, Maman, but there is just something about him that is a bit distant. I enjoyed speaking with him at dinner. He's charming and he made me feel relaxed without any glib pretence of being too slick. I wouldn't have any qualms about you working with him. I'm confident he is as honest as the day is long. But… there's just a *but*."

"So, why the hesitation, dear?"

"Not knowing anything about his background, I'd hazard a guess and say Tom was an orphaned child. I say that from an intuitive psych assessment. I think he really enjoyed being invited to dinner with our extended family because, perhaps, he never had that inclusive relaxed, warm family experience while growing up. He has instinctive high emotional intelligence, and finely tuned social intelligence skills that may not be innate but rather learned. Orphans make the best espionage agents because they have fewer links that can get in the way of working in a secret environment. That's why I sense he is more than a Deputy Chief of Police of the LAPD."

"Thank you, dear, for your straightforward analysis. I've no doubt you'll pass your practicum with honours at Fred's firm."

"I agree with your mother's assessment, Collette," Paul added. "You are already a talented forensic psychologist. I have complete confidence in Tom also and agree there is a reserved je ne sais quoi about his persona, yet no red flags."

After Collette left, Alexandra asked,

"Thoughts? What is Jean's assessment?"

"As I just mentioned to Collette, I'm comfortable. Jean said he had no reservations at all."

※ ※

WITH THIS FEEDBACK, ALEXANDRA AND PAUL MET Tom again and formally accepted his offer to engage in a business relationship.

"I passed the family acid test?" Tom responded with a chuckle. "I've checked out okay with all the psych assessments for honesty and integrity. Woohoo!"

His new business partners smiled in acknowledgement of his astute observations.

"You have also passed my acid test for thoroughness and caution," Tom retorted. "So, let's work out some details. I've taken the liberty of forwarding your files to my colleagues who are duly impressed with your collective accomplishments, integrity and diligence. Our focus now will be on gathering intelligence on the funding source for the Fourth Reich, what we perceive to be the stolen Nazi gold. This is what consumed most of your mother's time in French counterintelligence, Alexandra. You may find some comparisons with your mother's life."

She smiled. She felt closer to her mother now than she did when she was a child. Although she loved her mother and was confident that her mother loved her, there were those times when she felt abandoned. Reflections on those lonely times made her heart sink. She gained comfort from being close to Paul.

Tom continued, "We need to reach into the core of the neo-Nazi psyche in their world, which is devoid of ethical feeling and compassion. Their source of funding will be their Achilles' heel. Now, it's on to Langley."

As they parted company with Tom, Alexandra suggested they needed to call Sir James and confirm a date for a visit, just to relax. She felt safe behind the ramparts of his cottage and protected in his presence.

"We need to spend a little R&R downtime with him in Dover at his cottage overlooking the Channel. He left us an open invitation and I can hear the comfy chair in his sunroom calling me back."

"I agree," Paul replied. "He mentioned your mother found solace sitting in that chair and you found the same serenity when we first visited. We also owe him a more detailed explanation of the fate of Thon – how *la princesse, la chasseuse de dragon* – the princess dragon slayer, single-handedly saved the world from that monstrous murderer. In addition, I need to thank him for your amulet and for my ring."

"It was a team effort. I couldn't have done it without you and the Harley cavalry that came to the rescue."

"I'd like to stroll in his English garden again and hear more about his belief in the spiritual world of the Druids and Wicca. Since receiving his gifts and experiencing their powers, I'm now convinced, like Sir James, our lives are controlled by forces in our environment that are all interconnected. As my father correctly pointed out, the Pope is not always right."

"Let's go back to Luxembourg. My *shrew* is telling me we should sort through the box of rare books my mother left for me, before we go to Langley and before we visit Sir James. I've become more conscious of the fact that life moves in a rhythm, like the seasons. There is a need for balance between the past and the present, and the present and the future."

Paul reached for her hand. He was again humbled by the courage and wisdom of the dragon slayer. He quietly savoured the balanced unison he fleetingly experienced with her all those years ago in Montigny-lès-Metz before their puppy love had been abruptly interrupted. The experience of their first kiss was still as alluring today.

"Je t'aime, ma princesse," he softly whispered in a sincere expression of adoration, again sealed with a kiss.

"Je t'aime aussi," she quietly replied in a down-soft voice reinforced by an extended embrace.

Oh, how I missed this closeness, she reflected. In all their years of marriage, André had never spoken to her in such a genuinely loving manner. If she died tomorrow, her life with Paul, although brief at this juncture, would be fulfilled in every respect. She would never again experience the dreaded loneliness and paralyzing angst she had felt as a child and in her marriage.

"To bring more balance, may I suggest we move you into my apartment when we return to Luxembourg? It's more spacious. We can leave your place vacant for now. Jean and Collette can stay there when they come to visit, and perhaps Jo."

Alexandra wrapped her arms around him and as she kissed him she asked, "Does that answer your invitation?"

Why? she asked herself. She recalled the lyrics of the song by the same name sung by Betty Carter, perhaps made more famous by Louis Armstrong. Was her marriage to André a failure because of her shortcomings as a partner? She had often questioned her own inability to engage in a meaningful relationship because of her upbringing.

Although she loved her mother and believed her mother loved her, work took her away from home. Alexandra kept coming back to this doubt. Did her mother really love her? Did she really love her mother or is that something everyone said to avoid the reality? Growing up, she didn't know why her mother had to travel so much. It wasn't until she was well in her teens that she started to appreciate her mother's work and the sacrifices her mother had made in the service of the Republic of France. Yet, she still felt inadequate in relationships. Had her marriage to André dissolved as a result?

CHAPTER 5

"We're at a bit of a disadvantage, Tom," Alexandra commented. "You know more about us than we know about you. So, what's your background, if you don't mind me asking?"

"I don't mind at all. I could describe my life as nomadic at best. My father was U.S. Air Force and flew Mustangs during the war. He met my mother in England. In 1945, they had a daughter who died at birth. I understand my mother suffered severely from postpartum depression. After the war, they moved to Berkeley, California where his family was living. I was born a few years later. My father reenlisted in the Air Force when war broke out in Korea. He was shot down and killed by a MIG in 1953. On hearing this news, my mother curled up in a ball and died of a broken heart. I then moved in with my grandparents in Berkeley. My grandfather had been American Ambassador in Russia, Morocco, Algeria and France. He and my grandmother were fluent in French and Russian. So, in that household, I became fluent in both languages."

"I was wondering where you learned French," Alexandra remarked. "And may I compliment you on your pronunciation which is exquisitely continental. Most Americans destroy the French language!"

"*Merci beaucoup*," Tom replied with a quiet smile.

"I attended the University of Southern California at Berkeley where I completed an undergraduate degree majoring in Business Finance. In my final term, both my grandparents died within a few months of each another from lung cancer brought on by years of smoking. Being the only child and only grandchild, I inherited their estate and my parents' estate, which had been held in trust until I was twenty-one."

"That's very much like my situation with my aunt and uncle who raised me except they were killed in a car accident by a drunk driver," Alexandra confided, in acknowledgement of their shared experience.

"It's unfortunate we have that in common. My grandmother had been an avid reader and book collector. While in Moscow, she acquired first Russian-edition copies of Tolstoy's *Anna Karenina* and *War and Peace*, and Dostoyevsky's *Crime and Punishment*, *Demons* and *Brothers Karamazov*. They all became very valuable, as did her first French-edition copies of Alexandre Dumas' *Three Musketeers*, and *The Count of Monte Cristo*. She picked them up when they lived in Paris. She also acquired a first edition, first print of Charles Dickens' *Tale of Two Cities* in very good condition, in addition to a few other valuable collectables."

"Ah, now I know how you recognized my copies of *The Count of Monte Cristo* and *The Three Musketeers* from my mother's collection."

"Yes, but your copies are in far better condition than mine. Let me carry on with my tale of several cities. I'll get back to the book collecting that will tie into my life's adventures."

"I'm all ears. Curiosity is my middle name," Alexandra rejoined.

"I've ridden motorcycles since I was a kid. My first bike was a Honda 50 and then I upgraded to a Honda 90. I was part of the '60s California surfer scene. That's where I found my passion for motorcycles. The sun, the surf, the girls, it didn't get much better. But the Viet Nam war was at full throttle and I was attending university. I joined the California National Guard to fulfill my military obligation rising to Second Lieutenant. After graduation, I joined the California Highway Patrol because they had Harleys. And, yes, your Sophia was my CHP bike. After a couple of years of brainlessly giving out speeding tickets, I realized my career wasn't going anywhere so I joined the LAPD. Early on, I must have impressed someone because I was quietly asked to apply for the CIA, which I did. I think being fluent in both French and Russian helped, as we were in the midst of the Cold War. In addition to being trilingual, I was well read in French and Russian literature and culture."

"May I ask a more personal question, Tom? Were you ever married?"

"Yes. We met at Berkeley. Her name is Stephanie and she was a surfer girl from Jenner, a small town on the coast west of Santa Rosa. She wanted to return to Jenner after graduation and be an elementary schoolteacher. I wanted to travel. We separated when I moved to LA but briefly got back together. I actually thought we were over the worst. But then when I joined the CIA we separated again. Technically, we never divorced, which gives her my health benefits and she'd be the survivor for my pension. We've kept in contact over the years with the odd Christmas card. I have one of those non-descriptive post office box return addresses. I sense she thinks that I'm still distant."

"Have you ever thought of getting back together?"

"To be honest, until I met you and Paul, the thought never crossed my mind. I was too focused on the job. Domestic distractions can have fatal consequences in this profession as you can appreciate. However, seeing how happy and peaceful you are together has caused me to ponder the possibility as of late. But I came to my senses and realized my lifestyle is still just too unpredictable."

"I'm sorry to hear that but I fully appreciate your work and its demands. I understand from speaking with Sir James that you were a close associate of Major Mike Murphy. How did that happen?" Alexandra followed up.

"Major Mike was my CIA field trainer, so to speak. His background, as you may know, is French. His father had been an

American journalist who covered World War I and the Paris Peace Talks in Versailles in 1919. His mother was a French schoolteacher. Major Mike's early upbringing was in Paris where he attended school. Because of the French connection, Major Mike and I hit it off, speaking French much of the time, to the irritation of some of our unilingual CIA colleagues. He was also an ardent book collector as I discovered later. Apparently, his mother had many books, being a French grammar teacher and avid reader. Mike inherited her collection, which he left to me when he died several years ago. To my knowledge, he was never married and had no family."

"Interesting," Paul commented. "After our dinner meeting at Jo's, Alexandra and I went back to Luxembourg where we sorted through all the rare books Maria had left to her. In the box was a note on letterhead from Sir James referring to the Antiquarian Book Collectors Club, the ABC Club. He, Maria and Major Mike were founding members. They were the only three members as far as I can determine. Do you know what that was all about?"

"The plot thickens, *mes amis*. Let me back up a bit. I became Major Mike's protégé. He took me to Europe where I learned the tradecraft. Mike introduced me to Sir James and Maria, explaining they were the only two people he fully trusted. As you may know, Major Mike served with the OSS, the Office of Strategic Services, during the war. He was one of the Allied Intelligence officers in Northern France coordinating with the French Resistance, the *Maquis*, for the Normandy invasion in June 1944. That's where he first met your mother, Alexandra. She was a member of the French Resistance at the time. After the war, he became one of the initial members of the CIA in 1946. The Americans, British and French Intelligence Services were on the trail of the stolen Nazi gold and other treasures. Perhaps serendipitously, Sir James and Maria were also collectors of rare books. When you get the opportunity, have

Sir James show you his first edition collection of Charles Dickens' novels."

"We contacted Sir James and set aside some time to visit and just relax at his cottage in Dover after we return from Langley," Alexandra commented. "He mentioned he wanted to show us his collection and explain its value. I got the impression he was talking beyond just monetary. We're captivated, having examined my mother's collection, and now hearing the story about Major Mike's books which he left to you."

"Apparently Maria came up with the strategy that the three of them should form the ABC Club as a cover to locate art and other valuable artefacts which the Nazis had stolen. She figured some of those Nazi conspirators were filthy rich and would not want to convert their acquired treasures into cash for deposit in banks. If they did, it could easily be tracked. They knew there was a considerable number of stolen gold bars purported to be in some Swiss banks and the Vatican bank."

"Am I correct in saying these monies are still housed in a select few Swiss banks?" Alexandra asked.

"Yes, but we'll get to that later. Let me first take you back to your mother's strategy. She believed the now-rich Nazi thieves would arrogantly display and gloat over their stolen treasures, but only at their private estates. If Maria, Sir James and Major Mike presented themselves as antiquarians with considerable collections of rare and valuable books, they might be able to weasel their way into the inner sanctum in the clandestine realm of these ex-members of the Third Reich. That was the motivation to form the ABC Club. But Major Mike died before they could advance the plan. Sir James retired from MI6 soon after Mike's death. That just left Maria who was suffering from poor health by then."

"So, where does that leave us, Tom?" Alexandra enquired. "Do we want to resurrect the ABC Club as a means of intelligence gathering? Paul and I are committed to riding our Harleys as part of our retirement plans. Could you see us riding to antique bookstores and making it known we are in the market for rare collectables?"

"That's an option I haven't considered! You're a step ahead of me, Alexandra. Let's propose this to my colleagues."

"I have a question, Tom," Paul probed. "You are supposedly a deputy chief with the LAPD as far as Interpol is concerned. How?"

"Technically, I am a reserve police officer with the LAPD and hold the honorary rank of Deputy Chief. Few in the police community know otherwise. Thus, if anyone calls the department, they will confirm my status and explain I have been attached to Interpol."

"Now that's convenient. As you say, we live in a New World Order that requires new world strategies. The white-hatted good guys and gals need to become creative in order to increase the provision of security."

Paraphrasing the Chinese proverb, Tom added, "We live in interesting times."

"I'm not certain of the date of that proverb," Paul replied. "But there is a similar Latin expression dating back to the time of St. Ambrose – *si fueris Rōmae, Rōmānō vīvitō mōre; si fueris alibī, vīvitō sicut ibi* – if you are in Rome, live in the Roman way; if you are elsewhere, live as they do there. Colloquially interpreted, when in Rome, do as the Romans do."

"You're good, Paul. I need to hang out more with you and Alexandra to learn about the classics. Your collective knowledge would complement your cover of being intellectual antiquarians seeking literary cultural artefacts. One can't quickly gain the level of knowledge you have acquired over a lifetime. Combine that with your recently registered Black Hat Photography business, Paul, and you have an ideal intelligence gathering cover. You really are a diamond duo extraordinaire."

On their way to dinner, Alexandra thanked Tom for the candid exposé of his background.

"That helps us to gain a better appreciation of who you are and how we can best work together."

"*Je vous en prie, mes amis* – you are welcome, my friends," Tom enunciated in a cultured Parisian-flavoured accent, then turned to motion to the waiter for more coffee.

Alexandra quietly whispered to Paul, "My Collette is very perceptive. She sensed that Tom may have been orphaned and he was."

"Like mother, like daughter in more ways than one," Paul echoed in a soft voice. "She seems to have cast a spell over my Jean as her mother has cast a spell over me. I am a willing participant in your spells not just for the world of the Harlista."

Slightly more loudly, Paul said, "Now that Tom has placed the ABC Club in context, I'm really looking forward to talking more with our colleague in Dover. I'd like to get a clearer perspective of the ABC Club. What are your thoughts?"

Alexandra let the question hang for a moment before responding, aware of the diminished privacy of the public space.

"Every time I hear more about my mother, the more I find myself wishing I'd had greater awareness of her work. But then again, I might not have been able to appreciate the extent of the field had we not experienced Thon's threat firsthand. As she reminded me on several occasions, I had to have lived through a lifetime of constant alertness due to ever-present fear to understand the intervening variables operating in the environment."

"We can't live in the world of past what-ifs as you correctly identified, madame. We can only consider how to make the most of our present and future together." Paul gave her a gentle reassuring hug.

Tom nodded his agreement, accompanied by the subtle smile which had come to define his character.

CHAPTER 6

*W*e *live in interesting times and it's about to become increasingly interesting, je pense,* Alexandra considered with a silent foreboding, sensed but not felt, suggesting a fault line on the horizon. Red sky at night, a sailor's delight. Red sky in the morning, a sailor's warning. She had never been to sea, nor could she remember ever meeting a mariner and asking him about seafaring folklore. For whatever reason, this nautical verse resonated in her mind. *The premonition wouldn't be immediate but impending,* she thought. *Catastrophic when it occurred, as if linking aftershocks to a single abrupt shift in two tectonic plates.* Those in the trajectory of her orbit would be impacted by the enigmatic gravitational forces of quantum physics. All but one would rise on the flood tide.

She scanned the array of images projected on the monitor of her mind in the context of her intuition, her *shrew.* She thought about Paul whose radar was up but detecting nothing out of the ordinary. It just seemed odd. *Where could they be safer than in Tom's company in the CIA complex?* She had Paul. The omen seemed beyond the safety he could assure, beyond the power of the amulet which Sir James had given him to hang around her neck.

Your roots are those of Charlemagne. Your destiny Merovingian. In them, you will discover your strengths and unearth the truths, her mother had proclaimed. Her voice was not so much a warning but a challenge to seek the truth despite the omens, which would come her way. She questioned the inherent message. Was the fault on the horizon aligned with another beacon? She was still unsure of the path she was taking. Lately, she seemed compelled to second-guess rather than probe for answers. There was a difference. Her intuition had yelled out a warning when she and Paul had driven to Dieppe immediately after her mother's funeral to verify the facts regarding the murder of her mother's tenant, Madame Deschaume. This current sensation was a call to seek out the truth which, by its very nature, was shrouded in the cloak of the grim reaper.

Here you are again, Alexandra Vanessa, taking on the world single-handedly, she ruminated. *You have done it all by yourself because, although there were others like Jo, there was only one person I could trust: myself. It was less complicated, more predictable,* she supposed. Yet in those moments, especially at night, she yearned for the company of her puppy love. But it had been her decision to entertain those fantasies, which she could also dismiss with the same finesse as she could summon them. As long as she could keep reality and escapism separate, she would succeed. The adjustment from solo to duo was proving to be challenging.

Now, the self-talk. *There is Paul, your new business and committed life partner. So, when the questioning moments occur, like now, seek Charlemagne's truth with Paul.*

CHAPTER 7

*C*ordial *but cautious*, Alexandra deduced as she shook hands with Tom's colleagues. They all seemed to dress alike having shopped in the same Middle-America department store. Tom was the exception. His clothes were more continental as were Paul's. She hadn't noticed the variance before. In retrospect, she wasn't impressed but acknowledged her preference, perhaps bias, for quality and excellence in taste. That was one of the attributes that set Paul apart from other men – his dress, deportment and demeanour. For their own safety, she hoped that CIA agents working in foreign jurisdictions would be more attuned to environmental nuances and less inclined to comply with cookie-cutter standards. She would compare her first impressions with Paul's. For now, she sensed he was in accord with her initial assessment of their hosts.

"I'd like to introduce you to Helena LeDuc," Tom announced. "Helena is a member of the Iroquois Indian Band and holds dual citizenship from the United States and Canada as a result. She had an informal relationship with the Canadian Security and Intelligence Service in Montreal while attending Laval University. Then she completed post-graduate studies in political science at the University of Geneva which Henri, Grand Duke of Luxembourg, also attended."

Tom's director interjected, "Helena will be continuing graduate studies at Frankfurt University. Ideally, you may have an opportunity to become better acquainted."

Alexandra extended her hand in greeting, *"Je suis honoré de vous rencontre* – I am honoured to meet you, Helena." It dawned on her that none of Tom's colleagues had greeted her or Paul in French. An oversight or hubris intent? She recalled Tom explaining that his colleagues had taken exception when he and Mike Murphy had spoken in French. In contrast, all of Alexandra's colleagues were perfectly bi-lingual. Many were fluent in three languages, with a working knowledge of others. She wondered how Helena felt, surrounded by unilingual associates. It was readily apparent that she did not feel wholly welcome. She and Paul would take the opportunity to engage in conversations that mattered while Helena was in Frankfurt attending the university. In doing so, they would cultivate a contact, an informant, more willing to engage in conversations that mattered because of common cultural interests than business requirements.

Paul bowed slightly, following Alexandra's lead. "*Bonjour,* I too am pleased to make your acquaintance. Dual citizenship. Are you permitted to elaborate?"

"In Canada, I'm referred to as French Canadian and Iroquois First Nation because I was born to Iroquois parents and grew up in the Province of Québec. In the United States, I'm called an American Indian because Iroquois traditional lands are in what is now New York State. I hold dual citizenship because the traditional Iroquois Nation land base spans the current international border. Also, my mother was born in what is now called the United States of America and my father was born in what you call Canada."

"How do you wish to be addressed?" Alexandra asked.

"That's respectful of you to ask, Alexandra. Thank you. I prefer just Iroquois because that's who I am. I don't wish to be political but it's difficult to avoid."

"And I thank you. In continental French tradition, I bow in honour of your culture," Alexandra replied.

A warm welcoming smile rose from her lips to her eyes. "I never was a CSIS agent, instead a member of their watcher service because I supposedly didn't meet the qualification standards. Go figure with my background," Helena grinned with a sarcastic tone.

"I just reported what I saw, what my handler asked me to look out for. At an early age, I learned that I needed to adapt or die. Many of my people have not changed and, as a result, our people are dying." Her summary comments drew bored expressions from agents in the room.

"Helena has recently joined the CIA as an analyst," the director added. "She's here at this briefing because she will be joining Tom and, as I understand, possibly working with the two of you."

"I'm deeply honoured by this opportunity," Helena acknowledged. "Your mother, Alexandra, was an accomplished professional from all I hear."

"Only recently have I gained a better understanding of her work with French Counterintelligence and with the French Resistance, the *Maquis*, during the latter years of the Second World War. I have followed in my mother's footsteps." Alexandra couldn't help but notice some of Tom's colleagues become disinterested and withdraw from the conversation.

"I'm intrigued," Paul commented. "With your background, Helena, multi-lingual in Iroquois, English, French and German. I'm dumbfounded as to why CSIS didn't offer you employment. But as Tom has commented on several occasions, welcome to the new world order which requires new ways of dealing with new threats."

The formal briefing lasted all day with presentations from an array of experts on the Fourth Reich and the neo-Nazi movement, and its suspected and confirmed links with Middle East terrorist cells. Of greatest value was information on the surveillance and information gathering techniques that Alexandra and Paul would employ. They were reminded they were not employees of the CIA but instead confidential informants. They would be compensated accordingly.

Evening briefings were more relaxed with a greater opportunity for Q&A. Helena expressed interest in the ABC Club. Tom announced he had some business in Langley so wouldn't be returning to Paris with them. He would meet them after they returned from their trip to Dover to visit with Sir James.

Alexandra passed Paul a note suggesting they not debrief in their hotel room but go for a walk. He nodded, agreeing that the room could be bugged.

Once away from their hotel, Alexandra asked, "What do you think?"

"A foreign environment, not conducive to improving collegial relationships," Paul replied. "In brief, I wouldn't trust most of them. Tom, yes. Helena, probably. We need to re-think our business model. Everything Tom asks us to do we carefully analyze, knowing that direction comes from his superiors who have their own agendas."

"I agree. I remain confident that Tom would not knowingly set us up. But he has divided loyalties to his oath of allegiance, and to us by virtue of his connection to Major Mike and through him to Sir James and my mother. He might hesitate if push came to shove and that might have serious if not fatal consequences. We need to have a confidential conversation with Commandant Benoit Parent."

"And with Sir James," Paul confirmed. "His counsel, his wisdom are becoming increasingly indispensable." Sir James would be their Yoda, their Jedi Master and connection to the Force.

Alexandra reflected on her feelings of being left alone by her mother and having to become self-sufficient. There was Paul now to consider. He had confessed his love to her in the love letters he had written and again lately filling the gap left by her marriage to someone she didn't love, never did. But her mother had kept the old letters from her to Paul. Alexandra thought that if there was one person she should have been able to trust, it would be her mother. But her mother had betrayed her, kept her apart from her first love, or so she thought. All those years, she had dreamed about Paul. But as the years passed, he seemed to fade from her memory. Was she alone again, abandoned, having to be self-sufficient once more? This returning anxiety was making her wonder whether she could ever experience true love with a devoted partner. Was she just fooling herself? Should she express her doubts to Paul, suggest a trial separation just to test the veracity of their commitment to one another? Given the brevity of their reunion after all these years, could their relationship survive a separation? Was she projecting onto Paul her doubt regarding Tom's commitment to her, to them? Complete commitment seemed like a concept she had never known.

⊰ ⊱

"Bonjour, c'est Aulne." – *Hello, this is Aulne.*

"J'écoute" – I'm listening.

"Они возвращаются в Париж" – They are going to Paris.

"Да. Принято" – Yes. Acknowledged.

CHAPTER 8

As their Airbus A380 pulled into the gate at Charles de
Gaulle International Airport, the flight attendant welcomed
all passengers to Paris and advised that cell phones and other
electronic devices could now be activated.

"The flight has been a pleasant break from the e-addiction of
the cellular world that has dogged the latter years of our careers,"
Alexandra reflected.

"I agree, but best to check in with Collette and Jean to confirm
they're in the waiting area. I'm looking forward to hearing about
Papa's condition and how he's getting along. I was convinced six
months ago I would be writing his obituary by now. But the news
of Thon's demise and our reunion has brought him renewed energy
although the dementia is taking a toll on his memory. It seems to
have slowed in some respects but reversed in others."

"Got a message from Collette saying they're waiting for us,"
Alexandra commented. "She explained we were not to read any
newspapers or listen to any news until we speak to her first. That's
a bit bizarre."

"I have a message from Jean basically saying the same thing.
That is strange for sure. What's your sensation telling you?"

"They're okay but something has happened that involves them
both and potentially us, also."

As they approached the baggage claim area, Alexandra noticed
Collette and Jean waving.

"Why is Collette wearing a scarf on her head and sunglasses?
She has never worn a headscarf. Well, we'll find out soon enough."

"What's the cryptic message all about, Jean?" Paul asked
eagerly.

"One explanation and one announcement, Papa. First, Collette has to bring you up to speed on an incident she was involved in. Let's move away from the crowd – it's a bit confidential."

Alexandra and Paul transferred their perplexed attention to Collette and awaited her announcement.

"Late yesterday afternoon, I was jogging along boulevard Saint-Michel close to the Sorbonne when I was accosted, well, assaulted by a guy. But I'm okay."

Alexandra and Paul gasped in unison as they looked quickly at each other before returning their stare to her.

"I'm okay, really. He just tried to grab me. I recognized him from the université. He's one of the Saudi students who has gained a reputation for wanting to add more concubines to his private harem. He clearly hadn't done his homework. If he had, he would have realized I'm in training for my black belt karate competition coming up next month. I took him out with one well-aimed kick to the groin followed by a left hook to the head. He went down like a ton of bricks."

"What!" Alexandra exclaimed as quietly as she could.

"It gets better," Jean added, looking gleeful.

"There were two police officers across the street who witnessed the whole incident. They called for a paddy wagon which took the guy off to jail. This morning, he was charged with assault. Apparently, he is the son of a Saudi diplomat so the embassy is now involved. The media got wind of the story from their police scanners. The tabloids are reporting a five-foot three-inch petite Parisienne successfully fought off a six-foot Islamic pervert. There is a connotation of Islamic terrorism and a call for greater scrutiny of foreign students, especially from the Middle East."

"I'm speechless," Alexandra gasped.

With a smile, Collette continued. "So much for my reputation as a quiet psych student. It's a good thing my classes are over and I just have to complete my practicum for graduation. Because of the media attention, I may not attend convocation, but I'll cross that bridge when I come to it."

Stunned by the revelation, Alexandra and Paul froze in their tracks. They didn't want to create a fuss that might draw attention to Collette but wanted to hug her in an expression of compassion and support. In contrast to their anxiety at hearing this news, Collette and Jean were holding hands and smiling in what appeared to be controlled confidence. Their poised composure added to the astonished response of their parents.

Paul broke the silence. "If that's the explanation, what's your announcement, mon fils?"

Jean looked at Collette and then at Alexandra and Paul. "Two days ago, we got engaged." Collette brought up her left hand and proudly showed off her diamond ring.

With eyes wide, Alexandra and Paul stared at the ring. Hugs were certainly in order after this declaration.

Collette quietly whispered, "The Saudi has a permanent dent in the side of his head from the deep impression of the diamond. It will be a permanent reminder of his botched assault of a petite Parisienne!"

With pride in his voice, Jean quietly added, "In the warehouse where Alexandra was taken hostage and I was shot, I remember thinking when Collette burst in that she may be slight in stature but she is feisty by nature. She's a force to be reckoned with, like her mother. I couldn't be more blessed and honoured than to have her as my partner in life." He beamed with pride.

"Who else knows about your engagement, Collette?" Alexandra asked.

"No one else. We wanted to tell you before informing the world. We thought we would leave it up to you to break the news to Jo."

Dumbstruck by the news of the assault and still spinning from the announcement of their engagement, Alexandra suggested a celebratory dinner was in order for tomorrow evening at 58 Tour Eiffel Restaurant on the first floor of the Eiffel Tower. With everyone in agreement, Paul called and made reservations at 7:00 p.m. for four.

"We had planned to spend tonight at the Novotel Les Halles before returning to Luxembourg but we'll stay tomorrow night as well," Alexandra told them. "For now, can you drive us to Jo's? Paul and I need to brief you on our new working arrangement with Tom. It will affect everyone, not that the events of the past forty-eight hours haven't! Your news of the assault will also influence things. We'll have to figure out how we will individually and collectively navigate this New World Order. Let me call Jo now and ask her to put on a pot of coffee."

⊰ ⊱

JO COULD HARDLY CONTAIN HERSELF WHEN SHE heard the news of the engagement. She was aware of the assault, as was most of Paris with the coverage in the tabloids. Collette's name was not mentioned, fortunately. The overtones of Islam were readily apparent. The decisive action of the police was praised in defence of French culture and the reputation of a *petite Parisienne*.

"One more for the white-hatted good guys against the latest incursion of the black-hatted bad guy," Paul quietly chuckled.

Alexandra and Paul excused themselves from the gleeful celebrations and the wedding plans. They agreed the media coverage could have a bearing on all their lives in ways they had not envisioned. If the neo-Nazi Fourth Reich was funding Islamic terrorism, as had been strongly suggested in their briefing at the CIA headquarters, their cover might be compromised. They would have to update their strategy with Tom as soon as possible. Alexandra sent Tom an email with a news link to Collette's involvement and recommended they should chat as soon as possible. She would send Sir James a coded message, asking for his sage advice.

"The media coverage of Collette's assault did not link her with you," Paul noted. "Furthermore, her name had not been disclosed."

"I agree. Only Fred Jorgensen and Tom know of our familial relationship, in addition to Marc and André." After discussing it further with Paul, Alexandra immediately called Marc and André to explain that it was in Collette's best interest as a victim of crime if they did not speak to anyone. Marc confirmed that he was unaware of her involvement. Had he been, he would not have spoken with any of his friends and would not because, quite frankly, he was embarrassed and jealous that his sister was the center of attention with the tabloid exposé.

André was surprised to receive her call. He advised Alexandra that he wasn't aware of the incident, because he hadn't read the newspaper or watched the TV news. Like Marc, he was embarrassed by the revelation. He blamed Alexandra and her mother for encouraging Collette to take karate lessons. From his perspective, his daughter should not be out enticing young men but should be married and at home taking care of her family.

Alexandra was not surprised at Marc's male-chauvinist attitude as he was cut from the same dinosaurian cloth as his father. This was yet one more reason why she was so pleased to be divorced from André. She would not let their prejudice against women get to her.

After telling Paul about her phone calls with Marc and André, and André's sexist response, they re-joined the wedding plan conversation. Jo was being Jo, organizing and offering her home as a venue for a wedding shower. She was more excited about the engagement than Collette and Jean, who seemed content with her event planning.

"You have been rubbing your amulet on and off ever since we

left Virginia, and even more since landing in Paris. What's going on?" Paul enquired.

"Not sure. Perhaps I'm just suffering from jet lag. I'm not the 21-year-old jet setter I once was."

"Let's not shrug it off. Remember Dieppe and the black Mercedes. You told me you need to listen when your *shrew* is talking. So, listen to the sensations of your mind, as your mother would say."

"You're right. Caution is the operative word until I can identify the source of my concern. Thanks for the reminder," Alexandra replied.

Without mentioning the CIA, Alexandra and Paul explained details of their new business relationship with Tom. They drew a connection to Maria's work with French Counterintelligence. With that revelation, they reaffirmed the need for complete confidentiality.

"All right, the radar stays up," Collette said with a subtle smile. "Life with Maman is life with Maman in this New World Order. I figured as much. After our dinner with Tom, I sensed his life was different from most, like Grand-maman Maria's life, and your life, Maman, even more over these past few months."

"Hmmm," Jean murmured. "Life with Papa is life with Papa in this New World Order. I figured as much. Tom seems to be doing grey things with other non-descript people. With my secondment, I have received a few intelligence briefings that have come with cautionary caveats about heightened security and secrecy. The ominous undertones reminded me of what Collette described as warnings from her Maman and Grand-maman."

Jo just shrugged her shoulders and smiled. "Would I be correct in concluding there will be more requests to conduct discrete data base enquiries in the form of research requests and more 'Alexandra owes Jo one more IOU' nonsense? There had better be some face-to-face Ladies of Harley riding time in this new business arrangement."

"We'll schedule in those riding times, Jo," Alexandra confirmed. "But you may have to meet up in Luxembourg *chez moi*. There is room for one more Harley at my place."

"And if there isn't room at Alexandra's, you can park your bike at my place alongside Chuck," Paul smiled.

"One last point before we adjourn, Collette," Alexandra lectured in a stern mothering manner. "No more high-profile media incidents, ma chère fille. We need to be low key, so let's stay out of the news. Perhaps you can postpone your black belt karate competition until this whole matter blows over?"

Jean took hold of her hand and stood sentinel beside her. "I won't let her out of my sight. We'll be preoccupied every evening planning for the wedding. 'Out of the media' means us spending time with our folks in Luxembourg and walking along cobblestone lanes of the old city with Maria Vanessa. I understand Bichon Frise puppies are most welcome in the neighbourhood."

"I forgot to ask," Alexandra apologized. "How is MV?"

"She graduated at the top of her puppy-school class with *cum laude* distinction," Jean proudly announced. "We're now enrolled in an advanced puppy training class."

"Outstanding!" Alexandra exclaimed. "She has set the standard established by her human father and mother."

"Don't worry about not keeping up with your cardio training, Collette," Paul said. "I'm thinking of running another marathon so you can jog with me, if you like."

"OK, I'm clearly outnumbered here," Collette conceded. "No more jogging alone as I can't afford a mortgage, tuition and alimony all at the same time. In addition, I need to engage in some serious nesting activities in Jean's man cave."

Smiling at Jean, Collette blew him a kiss. "I love you dearly but your place does need a woman's touch."

"Get used to it, mon fils," Paul lamented.

"I have and I'm loving it, Papa."

"We old folks need our beauty sleep, so drive us to the Novotel Hotel, Jean. Thanks for the java, Jo. We'll be in touch."

Over a bedtime cognac, Alexandra enquired, "When did you decide to run another marathon and where will it be?"

"On the flight back, the thought crossed my mind. I had mentioned to you before that I ran all those other marathons over the decades with you on my mind. They were your marathons. When Collette said she was jogging to train for her black belt competition, I thought I would run one more marathon just for you. For the first time, you would be with me in reality. There's a marathon coming up in Palermo. What do you think?"

"I'll be there with you in body and spirit," she quietly confirmed as she snuggled up to him. "Those are my thoughts."

CHAPTER 9

"Sir James replied to my email," Alexandra announced, her lips pursed ever so slightly.

Paul looked at her with an expectant smile. From their first dinner together after Maria's funeral, he had learned that she often introduced a thought in a roundabout way. The pause that followed suggested she was mulling over the intuitive manifestations of her *shrew*.

"He said that I must have been reading his mind when I emailed because he had been lamenting the fact it has been too long since we first enjoyed the breezes atop the White Cliffs of Dover." She paused again.

Paul held her stare.

"He is anxious," she qualified. "And I am concerned."

Paul nodded slowly.

"I mentioned that we wanted to learn more about the Antiquarian Book Collectors Club. He seemed quite insistent we understand its importance and the hidden knowledge veiled in his collection of books. It was almost as if time were running out for him."

"And?" Paul replied, probing for the essence of what she needed to share.

"I'm a bit concerned that his health may be failing. As a result, he is feeling apprehensive – he might not have many more opportunities to tell us everything we need to know. He seemed particularly pleased that we have teamed up with Tom and visited the CIA headquarters in Virginia. He is interested in our impressions as if there were innuendoes we need to appreciate."

"Well then, let's plan to stay as long as he wants. We have nothing else more pressing on our schedule."

❧ ❧

Sir James answered the knock on the door.

"Welcome! I've been looking forward to your return to Dover. Please come in. Make yourselves at home in the sunroom while I put on a pot of tea. Would you prefer Earl Grey or a Jasmine green tea?"

"Green tea would be wonderful," Alexandra replied.

"And you, Paul?"

"I'm with Alexandra. Green tea would be excellent, Sir James."

"You have been hanging around together too much. Your taste in tea is in harmony."

"Where's your butler, Sir James?" Paul enquired.

"He had to return to Scotland to attend to some family business. He should be back this week. I find my biggest challenge in his absence is to locate where he has arranged things, like the cache of tea."

Alexandra and Paul strolled into the sunroom, warmed by the afternoon sunshine. The view of the English Channel was still alluring. The slight haze had not entirely obscured the French coast.

"Tea is served," Sir James announced.

"Allow me to help you with the tray." Alexandra spoke with appreciation for his hospitality. "I've been so looking forward to enjoying some downtime. My chair, my mother's chair, has been calling me. I can only imagine what she might have thought about when she sat here reflecting on her life. My heart aches knowing I never had the opportunity to learn more from her." She shifted her eyes from the vista of the past to the present and Sir James. "In one way, I feel so blessed to have met you and to have had this chance to get to know her through your eyes and your memories. But I feel a bit jealous knowing that you knew her far better than I did through shared experiences."

Sir James just smiled. As he sat in his favourite chair, he replied,

"And I have been looking forward to welcoming you. We have much to catch up on. I received your coded question regarding Alder. It is good that you have met and Tom has taken you into his confidence with a visit to Langley. When Major Mike, your mother and I were working together during the Cold War, we visited CIA headquarters. The intrigue was as shrouded in personalities as I have ever experienced, even more than the British Joint Intelligence Committee and the Government Communications Headquarters. From that visit, Maria, Major Mike and I reconfirmed our belief that we could only trust one another."

"I sensed the same level of disguised mistrust," Alexandra replied guardedly. "I don't know why I'm speaking so quietly."

"I found the same sense of caginess," Paul confirmed. "It was pleasant, collegial and welcoming on the surface, but distant. Perhaps Kim Philby still walks through those not-so-hallowed hallways."

"It comes with the territory," Sir James noted as he sipped his tea. "I knew Philby and never trusted him and neither did Major Mike, although he never met him in person. Philby was just too slick. You're not in the thick of it because you are just gatherers of intelligence. But you are intuitive enough to appreciate the danger of spies disguised as spies or as you so adeptly describe them, the black-hatted bad guys and girls masquerading in white hats. All is not what it seems to be."

"Yes, and as each day passes, I'm becoming more comfortable with the need to gain a more comprehensive understanding of my mother's world. I've been able to put in context the letter she left for me in her safe deposit box. As a result, I can commiserate with her anguish when she decided to keep Paul and me apart all those years ago. I was distraught and completely devastated when I first read about it but now have come to terms with her tormented emotions – and my own." She transferred her gaze to Paul. "And Paul's."

Sir James nodded, slowly conveying his understanding.

Alexandra continued, "I mentioned in my coded message to you that Tom had introduced us to a new agent, Helena LeDuc. What do you think about how we should proceed?"

"I trust Tom but with some hesitation only because I have not worked directly with him, only Major Mike, his mentor. I trust with equal reservation his level of judgement about others. But you need to make your own decisions. Alexandra, I recommend you use your intuition to judge Helena. And, Paul, use your analytical skills to judge your relationships. Go slowly and test the waters. I know you won't just jump to a decision without first considering all the factors. Confide in each other but be careful. I repeat, things aren't always what they appear to be."

"Advice heard and taken, Sir James. Thank you," Alexandra replied with a bow and a grateful smile.

Paul brought Sir James up to speed on how Alexandra, the dragon slayer, had defeated Thon.

"I couldn't have done it alone!" she replied.

"I'm not surprised," Sir James observed. "You have already started to earn a reputation as the diamond duo, a joint force to be reckoned with. Now let's talk about the ABC Club and how Maria saw it as a strategy for infiltrating the old Third Reich and the evolving neo-Nazi Fourth Reich structure. What did you talk about at Langley?"

Paul summed up the conversation. "At the CIA briefing, we discussed how we could resurrect the ABC Club to our advantage. Helena LeDuc expressed an interest in becoming involved and Tom endorsed her. Tom's superiors supported our proposal. Well, they were supportive of Maria's strategy and how we could incorporate it into our Harlista rides, which Alexandra and I have scheduled. Having said that, I left with the impression that the concept of the

ABC Club might have merit from their perspective but it wasn't a great strategy only because they hadn't come up with the idea."

"That sounds normal, consistent with American arrogance," Sir James commented. "In general, I don't get any bad vibes thus far. If you stay with Maria's plan, which Major Mike and I worked on with her, you should be all right. As a caveat, be wary of anyone who is too eager to become involved or anyone who wants to modify the details."

Paul remained guardedly optimistic about Helena's offer to become involved in the ABC Club. It was a cautiousness consistent with Sir James's reservation regarding anyone they did not know, regardless of Tom's endorsement; optimistic because of the credibility of its founders. He would first discuss his concerns with Alexandra. Her intuition would be a determining factor. After all, there was no pressing need for a decision.

Although he had consistently consulted with colleagues while working in the forensic lab, Paul's had been the final decision. It was refreshing to now have a true partner. Yet the situation was still novel. Their business relationship had not been tested. What would he do if they came to an impasse?

Such a circumstance had never been considered with his wife because he had never involved Suzette in any decisions. From the moment they met, she had rebuffed any and all offers to take any responsibility for decisions, even shopping for groceries or balancing the cheque book. She had been an impulse shopper with complete disregard for cost or consequence. An argument would ensue if he pressed the issue or even asked for suggestions. So, he simply made all domestic decisions. In retrospect, it was an insult to compare Alexandra with Suzette. They weren't in the same league. Lately, he couldn't understand why he had decided to marry Suzette. On a positive note, he used that criteria, or lack thereof, as a low benchmark for all subsequent decisions.

CHAPTER 10

"Tell us about your Charles Dickens collection, Sir James." Alexandra sensed it wasn't simply a collection of antique books. There was something more.

Sir James pointed to a bookshelf containing the complete collection of Charles Dickens on the top shelf in addition to other volumes on lower shelves.

"Paul, reach over to the bookshelf, would you? The fifth book on the third shelf from the top on the left is entitled, *The ABCs of Knowledge*. Bring it to me. Also, bring me the third book on the fifth shelf."

Paul retrieved the books with spines which appeared to be antique but, on closer examination, were new. Looking curious, he passed them to Sir James who opened the first book to chapter seven and then passed it to Alexandra.

"Read the first paragraph."

As she did, her eyes widened in astonishment. "My mother wrote this. I recognize her composition style."

"You are correct, my dear, she did write it, and with such elegance that it flows flawlessly. The first six chapters are just malarkey as are all even-numbered chapters. Chapter seven is Maria's full description of the ABC Club as she envisioned it. All subsequent odd-numbered chapters are the explanation of how she, Major Mike and I were to carry out the strategy."

Alexandra looked at Paul and then at Sir James. "I can understand why you wanted us to see this."

"Now open this second book to the seventh chapter," Sir James instructed. "Likewise, the first six chapters are just the meaningless rambling of poetic rhetoric as are all even-numbered chapters thereafter, and the first page of all odd-numbered chapters. Starting with the second page, the odd-numbered chapters, seven, nine, eleven and so on contain all your mother's codes which she developed for herself, Major Mike and me to use when communicating about the ACB Club. They refer to passages in our respective antiquarian collections that we were to use for coding and decoding. It's all there. I doubt the decoders at Bletchley Park or even the enigma machine could have figured it out. Last time we spoke, I promised Maria I would pass it on to you. It's the brilliance of your mother, Alexandra. This is who she was."

"I'm stunned. Each time I learn more about who she was and what she accomplished, I'm amazed I never picked up on any of it. I'm learning more about myself and Collette with each revelation," Alexandra conceded.

"Perhaps now you can understand why she did what she did to protect you. Not only was there the real threat from Thon but also the even greater threat of this information falling into the wrong hands. We knew that others like the Russians and Chinese were aware that a super code was out there somewhere. But they didn't know where it was or who had created it. Now being aware of it and where it exists puts you and Paul, and Collette and Jean, at an even higher level of risk in the New World Order. It will be your decision to share it with Tom or others including Helena LeDuc. I pass the codes on to you. My default advice is to trust no one unless you know them as well as you know each other. Tom maybe. I trust Tom, with reservation because he works for and with people who cannot be trusted. Certainly not Francine. If it gets out that you have the codes, the black hats will stop at nothing to get them, including killing you, Collette, Jean and anyone else associated with you."

"Thank you for that counsel. We'll keep things to ourselves for now," Alexandra replied. "I keep hearing my mother's warning to be very cautious about what you say and especially to whom."

Sir James added, "The rest of the books in the case are just my antiquarian collection. Here's a list of all the titles, authors, dates published and values of each as of this year. Add them to your list for the ABC Club to entice possible nefarious Nazi collectors."

"We are most grateful for your gifts. They will augment my mother's collection."

"To pass yourselves off as professional antiquarians, you need to be well read. Here is a summary of the Charles Dickens collection that I recorded. For example, there are two editions of the original *Pickwick Papers* in my bookshelf. One is a two-volume set but the other is just one volume. Note that Dickens stopped writing this first book to write *Sunday Under Three Heads*, which he published under a *nom-de-plume* – Timothy Sparks. Seymour was his first illustrator and Brown was his second. Not surprisingly, you will see slight variations in the illustrations. If you look at the sagacious dog illustration, for example, you will notice that one has a trigger on the rifle while the other does not. There are 128 points of issue like this. You will need to know them. I've described them all. So, study carefully, my children."

"We will be your prize students," Paul confirmed. "We are the sorcerer's humble apprentices."

"You can leave them here for now if you wish but take the two code books with you."

"Thank you, Sir James. We'll add them to our inventory, which is impressive, especially with what my mother left me. They should catch the attention of a few potential black-hatted customers."

"You're welcome. In my modest opinion, an e-book collection is ephemeral, temporary, transient, and has no value. You can only appreciate the richness of an actual printed copy, especially first editions. You can hear the authors speaking through the sensation of the printed words. Books are one hundred percent loyal to their readers and owners. E-books are faithful to no one."

"Once again, Sir James, you express your wisdom eloquently."

"Know that I have left all my books to you in my Will with all the titles listed. Here is the name of my lawyer. The original Will is in his law office."

"You are too kind, Sir James," Paul replied. "But we hope we don't have to go down that road for a long time."

"I mentioned to you last time you visited that I have no family to leave anything to. You two are now my adopted children. So, my children, enjoy."

"We are grateful you think of us this way. I'm sure my mother is smiling down on you."

CHAPTER 11

"Now let me tell you about my butler, Walter Burns. He was my sergeant when I was with military intelligence from 1944 to 1945. That was after I transferred from flying Mosquitos with the RAF. After the war, Walter returned to Scotland where his family had been established in the distillery business in Edinburgh. Walter chose not to join the family business but instead serve as a concierge in one of the major hotels. He had seen too much during the war and just wanted a simple life, to serve others. He married and had two sons, one of whom died in a car accident in his late teens. The other son works in the family distillery business. About fifteen years ago, his wife died of cancer. Walter contacted me and asked if he could come for a visit, to get his life back in focus. He never left and has been my butler ever since. He is independently wealthy from his family inheritance and refuses to accept any salary from me. He just wants to serve. He is aware of the book collection but has no interest in it. He knows nothing about the code books, Maria, Major Mike, Alder, or anything about my life at MI6. All I have told him is that I retired after a distinguished career as a professional bureaucrat. He is as loyal as the day is long and would give his life for God, Queen and Country if called upon again to do so. He can be trusted, but on a need-to-know basis only."

"Thank you so much for telling us," Paul acknowledged. "Now while there is still some warmth in the afternoon sun, I'd like to walk with you in your garden and talk about your Druid beliefs. But before we do, I need to thank you for the gift of the ring and the amulet."

Alexandra followed Paul's expression of appreciation with

sincere gratitude. "I could not have slayed the dragon without my prince and the power of the amulet you gave me. For that, I will always be indebted to you. It hangs over my heart that is now at peace."

"There is a Druid expression. 'Those that guard and those that bless share, in time, life's timelessness.' You are the guards and you have the powers to bless because you have been blessed, my children."

Paul replied with a verse from Kahlil Gibran: "'The timeless in you is aware of life's timelessness. And knows that yesterday is but today's memory and tomorrow is today's dream.'"

"And I thank you for the ring," Paul said with sincere gratitude. "As you mentioned, over time it has brought me the strength to deal with my demons. I've been able to bury the ghosts before they buried me."

"As I told you, Paul, our universe has been pre-destined. We were meant to meet. You were meant to be together at this time, to take up the standard to fight against the forces of evil. Know that you will be successful together. You also have the responsibility to pass this torch on to others. Trust your intuition to identify these people. Listen when the spirits speak."

Alexandra glanced over at Sir James and then at Paul. She felt there was something ill-omened about his urgency in passing along this information, as if from a spiritual realm.

Paul met her contemplative look with a stare as if to say, "I'm detecting uneasiness with you, ma princesse. We will talk."

As Paul and Sir James rose, Alexandra explained that she wouldn't join them in the garden but would relax in her chair, her mother's chair. She could not help but notice that Sir James was moving more slowly than normal as he stood up from his own chair.

"That is most acceptable, my dear Alexandra. We can chat about

Thon and your work with Tom over dinner with Pinot Noir from the Côtes du Rhône region. I also have a bottle of Rémy Martin that has not yet been opened. I understand that those have become your favourites."

"Your intelligence sources are accurate, Sir James," Paul responded jovially.

⊣⊢

THE EVENING'S CONVERSATION WAS AS WELCOMING AND agreeable as the cognac. Sir James bid his guests a good night as he retired to his room.

"I shall sleep well knowing that you are here and that you are in possession of the code books. That is the last commitment I made to your mother. I know you and Paul will consider your decisions wisely."

Pillow talk for Alexandra and Paul meant examining the events of the day. Paul picked up on the comment that Sir James had made and was as mystified as Alexandra regarding its implication. "He didn't say that he looks forward to more visits in the plural but just the next visit as if there may only be one more. And the explanation of his Will had an ominous ring to it also."

"I sensed the same thing. For whatever reason, I felt he needed to meet us to pass on all his knowledge because this might be our last visit, or perhaps our last if we don't return soon," Alexandra whispered.

"Yes, that was my impression. Let's put it into context as we visit and talk more. We can compare notes again on what we feel."

⊣⊢

"GOOD MORNING, SIR JAMES. HOW DID YOU sleep?"

"Best sleep I've had for a long time, Paul. That might not be saying much about my memory. And yourselves? Did you sleep well?"

"It must be the seaside air that is so calming to the soul. Alexandra is still in bed so she must have been tired."

"No, I'm up. One day soon I will turn off my cellphone. Tom sent me, well Paul and me, a request to return to Paris as soon as we can, as there has been a new development. It actually came from Alder which indicates a high priority. No rest for the retired or semi-retired seniors. But we will be back as soon as possible. Will you be all right without Walter?"

"That's no problem. Walter called. He will be back in Dover this evening, so don't worry, my children."

"Although Tom's message was marked urgent, it can't be that pressing to get in the way of a cozy continental breakfast on the White Cliffs of Dover. Why don't you relax in the sunroom, Sir James, while Paul and I prepare a *petit déjeuner* to start your day."

"I'll take you up on your offer," Sir James replied. "I shall retire to the sunroom while I await your culinary creations."

"What was Alder's or Tom's urgent message?" Paul asked as they started preparing breakfast.

"It said he was in Paris with his new business associate, which I took to be Helena. A safety matter had been brought to his attention. He said I should check my emails about a recall notice from the Harley-Davidson dealership where I purchased Sophia. The recall was for a clutch cable that was on warranty. I was to enquire at the dealership with the new service manager. But Sophia is well beyond any warranty."

"Back to Paris we go. I'll make reservations while you finish making breakfast," Paul replied.

After the dishes were washed, Paul and Alexandra bid Sir James *adieu*. "We will be back to visit again, Sir James, as soon as we can. Stay well."

"With Walter here, I will be well attended to, my children. He fusses over me like a true British Army batman. Let me know what you are up to. I can still decode Maria's messages *sine vitium* – without error."

Alexandra packed her travel bag for the return trip to Paris as she always had. Her mother ensured she follow a routine so she would not forget anything. "Leave it cleaner than when you arrived," her mother would remind her when, as a child, she accompanied her on those business trips to Metz in the Moselle Valley and Dieppe on the Normandy coast. Just before leaving the hotel room, her mother would conduct a final inspection, following the trace of her hand as it floated over all surfaces, a housekeeping sweep. Like many of her mother's teachings, Alexandra never found out until later in life what the true purpose of the lesson was. Discipline in cleanliness was about not leaving any traces of your presence, essential behaviour for espionage and counterintelligence.

Packing and unpacking and staying in hotel rooms was a constant reminder of the transient nature of her own life, and of her mother's. Alexandra longed for the brief yet cherished quiet times they had spent together. She dreaded the sight of her mother's travel bag that was a constant at the front door, ready at a moment's notice, never stored in a closet out of sight. When her mother walked out of the door, Alexandra had cried a thousand tears and hated her mother for abandoning her once again.

What had Collette thought when we travelled while I moved from university to university and while working as a forensic psychologist on all those cases at police precincts? Growing up, did Collette mind the stability of a constant home life? Alexandra never broached the topic with her own mother, nor did she ever talk to Collette about the impact. When she and André unofficially separated, Marc stayed with his father and Collette stayed with

Alexandra. It was a topic she and André never discussed. The constant, throughout, was the travel bag at the front door.

She now dreaded having to leave Sir James. Would he hate her for being transient, for leaving him? As a penultimate gesture, Alexandra conducted a cleanliness inspection. Her hand hovered over all surfaces she might have touched in the Dover cottage. She then gave Sir James a warm hug and whispered her mother's words, "I love you. Don't hate me for leaving."

Sir James replied, "I love you too, my dear Alexandra. I don't hate you for leaving. Where would I get such an idea?"

She retrieved her travel bag, which she had left at the front door of the Dover cottage. She detected her mother's regret for the conversations they never had, the explanations that never were, the absences that could never be replaced, the pain that was never soothed.

Alexandra knew that no volume of text messages or emails could ever replace the emotion of a personal hug or a loving voice. She would make a special trip to Paris to be with Collette, to have long hugs, to tell her how much she loved her and how much she missed her, and to ask her how she felt about the transient life they had lived.

CHAPTER 12

Alexandra and Paul entered the Harley-Davidson dealership where she had purchased Sophia years ago. The service manager handed her a note when she enquired about the warranty on the clutch cable. It directed them to call the service representative. After verifying the make and model of her bike, Alexandra was provided with an address where she could pick up the cable. At that location, they were ushered into a meeting room where Tom and Helena were waiting.

"Welcome. I'm glad that you could make it so quickly. I apologize for the intrigue. Let me explain," Tom announced.

"We figured that something was up as your email was from Alder. You used that name when you asked us to return from our inaugural bike trip to brief us on the synagogue attacks in the U.S."

"You're correct. When Alder calls, it is high priority. Helena is up to speed on this case and will be working with me. Let me explain. Someone broke into the jewellery shop in Luxembourg, the shop with the safe room above where your mother had stayed before she died. The shop and the apartment were ransacked. Fortunately for us, a guard on duty at the palace observed the B&E and called the police who arrested the perpetrator. He wasn't all that intelligent because he didn't realize there was only one entrance and exit. He has been identified as a Fourth Reich neo-Nazi member connected to the Munich cell. He had a gothic tattoo on the right lower side of his neck with the initials VR for *Vierte Reich* – Fourth Reich. This was the same tattoo proudly worn by the neo-Nazi who was arrested at the awards ceremony at the Élysée Palace when Paul was made a Commandeur de la Légion d'Honneur."

"How can anyone forget that gala evening of honour?" Alexandra exclaimed. "Had it not been for Jean's heroics, Collette and I would not be here."

"I agree," Tom replied. "Intelligence has connected this Munich cell with a Fourth Reich cell in southern Brazil with links to terrorists in the Middle East. The Nazis have been active in South America since before the war. For your information, here is a newspaper article published in the *Sydney Morning Herald* dated 14th December 1939, and other related documents. It reveals the extent of Nazi shipping in that region in the 1930s."

"I was aware of the Nazi connections to South America after the war, to Brazil, Argentina and Chile, especially ex-SS figureheads like Klaus Barbie and Adolf Eichmann, but not to this extent," Alexandra commented. "The breadth and depth of their roots never ceases to amaze me."

"The plot thickens, mes amis," Tom continued. "At the time of the synagogue attacks, a neo-Nazi cell in the U.S. advised that there would be further attacks. This Luxembourg B&E may be a prelude. For your info, other international intelligence agencies, particularly Mossad, are picking up increased neo-Nazi traffic. We are expecting other attacks at any time. Further, some funds seem to be moving through two Swiss banks, one being a bank in Geneva with ties to the Middle East and the other in Zürich. We suspect Al Qaeda terrorists. It seems all perfectly legal on the surface but troublesome nonetheless, given the increase in terrorist activities. There is some money moving in Paris, also, in the form of a German bearer bond that had been looted from the Reichsbank in 1945 by the Russians. Another bearer bond recently surfaced in Rome. Each was sold on the black market."

"Where is the neo-Nazi who broke into the apartment now?" Paul asked with heightened concern. His arrest in the old city was too close for comfort.

"He was released on bail and disappeared shortly thereafter. I understand he is wearing florescent green coveralls and ankle bracelets in a hot climate," Tom replied. "Nothing to worry yourself about."

"The New World Order," Paul acknowledged with a smile. "So, what would you like us to do?"

"Helena, would you take over the briefing please?"

"Thanks, Tom. One of the Munich cell members by the name of Dieter Bayer runs an upscale antique book shop that has a well-stocked collection. We would like you to visit the shop and present yourselves as antiquarians. Start to develop a relationship with Herr Bayer and just report back. It would be great if you could get a list of books this establishment carries, especially those that are not displayed but reserved for special clients. Long-term relationship building is your primary and sole goal at this time."

"That sounds easy enough but do you want us to make any purchases if we see any interesting editions?" Paul enquired.

"You may or may not wish to make a purchase right now. We leave that up to you to decide. If any books are on consignment, it would certainly be of interest to identify the owners. We may be able to cross-reference their holdings with known stolen property. Here is the address of the target store and the addresses of other antiquarian bookstores and antique shops in Munich. Check them all out so the owner of our target shop won't be suspicious that you are only shopping at his store. Here is an advance on your expenses. It's in Euros cash so no cheques will need to be cashed. Just sign here with your John Henry."

"I guess that means we are officially on the unofficial payroll," Alexandra said as she signed her Jeanne Henri. Paul followed with his Jean Henri.

"From this point on, we will only meet in private due to the need for increased levels of security," Tom stated emphatically.

"All future contacts with you will be established through Alder. We will keep all future e-traffic to an absolute minimum."

"Are there any reverberations from Collette's encounter with the Saudi student that we should be aware of?" Alexandra asked.

"We have no intelligence indicating that anyone suspects either of you. Just carry on as normal going about your Black Hat Photography business, Paul, and your semi-retired lifestyle. If you need to contact us about any suspicious activities, do so through the service manager at the Harley-Davidson dealership here in Paris where Alexandra purchased Sophia. Or make contact through the waiter at the Café Kaempff-Kohler, in the old city of Luxembourg where you first dined after Maria's funeral. Any questions?"

Paul and Alexandra looked at each other and then back at Tom and Helena. "No questions at this time," they individually replied.

Paul commented, "Where the weather is a bit cooler these days, we'll drive to Munich in my Jaguar. That should suggest some availability of funds to purchase classics."

"Sounds like a plan," Tom sagely nodded. "I shouldn't have to remind you but I will as this is your first official foray into black-hat country. Always keep your radar up, safety first, safety last and safety always. Remember that your sole purpose is to gather intelligence and report back. Back out if you have any sense of danger."

"You mentioned two Swiss banks, one of which was in Geneva," Alexandra added. "I have a colleague with family connections in the Swiss banking system in Geneva. Would you like me to make some general enquiries with him? I trust him completely. The Gestapo SS had persecuted members of his family during the war so there is no love lost. He would be a willing ally."

"That would be fine but keep details out of any conversation at this time. I'll enquire further at my end to identify which banks are suspected. We can talk again after you return from Munich."

When Alexandra and Paul left, there was a different air about their new business partnership. Money was flowing without invoicing from the Black Hat Photography. The need for vigilance was rising correspondingly.

"Right, we need to rehearse our story as we planned for our covers. This is for real with a danger level approaching that of the hunt for Thon," Alexandra confirmed. "We're antiquarians and newlyweds on our honeymoon, holding hands, exchanging smiles and occasional secret kisses."

"Got that, partner," Paul confirmed. "There's just one important part missing. I think we should have rings because we are newlyweds. If we were as young as Collette and Jean, rings would not be an issue. But we're older and from a more traditional era. Thoughts, madame?"

"You're absolutely right. I couldn't agree more. What do you suggest?"

"When we visited my father the first time after your mother's funeral, you will recall that he asked if you could leave us alone because he had something personal to discuss with me. He told me that we were meant to be together, to be married."

"Yes, I distinctly remember your telling me that."

"What I didn't tell you was that he handed me my mother's wedding ring. He gave me permission to give it to you. Usually, married couples exchange rings just before they say 'I Do' and are pronounced husband and wife. We have the cart before the horse due to time and circumstance. I've had my mother's wedding ring cleaned and polished. Would you be comfortable wearing her wedding ring now? I know we haven't formally talked about getting married. It's just been out there. We should have that conversation soon. But for now, we at least need a ring for you. Let's go back to Luxembourg, get the ring, get packed and drive to Munich."

Paul lamented that this was not the romantic proposal he would have preferred under less pressing circumstances.

As Alexandra stood still for a moment, she considered that this was neither the time nor the occasion for a full emotional embrace in celebration. A delicate kiss conveyed the full magnitude of her sentiments. "I've never been so happy," she whispered into his ear as she squeezed his hand and leaned closer to him than ever before. "I agree that we need to talk soon, very soon. The significance of the ring you are suggesting I wear is beyond my feelings right now. I think you know that I won't be *acting* the part. Instead, it will be coming from the deepest depths of my heart. Yes, I do. Let's go home."

⊣ ⊢

"Bonjour, c'est Aulne" – *Hello, this is Aulne.*

"J'écoute" – *I'm listening.*

"Они едут в мюнхен" – *They are going to Munich.*

"Да. Принято" – *Yes. Acknowledged.*

CHAPTER 13

As the Eurail left Paris for Luxembourg, Alexandra noticed a middle-aged couple who occupied the knight's seat across the aisle. They were overtly cold and formal with each other and seemed not to meet each other's gaze. Instead, they persistently looked blankly in opposite directions. They presented contrived expressions as if they were ventriloquist's dummies. *Was their motivation to respond to one another in circumstances similar to her own with André*, she mused? Yet with Paul by her side and the anticipation of wearing his mother's ring, soon to be her wedding band, she felt more secure than she had ever been. In contrast to what she was seeing, her *shrew* was crying out for caution: a threat akin to Thon. *Was this couple acting out a charade*, two sets of surveillance eyes? She trawled through the Rolodex file of her memory for their faces. None appeared.

"I'm sensing your unease, madame," Paul whispered.

"That couple do not want to appear to be what they are not. Not married. Not a couple. Perhaps partners. Regardless, not happy. Accordingly, I conclude a tad Russian. I feel they are watching us, keeping us under surveillance. My emotions are high in anticipation of wearing your mother's wedding ring, soon to be my ring, so perhaps I'm reading too much into this."

"You have never been wrong," Paul murmured. "I've had a feeling we have been followed several times before, even before Thon was killed. If they are not what they appear to be, then they are long-in-the-tooth professionals from the arcane world."

Russian, maybe? Am I my mother's child? The daughter of a French counterintelligence agent with many secrets not yet revealed? she thought.

"Maria cautioned you to always be wary. She repeated that the truths of those times are masked in the mists of the Moselle. If your *shrew* is correct, that they are Russian agents, then we truly have been drawn into her vortex, her world of intelligence, of codes and intrigue."

"For now, let's just watch them," Alexandra whispered.

Within moments, the couple got up with luggage in hand. The man walked toward the front of the car while the woman left the coach via the back door.

"The reincarnated ghosts of Thon live on, *je pense*," Paul suggested with a sour face. "I regret I omitted to drive a holly stake into his heart and sprinkle his body with Transylvanian garlic."

"Perhaps not Thon but other ghosts of my mother," Alexandra muttered with an equally acrid forewarning. She sat quietly. Her muscles became taut. Her heart hung heavy. Her complexion paled. Images appeared on the monitor of her mind. "Run. Run," her mother's voice rang out. "That was an impossible shot." Her mother's stare was riveting.

"What's wrong?" Paul asked.

Alexandra stared straight ahead either not hearing or choosing to obey her mother's words: "Some things you cannot talk about, not to anyone."

She slowly turned and stared at Paul. "Something my mother said." She paused. "I can't remember exactly what it was or the context in which she said it. It is a reoccurring nightmare without clarity in sound or sight."

Paul reached over to hold her hand but could not loosen her vice-like grip.

"Your hand. Your grip. What are you gripping?"

She stared down. Realizing the tightness of her muscles, she concentrated on relaxing her fingers. Paul rested his hand on top of hers and gently rubbed her fingers. He did not speak. Instead, he awaited her response.

"I don't know," she whispered. "That has never happened before. At least not that intense."

"What triggered it?" he asked.

She sat quietly reflecting on everything but not examining anything in particular. Her mind flashed back to events in her childhood to the moments preceding her blank glare into the abyss. She was drawn to her mother's words. She recalled them in detail but couldn't define the context.

"I don't know," she said, somehow calmly detached from what had just happened.

"We had been talking about the mysterious passengers who were sitting across the aisle, if that helps. Was it something about them that triggered it?"

After a moment of reflection, she replied, "It could have been. I heard my mother's voice telling me, yelling at me to run. But I can't remember why she was yelling those words. She said that it was an impossible shot."

"Perhaps it was related to sitting in her chair in the sunroom on the coast of Dover? Perhaps talk of wearing my mother's wedding band? Or both? Somehow linked? Is there a common denominator?"

"I don't know," Alexandra replied stoically as if the incident was just a matter of routine. Clearly, there was nothing routine about it. "Whatever it was, my mother warned me never to talk about it to anyone. If I can't recall the context, it is deep in my psyche. It's something that occurred in my childhood, something traumatic, life-threatening. Next time we are in Paris, I'll make an appointment to chat with Frederik Jorgensen."

She held tightly onto Paul's arm and leaned her head against his shoulder. His closeness brought a sense of reassurance yet apprehension, of security yet trepidation. "Some memories are arctic wolves," she murmured. "You can lock them up but you cannot silence their haunting howls."

As she relaxed, her mother's words returned to her as a cautionary caveat, their context shrouded in the impenetrable mist of the Moselle. "Run, Run. You took the impossible shot. You saved my life. It was not your fight. Because you are my daughter, you have been drawn into my world at far too tender an age. Ironically, it is an age when I entered into the *Maquis* vortex as a French Resistance fighter. That defined my future, our future, now your future. Your roots are those of Charlemagne, your destiny Merovingian. In them you will discover your strengths and unearth the truths."

⚑ ⚑

"Bonjour, c'est Aulne" – *Hello, this is Aulne.*

"J'écoute" – *I'm listening.*

"Они едут в Они едут в люксембург "– *They are going to Luxembourg.*

"Да. Принято" – *Yes. Acknowledged.*

CHAPTER 14

Alexandra's eyes welled with tears as Paul slipped the wedding ring on her finger. Words would have been meaningless. This moment was the zenith. She wished she could have held his hand for all the years gone by. She caught herself staring at his lips. His intentions were muted by her thoughts of kissing those lips for hours, for days, forever. For her, it was all about his kiss. That is what she had missed the most, the kiss.

"I have something for you." Alexandra led him into the bedroom where she opened the wooden box that held all the magical ribbons she had played with as a child. She carefully withdrew a ring. "This was my father's ring. My mother left it to me in her safe deposit box. It is the only tangible possession that my mother had of Philip. It is now the only link I have to him. I would like you to wear it." As she slid it on Paul's finger, she whispered, "Yes, we have the cart before the horse. All these years, I have been your betrothed. And, yes, I will be your wife."

The moment their eyes locked, waves of deep emotion rushed through her. She gasped for air. His eyes could say so much in an instant, a deep knowing, caring and understanding. They became lost in the moment, forgetting all the problems of the world and everything around them. Once the trance was broken, the awkward shyness of their first kiss in Montigny-lès-Metz all those years ago consumed them both. The fullness of their embrace conveyed all that needed to be expressed, till death do us part.

Alexandra gazed in silence at her father's ring now on Paul's finger. What had it meant to her mother? What had it come to symbolize? Her mother's relationship with Philip was tormented because of the forced separation yet she loved him so dearly.

Lately, her relationship with her mother was a cascade of contrasts. As a child, she loved her mother and cherished their relationship but hated the days Maria left her with her aunt and uncle. When she read the letter her mother had left in the safe deposit box explaining why she kept the letters Paul had written to her and hers to Paul, she had hated her mother. More recently, reflecting on the reason Maria had kept them apart, she forgave her but the depth of the regret remained. Today, what was her relationship with her own daughter? Did Collette have regrets about their relationship as they lived apart from André and Marc? She had never had that conversation. Now she had Paul and had moved to Luxembourg away from Collette. Was history repeating itself? It was all about commitment to relationships.

She and Paul were in a committed relationship. They had been since their first kiss all those years ago. They were not two peapods on the same vine, not two peas in the same pod. Instead, each was half of the same pea in one pod. Without the other, there was nothing.

They had a quasi-professional relationship with Tom but a greater one as patriots of the Republic of France. The issue was loyalty of commitment to the same philosophy but through complementary stakeholders. The loyalty between the two was crystal clear. There was no conflict of interest. It was genetic, rooted at conception, confirmed at birth and forged in the crucible of their culture and now reinforced in practice with the exchange of rings. The ultimate challenge would be to chart the less-known path with one contractual partner aware of the other but not necessarily vice versa. It was a balance of subduction and seduction. Their success in the upcoming mission was incumbent on having the false façade of details known to the bare minimum of players.

The template for the realization of each mission was standard, based on flexibility to accommodate the unknowns. Paul and

Alexandra followed a similar disciplined format. They were chosen for that reason. The detail was in the preparation, physical yes, but more importantly the mental and the emotional. With their relationship now confirmed, there would be one less intervening variable to contend with.

CHAPTER 15

As they took the autobahn exit to the Olympiastadion in Munich, Alexandra commented that she could still remember the massacre of the Jewish athletes as if it had happened yesterday. "Not much has changed since the 1972 Olympics. Middle East terrorists are still targeting Jews. Munich may be a progressive city today but it will always have this stigma attached to it like the disfigurement of smallpox scars."

"Anti-Semitism hasn't been restricted to Munich, madame," replied Paul. "It's been in the Paris landscape for centuries. We just have to reflect back to the Second World War with the facilitated export of Jews by the Vichy government and the murder of Georges Mandel in the summer of 1944. Going back further, we have the Alfred Dreyfus scandal in the 1890s."

"Yes, and here we are gathering more intelligence on the Nazi Fourth Reich, the Thousand-Year Reich," Alexandra quipped satirically. "The truth has been lost somewhere along the way. It makes me wonder whether it will ever end. A strategically, loftier truth is known only to a very few."

"So, in applying the black-hat mentality to our white-hat covers, what do you suggest?" Paul queried.

"Perhaps we can do the tourist thing and visit for a while. You can take copious photos. I'll pose. That will reinforce our guise as Black Hat photographers."

"And while we're here, we could take in the Oktoberfest and the beer gardens," Paul exclaimed gleefully. "I'll wear lederhosen if you'll wear a dirndl. It's all about ruses and ploys."

"That's what newlyweds do. You're on. We could ask Dieter Bayer, the bookstore owner, for recommendations. That would fit well in our cover. I like this honeymooner routine, especially when someone else is paying the bills," She chuckled with a mischievous edge in her voice.

"The hotel where we are staying is central, within walking distance of our target bookstore and a few other antique shops on the list. The University of Munich is also close by. We can take a taxi to the Oktoberfest."

Over dinner, they reviewed their strategy for the bookstore visit. They agreed to tell Dieter Bayer, the bookstore owner, they would return for a more in-depth examination of the inventory if certain books became available. They would also bring a couple of their own books to offer as bait for sale or trade if they noticed the shopkeeper didn't have those titles.

"I'm contemplating Dom Perignon and Bolero, *ce soir, mon colonel.*"

Paul smiled.

⊐⊏

A SMALL BELL JINGLED AS THEY ENTERED the bookstore, located on Leopoldstrasse, a short taxi drive from the university. In the background, Richard Wagner's opera, *Der Fliegende Holländer* – The Flying Dutchman, played softly. *A requiem to the Third Reich,* Paul thought. Shelves from floor to ceiling covered every square centimetre of the walls. The top shelf was beyond arm's reach. Inventory was organized into fiction and non-fiction, biographies and autobiographies, religion by sect, poetry by genre, and history by region. All were in alphabetical order. Every title had a category. There was no miscellaneous section that might reflect the mind of a disorderly proprietor.

Alexandra said quietly, "I'm just going to read some spines." She pressed her lips together, contemplating the titles.

Paul browsed the collection of contemporary fiction. He then moved over to Alexandra's side, snuggling and stealing a kiss, as rehearsed with attention to detail equal to the meticulously arranged books on the dusted shelves. The silence was accentuated only by the metronomic tick of an antique chalet cuckoo clock.

"*Guten morgen*," a well-groomed gentleman wearing a tailored werdenfelser jacket uttered in a welcoming Bavarian baritone. "Can I help you?"

"Yes, we're looking for some collectables," Paul replied.

"Any particular authors or genre?"

"Perhaps eighteenth, certainly nineteenth and early twentieth century, ideally before the 1940s. Fiction mostly, pre-French First Republic political philosophy, perhaps Fyodor Dostoevsky, Leo Tolstoy, or Johann Wolfgang von Goethe," Paul suggested reflectively.

"I'm certain we can show you a few titles. We have some on display. Would I be correct in surmising that you are book collectors? Do you currently have a collection?"

"Yes, we are and we're looking to expand our holdings. Mind you, we have a few which we would be prepared to part with should we be able to come to a mutually beneficial arrangement. We have some very rare collectables which we keep offsite in a secure location," Alexandra commented. "One in particular is a first edition near mint *Count of Monte Cristo*."

"I'm always interested, *Frau*, or is it *Fräulein?*" The latter had overtones of a compliment yet its undertone was clear. He had glanced at the polished ring on her finger that glistened in the single ray of sunlight that shone on the counter moments before he posed the disguised question.

"*Frau*," Alexandra replied. "We are on our honeymoon."

"Congratulations. Perhaps in celebration, I could show you a few very fine volumes. If you don't see what interests you, I can make arrangements with a few of my colleagues who are also collectors to provide a list of books in your genre and vintage. How long will you be in Munich? Perhaps you could leave me your names and the name of the hotel where you are staying. I could get back to you by tomorrow."

"How kind of you. My husband and I would be very interested. We first met at the London International Antiquarian Book Fair a couple of years ago. We met again in the United States at the Seattle Antiquarian Book Fair. And the rest is history, so they say."

Paul noted, "We will be in Munich for a few days attending Oktoberfest. Perhaps you could recommend a clothing store where we could purchase lederhosen and a dirndl."

"Ah, you are within walking distance of an excellent clothing store, just one block south. They have a large selection."

"Thank you. And we would appreciate the opportunity to review your list of holdings. We'll be visiting a few other bookstores and antique shops in this district. And your name is?"

"I am Dieter Bayer. I own this store. And this is my wife, Katrina."

Alexandra and Paul returned the introduction with a firm handshake.

Alexandra had already begun her assessment of Dieter. The forensic psychologist versus the bookstore owner. The member of the *Maquis* lineage versus the descendent of the Nazi Third Reich. The white hat versus the black hat, at high noon as the sagebrush and tumbleweed rolled past, driven by a wary wind not yet spent. *De l'audace, encore de l'audace, et toujour de l'audace* – audacity, more audacity and always audacity, she murmured silently to herself. She was her mother's daughter at this moment.

Paul's faint smile said it all. He was by her side as she crossed the Rubicon from merely intelligence gathering to deliberate, probing engagement with the old enemy. The elegant lady had transformed into the biker, a formidable foe for anyone foolish enough to cross.

Dieter met and held her stare. But almost imperceptibly, he leaned back as he ever so subtly drew in a slow breath with nostrils flared. His senses were en garde. Learned investigative techniques from initial graduates of SS Gestapo officer training in the Wewelsburg Castle were activated. *Who was this sophisticated lady? She is not exactly who she presents herself to be, I am sure of that. She is not just a newlywed, a quasi-experienced antiquarian. She is too accomplished.* He concluded that something about her had changed since she first entered his store. Or had his mindfulness been raised for some other reason? She was neither simple nor simplistic.

"Well, that's settled. I'll leave a message for you at your hotel. Enjoy the Oktoberfest." Unlike his introduction, this time Dieter's ascetic face was more stoic and his voice more cautious. He was measuring his customers minutely with marksman's eyes.

"Thank you," Paul replied appreciatively.

"One clarification, if I may enquire," Dieter posed. "You said pre-Second World War. Any particular reason?"

"Yes. I have found that pre-war authors have a certain elegance in their writing style that you don't find in what is referred to as post-modern and contemporary writings. Even the quality of the pre-war 19th and 18th century bindings spell excellence in workmanship."

"I would agree with your assessment and commend you on your selective interest. There is no substitute for quality," Dieter responded in a tone of contemptuous tolerance. He gave Paul a withering gaze. His target did not wither.

As they left the store, Alexandra whispered loudly enough for Dieter to overhear, "I'm confident that we'll be able to add to our collection."

Paul nodded and gazed back at Dieter and Katrina with a reassuring smile in contrast to their pose of professional courtesy.

Dieter continued his reflection, this time on Paul. *Who is he? He seems too cool under fire. His mettle had been tested and found to be invincible although not without scars received under fire. He knew combat.* Together, they were an exponential force, perhaps a threat to be reckoned with. Dieter pondered his options and concluded he should introduce them to an old colleague, an older antiquarian, a seasoned graduate of the castle of his father's vintage, all of whom bore the two-letter gothic tattoo under their right collar. He concluded he might need a more experienced evaluation that had been honed under fire.

As they walked toward their hotel, with no one within earshot, the honeymooners began to de-brief.

"I sense you crossed over the point of no return, ma princesse, to peek into the inner workings of the dark side of the Nazis. Caesar is supposed to have said, *alea iacta est* – the die is cast – when he crossed the Rubicon River."

She smiled in agreement. "The opportunity presented itself. I wanted to test the waters, so to speak. It's a new world and a new game. A calculated, deadly game but a game nonetheless."

"And what did ma princesse surmise? What's your *shrew* telling you?"

"He's not just a bookstore owner. He's one of the black hats, without doubt."

"I agree. But he may be warier of us now. He might not know exactly what we're up to, but we have tweaked his interest."

"And thanks for your support." She leaned over and kissed his cheek. "That is just in case Dieter is still watching." She paused. "And because I love you, more than you may ever know."

"I'll follow the dragon slayer anywhere, anytime. You are

perfectly French, mysterious and alluring. Retirement has never looked so promising."

Alexandra reached for his hand and snuggled closer. "We need to present ourselves as newlyweds."

At the same time, Paul noted, "It's mid-morning, mid-week, we were in the bookstore for about half an hour, and no one else entered. We are within walking distance of other bookstores and businesses. Is this merely a slow day at the office? How does a store like this in the upscale university district show a profit? There has to be money coming from somewhere other than book sales. Thoughts, madame?"

"Astute observation. This street is bustling with pedestrian traffic. But you're right, no one entered the store. Citing the immortal Lewis Carroll, 'curiouser and curiouser, cried Alice.' I estimate that they'd need to turn over approximately twenty books per day given the profit margin, just to break even."

"Let's file that with another observation," Paul commented. "Dieter asked for clarification of my request for pre-war editions. My sense is he was testing us."

It was Alexandra's turn to reflect. "I agree. And your explanation seemed to satisfy him. The only reason he would be suspicious would be if he had something to hide. So, partner, we need to be prepared and rehearsed for all future communiqués with Herr Dieter Bayer. We need to balance the innocence of newlyweds, the professionalism of antiquarians and the stealth of intelligence intelligentsia."

CHAPTER 16

"Let's just do a bit of window shopping," Paul said. His tone alert, his demeanor guarded.

"I didn't know you liked to window shop," Alexandra replied gleefully. *Men usually do not like to window shop. Another characteristic I can admire,* she pondered.

"Humour me on this, *meine frau.* I think we are being followed. Can you see the reflection in the window of the man in the black coat and horn-rimmed glasses? Does he look familiar?"

Alexandra examined the slightly distorted reflection in the window for a moment. "Ah... a ghost from Versailles and the warehouse." She grasped Paul's arm while reaching for the amulet hanging over her heart. "It's not the suspicious man from the couple on the Eurail whom we suspected were Russian agents. The image in the reflection of the window appears to be much shorter. Could Herr Dieter Bayer have dispatched one of his associates to follow us?"

"Possible but I don't think so. We just met Dieter," Paul replied.

Paul got out his camera and started to scroll through a series of images on the back-lit screen.

"I have every picture I've ever taken of you including the ones I took in Luxembourg in front of your mother's house. There were a few that I really liked but they were spoiled by some people walking on the edge of the frames. Here, look. This one looks very similar to the guy following us. Look at the horn-rimmed glasses and what appears to be baggy eyes accentuated with dark shadow-like discolouration. If this person was female, I would conclude that her mascara was running."

Alexandra squinted at the image on the back-lit screen and then at the man reflected in the window. The resemblance was striking. The image of Thon was all she could think about, but he was dead. She had witnessed his henchman pull the trigger, Thon collapse to the concrete floor of the warehouse, and blood ooze from his temple and his budging eye.

"Adapt and improvise in order to achieve the objective," Paul announced in a low but command-and-control declaration.

"What do you mean by that?"

"A military term taught at the Staff College which means be flexible and deviate from the primary plan, if needs be, in order to get the job done. And needs be now. Plan A, I want you to continue to look in the window. I'm going to walk back to a store window a couple of stores away. As soon as I stop, I want you to enter this store and wait at the first counter. I'll watch our friend. If he moves in your direction, I'll retrace my steps and come in behind him. Come back out as soon as you see me. Plan B, if he doesn't follow you, I'll cross the street and move in his direction and see if I can spook him while I take some quick pictures."

"I'll follow your lead," Alexandra replied. Her confidence had been briefly shaken by the close proximity of the man following them. It had also been ardently reinforced by Paul's call to action.

As she entered the store, the man hesitated. Paul immediately crossed the street to move in his direction. The target hurriedly skittered across the street like a feral cat about to pounce on its prey. The man stopped and stood by the window staring in at Alexandra. Paul rapidly closed the distance. The predator had become the prey. Seeing Paul in the reflection of the window and feeling him stealthily grab his black jacket, the man froze. Alexandra quickly exited the store. The trap had been sprung. The target had been caught in a pincer movement. He was cornered, unable to escape the pressure of Paul's full weight wedging him against the window.

"Do not attempt to escape or you will find yourself propelled through this windowpane into the display," Paul ordered in the voice that left no room for negotiation.

"I strongly recommend you do as he says unless you want this to be your last moment alive," Alexandra directed in as stern a voice as she could muster. "Now who are you and why are you following us?" she demanded.

"Can we go somewhere and talk?" the man requested. His voice was weak. His knees trembled. His posture sank. Had Paul not been holding him against the window, he would have slithered to the sidewalk.

Paul and Alexandra were surprised. This was not the response they were expecting. Sandwiched between Paul's powerful weight and accompanying grip, and AV's piercing glare, they moved to the side of the store and into an alley where a delivery van blocked any opportunity for an easy escape even if one were possible.

With his face pressed stiff against the cold coarse brick façade, he wheezed, "My name is Rudolf Heydrich." With that utterance, he felt his throat tighten, almost cutting off his breath. "You knew my father from a brief personal encounter. He was killed in the warehouse in Versailles where he took you hostage, *frau*." His throat tightened even further. He swallowed hard and swallowed again in a vain attempt to fight back his tears. "I deeply apologize for my father's actions and for the terrible stress he must have caused you."

Paul and Alexandra were stunned. Their submissive captive seemed to be both fearful and apologetic at the same time. His general stature was like Thon's but the resemblance ended there. His demeanor was in complete contrast. Thon's eyes were black and intimidating, filled with psychopathic hatred. This person's eyed were blue and timid, filled with tranquil intentions. Thon was arrogant. This person was respectful.

Sensing their astonishment at his candid introduction, Rudolf continued, "Can you release your grip a bit? I don't like violence. You may find that difficult to believe given my father's murderous rampage. But you must understand I am a peaceful person. I do not believe in violence. In fact, I find it to be abhorrent."

Paul found himself responding to the passive plea. He seemed to be sincere. Paul loosened his grip in response.

"Thank you, sir. Ever since I was old enough to understand, I have felt terribly guilty being one of the Führer's children as we are called, the offspring of his SS officers and Hitler's other henchmen, like my father. Through no choice of our own but only by virtue of birth, we have been condemned to bear the guilt of the horrendous deeds of our fathers. Some of my friends have committed suicide because they were unable to reconcile the sins of their fathers. I continue to struggle with my demons." He paused as he attempted to recompose his emotions. "I have wanted to meet you, Alexandra, and the family members of my father's other victims, to apologize. This unfinished quest has kept me from ending my life."

Rudolf seemed petrified but calm, feeling sorrow but relief, apprehensive but assured, as he spoke quietly. The man and the emotion were strangely connected yet distant. Not two distinct personalities but two emotional dispositions in conflict with each other.

Paul relaxed his grip a bit more as he glanced at Alexandra. He seemed as bewildered as Alexandra. She subtly shrugged her shoulders suggesting they should follow along with the changes in their captive's behaviour.

Feeling Paul relax, Rudolf stared at his captors with tears in his eyes. "How do you say that you are sorry for deeds you did not commit yet feel responsible for?" Rudolf asked in a quivering voice. "How do you plan for this moment? I have wanted to make amends for a long time but never knew how. I have sought advice from my psychologist. It was easy enough for him to make suggestions but he isn't here now. I'm at a loss for words although I have rehearsed this moment more times than I can remember. All I can say is that I am so sorry. I feel so guilty for being one of Hitler's surrogate offspring."

Alexandra was the first to break the silence lingering in the emotional abyss created by Rudolf's confession. She placed her forensic psychologist's hat on, dissociating the objective facts of the chronicle from his subjective admission and plea for forgiveness. His apology overwhelmed their expectations like a torrent of raging water unexpectedly released from a dam. "Would you like to talk further, Rudolf?"

He nodded. His increasing emotions holding back spoken words.

Alexandra looked at Paul and motioned for him to relax his grip further still. Her expression of compassion reassured Paul of her sincerity and confidence that her *shrew* had communicated. Paul frisked him for hidden weapons. There was none. Rudolf was not an immediate threat.

"There is a *kaffee* next door. Would you like to sit and tell us your story, Rudolf?" Alexandra prompted.

"Yes, I would like to explain," he replied with a fragile trembling voice.

Although confident in Alexandra's appraisal of the situation, Paul stealthily held on to Rudolf's jacket as they entered the *kaffee*. He would not relax further until he knew Alexandra was out of danger. Seated beside Rudolf, he adopted a sentinel posture.

What transpired was surreal. The level of Rudolf's emotional release was akin to their own when they had read and re-read their respective love letters which Alexandra's mother, Maria, had intercepted and stored in her safe deposit box.

Rudolf explained that he had grown up in Nuremburg where he was schooled in neo-Nazi doctrine, the archconservative politics of the Christian Social Union of Bavaria, the CSU, with its clandestine neo-Nazi cells. His father had insisted he be a strong, active member of the Fourth Reich headquartered in Munich. Yet he was the complete opposite. He found himself constantly conflicted by this right-wing secretive and very violent organization. Ever since he could remember, this group had been his financial lifeline and sole social support network. Yet, he had been bullied by others in this tightly-knit fraternity for being too weak. He saw no escape from his depraved birthright.

He never knew his mother. His father had explained that she had died in an accident. He later found out that his father had murdered her. His motivation to leave the neo-Nazi movement and work to expose it and all that his father stood for was driven by this revelation. His mother had been the daughter of a member of the French Resistance, the *Maquis*, one of his father's intended victims. For whatever reason, his father befriended her long enough for her to give birth to a son, before the father ultimately poisoned her. Had he been born a girl, Rudolf was confident his father would have killed both mother and daughter.

Rudolf ended the story of his life with a committed offer to help the authorities in any way he could. He knew he would not be able to approach an intelligence or policing organization in Bavaria because the black and brown plague had tentacles reaching everywhere. He didn't know who to trust or how to contact anyone who might be in a position to help. Alexandra was now his lifeline, ironically.

Alexandra directed Rudolf to travel to Paris. There he was to register at the l'hôtel Trianon on rue de Vaugirard. They would leave a message for him. He assured them he would be there by the weekend.

After parting company with Rudolf, Alexandra sent a message to Sir James requesting advice and direction. She then sent a message to Alder, via the Harley-Davidson service manager, requesting a meeting in Paris. They would be back by the weekend also.

They then visited a few other bookstores in the region, again leaving a list of titles they were seeking. Dieter Bayer had left a message at their hotel by the time they had returned from their deceptive errands. It would be an early night, after a visit to the Oktoberfest activities. They would need to have their wits about them for their second morning intelligence-gathering mission at Dieter's bookstore. A visit to the Olympiastadion would have to wait for another time.

Not wanting to appear too eager and to add to their Oktoberfest cover story, they arrived at the bookstore mid-morning. They apologized to Dieter for their tardiness suggesting they were still a bit hungover from one too many Löwenbräu. The final strategy of their cover was a picture of themselves in full Oktoberfest attire hoisting beer steins. Dieter complimented them on their traditional festive apparel.

They spent the next half hour mulling over the list of books Dieter had amassed. This was followed by a discussion of which books they would be prepared to bring from their own collection on a subsequent visit to Munich. Finally, they confirmed they would return to inspect a select few of the books on Dieter's list. They would first call to confirm a date. All transactions would be in cash, in Euros. In a show of good faith, they purchased a 1790 first edition of *Faust, ein Fragment* by Johann Wolfgang von Goethe. Alder might shudder when they submitted their first expense account.

The recent encounter with Rudolf brought back nightmarish images of the still-raw events leading up to Alexandra's violent kidnapping and her forced transportation to the warehouse in Versailles. Rudolf's squinting eyes framed in his horn-rimmed glasses brought back threatening images of the gun pointed at

Alexandra's head. His face and short stature were the exact replica of his father which made her dreams more frightening. Only Rudolf's peaceful demeanour separated him from his psychopathic father who, for decades, had stalked and murdered ex-female members of the French Resistance, the *Maquis*, and their daughters.

Neither Alexandra nor Paul slept. Instead, they walked the floor of their hotel room, again describing to each other images and subsequent emotions which had gripped them in those final moments before Thon's henchman moved the pistol away from Alexandra's head to Thon's and then squeezed the trigger. The most horrifying image was the bullet that had passed through the right temple before exiting the left side of Thon's head. Paul had been torn between caring for Alexandra and for Jean, who had been shot by the henchman as he escaped through the side entrance. Paul would have given his life for both his teenage puppy love and his son.

"I didn't attend any pre-retirement seminars, like you," Paul acknowledged. "I just assumed I would naturally fall into a routine of rising late. I would join a morning coffee group of other retirees, play a little chess, perhaps learn to play golf, and catch up on my pile of books to read. Instead, I have chased after a serial killer, been shot at, almost suffered from a heart attack having witnessed you almost murdered after having been taken captive, witnessed Jean being critically wounded, joined a gang of Harley-Davidson motorcyclists, become a partner in a private sleuthing duo under the guise of a Black Hat Photography business which I formed, partnered with French police intelligence, gained the confidence of a CIA agent in order to find out what that organization was doing in France, forged a close relationship with a retired MI6 agent, and moved to Luxembourg. In addition, I fell deeply in love with you again after almost forty years, if I ever fell out of love with you, which I never did." He chuckled at the growing list of daring deeds. "And I have recently committed to chase after Nazi stolen gold held by ruthless members of the Fourth Reich. Did I mention that I am not yet officially retired because I'm still using up the banked holidays I amassed over my career plus the retirement leave I am owed? Have I forgotten anything?"

Alexandra blinked her blurry eyes as she smiled. "That pretty well sums up the major highlights."

"Remind me again why I want to marry you and try to make up for all those years we have been denied!"

Alexandra tenderly wrapped her arms around his neck as a reminder. "Have I told you lately how much I love you?" she whispered. "Think how boring your retirement life would be if I were not in your life."

He returned her adoring embrace and passionate kiss. "Balance, ma princesse, balance. We need to find a balance. Just thinking about you, let alone touching you, keeps me excited. I don't need bullets and black-hatted bad guys chasing after us to raise my blood pressure."

CHAPTER 17

"Good to see you again, Helena," Alexandra opened the conversation. "We have two items to report, Tom. First, we purchased one antique book from the target bookstore in Munich as an expression of good faith. Sorry about the price but we felt that we needed to make a strong commitment."

"No problem. Just keep the receipts so we can keep the accountants happy at the end of the day," Tom responded nonchalantly.

"Dieter Bayer gave us a partial list of books that other patrons of his bookstore might be willing to sell, or trade with a commission. We got the impression there are more," Paul clarified.

"What do you think your next step should be?" Helena enquired.

Paul elaborated, "In Greek mythology, Homer writes in the *Odyssey* about the Trojan Horse and the concept of the fifth column. I think we could bring a few of our more collectable books when we next meet the storeowner. But first, we'd have you place a GPS tracking device in the spine. That would be the fifth column, the Trojan Horse. You could then track it to the new owners. What do you think?"

Helena looked at Tom and then back at Paul. "Brilliant idea. We'd put the bug in a couple of books but not all you offer. That way if they find it for any reason, they might conclude that someone else had inserted the bug and not you. In order to complete the ruse, you could offer to leave your traders with Dieter on consignment. We'd have to set the bait in really rare and desirable books. If you don't have any rare attractive books, we could get a couple locally."

"Alexandra and I could review our current holdings and, if need be, purchase a really rare collectable from a Parisian antiquarian.

We'd let it be known that we just made the purchase. The word will spread fast within the community. Antiquarians, like other ardent collectors, tend to talk among themselves, especially if they have found a treasure."

"Sounds like a plan," Tom chimed in.

"Can we get another advance from the piggybank?" Alexandra asked. "I'm talking a significant amount."

"Not a problem. Just keep your records up to date for the bean counters," Tom directed. "The benefits of infiltrating the Fourth Reich and preventing another attack on an exponential scale akin to what we recently experienced with the nine synagogues, or worse, will outweigh the cost at this juncture. Now, you said you have two items to report on."

"You may find this hard to believe, Tom," Alexandra said hesitantly. She paused briefly before relaying the details of the meeting with Rudolf. "We just explained to him that he might want to speak to the police officer from the Police nationale who worked on the case of his father's murders. We didn't give any names. Instead, we emphasized that this police officer offered to assist us if we ever needed anything. We told Rudolf we had moved on in our retirement and were simply antique book collectors. I don't think he suspected otherwise. He was too consumed with his own emotions after confronting us and was overwhelmed by the reminder of the atrocities committed by his father."

Tom asked, "What does your intuition tell you, Alexandra? And what about you, Paul? What is your sense?"

"I got the feeling he was telling the truth," Alexandra said with a confident nod. "I'm convinced he doesn't like violence. The straw that broke the camel's back for him was the discovery his father had killed his mother and the realization that his father would have murdered him had he been born a girl. He was in a psychological state of acute anxiety and depression because he is thought to be one of Hitler's children similar to the Lebensborn children bred to lead the pure German race. He wants to make amends, somehow. He has had thoughts of suicide and is still in a fragile state but looking for relief from his internal conflict."

"Your thoughts, Paul?"

"I agree with Alexandra's assessment. When I realized that Rudolf was intent on talking to Alexandra, I was ready to do whatever I had to in order to protect her. Even now, I'm nervous for her safety but I have complete confidence in her judgement."

After further deliberation, Tom replied, "I trust your assessments. But we need to be sure. I suggest you contact Capitaine Dominique Roland at the Police nationale and request a meeting with Commandant Benoit Parent of their Counterterrorist Unit. Recommend to Dominique that one or both of them meet Rudolf. Let them take the lead on this. Our focus must remain the Fourth Reich, the stolen Nazi gold, and their link with Middle East terrorists who pose an immediate threat to Western interests. Just keep Helena and me in the loop."

"Agreed," Alexandra confirmed.

"On a related matter, Alexandra, we have intelligence indicating that the Fourth Reich has been moving cash through an Arab bank in Switzerland. You mentioned you had a friend. I think you said his name was Franz and he had a cousin in Geneva in the banking business."

"That's correct. He and his family despise the Nazis for what they did to their fellow countrymen."

"Can you re-establish that relationship and see what you can find out? Remember you are just collecting intelligence, not necessarily hard evidence. You are not to become more involved than that. This New World Order can be deadly. Let others deal with those armed elements. Understood? You are too valuable…" Tom stopped short. They knew what was intended.

"Understood," Alexandra replied.

"And you, Paul?"

"Understood, Tom. Know that my sole *raison d'être* is to protect Alexandra."

"To add to the mix, some stolen gold and treasury bills have surfaced. They were thought to be hidden in Paris in the fall of 1944, just as the Nazis were preparing to retreat from Paris. We believe the mastermind behind the thefts was Reichsmarschall Hermann Göring and his colleagues who, as you know, were responsible for the theft of still unknown quantities of priceless Parisian art and other treasures. The items that have surfaced have been traced to the St. Denis region north of Paris. We are still tracking the exact source. We're close and will let you know as soon as we can confirm. So, mes amis, be very careful out there," Tom re-emphasized. "Any questions?"

Alexandra and Paul replied in unison, "No questions."

Paul added, "No questions regarding your direction to gather intelligence and not necessarily hard evidence but more an observation. You mention the St. Denis region of Paris as where the art, treasures, bonds and gold stolen by Reichsmarschall Göring were stored. Assuming we identify intelligence leading to the recovery of these properties, where will it be held? I agree we do not want it being used to fund Middle East terrorism. But where does it go? If found in sunken ships, the law of the sea as it relates to ownership is quasi-clear. Am I correct in saying that monies and treasures located in St. Denis would be turned over to the Banque de France?

Tom nodded. "Exactly where it will be held is up to the lawyers to determine," he said without hesitation. "To reconfirm, we don't want it funding terrorism."

Paul considered Tom's response. It seemed to be an affirmative response, tagged with an unstated but… he paused, unsure of how much more he believed was necessary to express his intent.

Alexandra followed up. "The provenance of art is easier to trace and return. Gold and bonds less so. In advance of the German invasion, Dutch and Belgian monies among others from their respective national banks were moved to the Banque de France for safekeeping. Gold bars with national stamps embossed would be easier to return. Less so, the supposed Nazi gold. I say less so because the Nazis were infamous for melting down stolen gold into bars and placing their seal on it. Recently, at least one of those bars embossed with the Nazi insignia was reported to have been found in the Bank of England. It was kept there." She maintained Tom's gaze.

"Again, lawyers would determine ownership," Tom replied. "Our purpose is to keep it out of the hands of those whose intention it is to harm the West."

"Thanks for the clarification," Alexandra replied with a thin smile. "No other questions. And we agree that monies destined for terrorism need to be kept secure."

As they parted company with Tom and Helena, Paul said to Alexandra in a loud enough voice for Tom to hear, "Time to strategize regarding our follow-up trip to Dieter's antique bookstore."

Once out of Tom's hearing, Alexandra summarized the intent of Tom's communiqué. "In the final months following the German surrender which was formally signed by Admiral Dönitz who briefly succeeded Hitler, Americans seized large quantities of gold and other monies found in underground mines. It had been moved there after the Allies had bombed the Reichsbank early in 1945. What was found and what supposedly remained in Germany varied. A significant amount seemed to have disappeared, as did other monetary property. Allied nation states complained and continue to challenge Swiss bankers regarding holdings in their financial institutions deposited by the Nazis but unclaimed. We need to ensure that any treasures, art and other valuables found in France remain within the borders of the French Republic."

CHAPTER 18

Paul nodded in concurrence. "At our next coffee meeting with Commandant Parent, we need to pass on Tom's comments. I trust Tom. I'm worried about his superiors though and their masters who, I am convinced, would seize monetary properties under the premise that possession is nine-tenths of the law. Tom is long in the tooth and nobody's fool. I suspect he is aware that he has not been told the truth, the whole truth and nothing but the truth regarding the final disposition of monies located. I have no doubt that his superiors would transport cash, bonds and other easily moveable documents to American military establishments like Stuttgart or Frankfurt and fly them out of the EU as expeditiously as possible. They would do the same with as much gold as could be moved without detection. If not immediately possible, I'm convinced that they would hide it elsewhere for transport at a later date."

"The demarcation between espionage and intelligence gets fuzzy at this juncture. The Cold War is not over and neither is the Second World War," Alexandra added. "We are back into my mother's world – if we ever left it. In retrospect, I am convinced the two people on the Eurail sitting across the aisle were alien agents, more than likely Russian. One would have been deployed to follow you and the other to shadow me. Their purpose is to find out what my mother was working on, perhaps to find her code."

"You are your mother's daughter and I am your partner. There are the new guard, those whom Tom alluded to and those Sir James warned us about, including the new kids on the block like the Chinese and Middle East terrorists."

"But what else? There has to be more," Alexandra conjectured. "Why did my mother spend so much time in the Moselle Valley around Metz and on the Normandy coast around Dieppe? The Nazis were too strategic to have built new concrete battlements and buttresses along the Normandy coast and reinforce existing French fortifications of the Maginot Line with a single purpose in mind. It was an underground labyrinth of connecting tunnels and sub-surface buildings several stories deep in places. Ask yourself, if Hitler's vision was a Thousand-Year Reich, he must have believed the Nazis would win the war. He built these self-sustaining underground metropolises as the nexus and nucleus of the New World Order for his pure Aryan master race. Such a society would need financial institutions filled with gold in a secure location. What better place?"

"He wasn't the only one with a vision of a post-war world," Paul added. "In 1944, the Americans summoned most of the Allies to Bretton Woods, New Hampshire to discuss the post-war world. Those in attendance signed the Bretton Woods Convention. Its purpose was to establish a system of monetary management, rules for post-war commerce and financial relations, led by the United States. The IMF, the International Monetary Fund, was created as the management vehicle for currency conversions, among other purposes. This would be established by linking all currencies to gold and the U.S. dollar. Whoever held the most gold would rule. At that time, it was the United States that held approximately two-thirds of the world's gold. In 1971, the U.S. unilaterally ended the link of the U.S. dollar to gold, thus negating the Bretton Woods agreement in its intent because it was to their advantage. They did so at this juncture because it had become disadvantageous for the U.S. dollar to remain tied to the gold standard."

Alexandra nodded. "The Americans hold their stash of gold in Fort Knox, guarded by the U.S. Army. What if Hitler's plan was to hold all the world's gold he could steal in his subterranean bank and guard it with the army of the Third Reich, today the Fourth

Reich. My mother must have figured it out. That was the sole *raison d'être* of her work in the Moselle Valley and Normandy, which she referred to as her business trips, some of which I accompanied her on as a child."

"Serendipitously, we first crossed paths in Metz," Paul commented. "Our destinies were cast in that crucible."

"My mother told me on several occasions, 'Your roots are those of Charlemagne and your destiny Merovingian. In them you will discover your strengths and unearth the truths.' Sir James said we were destined to be together, to work together, to take on the mantle which he, my mother and Major Mike had carried. It all makes sense. My mother's idea of the Antiquarian Book Collectors' Club has to be the key or at least the compass bearing to the key."

"Where is all the stolen gold? Who is controlling it today? Who is involved in this master cabal?" Paul asked.

Alexandra thought hard. "I have to believe that some of the Allies, especially the U.S., the Canadians and the British were and remain involved in the search. Metz has to be a common denominator."

Paul's inquisitive look urged her on.

"Until 1966 when President Charles de Gaulle withdrew France from NATO, both the U.S. and Canada had military bases in Metz. There was no other location anywhere in France where post-war occupational forces from two previous Allies co-existed. Just Metz. Ask yourself why? When the U.S. and Canada withdrew, they relocated to Germany as close to the French border as possible – Frankfurt and Stuttgart among others for the Americans and Lahr for the Canadians, who also maintained two air force fighter wings in Baden-Soellingen and Zweibrücken on what was the Siegfried Line where Canadian and American air forces shared the same airport. Also, ask why the Russians pushed so hard in the final weeks of the war to take Berlin. To push the communist doctrine?

Supposedly. Or get hold of the stolen gold in the Reichsbank, quickly moved to underground mines in the surrounding area? It's about the gold, what it stood for, and what it has become. So, again I ask, who has it and where is it? Still in the labyrinth of Hitler's subterranean metropolis? The war has been over for decades yet these old Allies still have military forces in southern Germany, particularly the United States. The U.S. bases in Frankfurt and Stuttgart, closer to the Maginot Line, are predominant."

It was Paul's turn to ponder. "Whoever it is, it's an old consortium, a very tight group of individuals who have their own master plan. Bankers must be involved at some level. Your mother with her brilliant mathematical mind was close to figuring it out but didn't have all the details. The letter she left you in the safe deposit box in her bank in Luxembourg alluded to this."

Alexandra and Paul paused in contemplation. She was the first to break the silence. "As Tom advised, our job is to report intelligence only. We leave the heavy lifting to others. So, we report to Commandant Parent and the Republic of France. We leave the heavy lifting of property found on French soil to French hands."

Paul agreed. "For now, we shall meet Capitaine Roland to deal with the immediate priority – Rudolf."

CHAPTER 19

"Dominique, this is Alexandra Belliveau. Do you have a moment?"

"Alexandra! Good to hear your voice. I trust you are enjoying your new house in Luxembourg and that Dr. Bernard is well. How can I help you?"

"I'd prefer to chat in person and in a quiet offsite location rather than explaining on the phone. Can we meet for coffee, perhaps at the Pause Café on boulevard Henri IV, close to the intersection of rue de Lesdiguières? It's just west of the Place de la Bastille."

"Certainly. I can be there in about ten minutes. I'm just at the Central Police Station of the 4th District. I have the feeling that Alexandra is not fully retired. Is there some irony in the fact that the barracks of the *Garde Républicaine* is just down the street from the Pause Café?"

"You are as perceptive as ever, Dominique. And Dr. Bernard is very well. Thank you for asking. He will be joining us."

After relaying the story of the encounter with Rudolf in Munich, Dominique agreed to discuss the event with Commandant Parent and then meet Rudolf. In the interim, she would make preliminary contact with Rudolf to set up a meeting.

"Whether he is a Fourth Reich agent probing our intelligence or truly sincere about his intentions, his contact re-opens this file with a new and intriguing dimension. I'll get back to you one way or another," Dominique concluded.

"Thank you. I look forward to your call," Alexandra replied. "And how is Francine Myette?"

"We haven't had an opportunity to work on any cases together since the Thon file. I'll pass on your best wishes when next we cross paths."

After Dominique was out of hearing, Paul whispered to Alexandra, "You are fishing, ma princesse. Capitaine Roland didn't answer your question about Francine directly."

"Quite true. At our final debriefing on the Thon case, as Dominique describes it, I mentioned to you that I didn't completely trust Francine. My *shrew* was telling me there was more than a working relationship between them. Dominique's indirect response just now confirms my suspicions. I'd say that the connection is personal and, perhaps even intimate. It's just a woman's intuition, a je ne sais quoi interpretation."

"I agree, from a male perspective. This is the first time that we've had an opportunity to meet Dominique alone and not on her familiar turf. Until we know more details, I think we need to be guarded around them both."

"No argument. Let me share something that has been gnawing at me," Alexandra added. "At the debriefing of the Thon case, Commandant Parent spoke a bit of Russian to Dominique when he entered the room. He said, *'Zdravstvui'*. It's a greeting expression between old friends that loosely translates as good health. I saw Francine twitch and flick an eye at Dominique when she heard it. My intuition tells me that Francine may have a Russian connection somehow. So, partner, give me your male interpretation of the circumstances. What is the testosterone saying?"

"I heard somewhere within the bastions of the kingdom of male-dom that Russian women have big breasts and small necks. British women have small breasts and big necks. And French women, well they are just French, *parfait* – perfect."

"I guess I should be flattered, being perfectly French. But Francine's physique is certainly more French than Russian under that magnifying glass."

"Yes, I agree. And that, I suggest, would tend to make her a perfect Russian agent in France. It's just my male intuitive assessment. Francine has a shapely French physique. She is natural blonde with a fair, freckled complexion. This tends to make her too perfect. The operative words here are – *tends to make her*. There are blue-eyed blonde slim Russians in the south of Russia around Rostov close to the Ukraine, for example."

"And that makes her Russian?" Alexandra challenged.

"Yes. That's my point. She's too opposite in that dimension. Let me add to the analysis. French women are not just beautiful but mysterious. French women cultivate mystery, more than I may ever understand. That's what keeps them interesting, sensuous and alluring. Francine doesn't do this, at least not consistently. Therefore, I suggest she may not be authentically French. She is too much of an open book. Also, Francine seems sinuous at times, not sensuous as in sleek, svelte. She's fibrous as in tough like a gristly steak, and that tends to suggest Eastern Bloc influence."

Alexandra gazed in amazement at Paul. "You should be the forensic psychologist, partner, not me." She now had one more trait to add to his constantly growing list of remarkable attributes that she admired.

"A final point, madame. Russians do not smile because when they smile in Russia, others get defensive. Instead, they merely blink and nod rapidly without smiling if they are with friends in public. There is a Russian proverb, 'A smile without reason is a characteristic of a fool.' Francine has a constant smile but it isn't sincere. It's put on. She doesn't smile with her eyes, just her mouth. Therefore, I would deduce that she is not French but Russian by cultural influence and upbringing. Or formal professional training. It's just sometimes but not consistent, and that is worrying. It cries out for caution, as a result."

For a brief moment, they sat looking at each other as a waiter enquired whether they needed additional service. Alexandra dismissed his offer with a gesture of her hand, a cordial French smile and softening voice, "Non, merci."

Paul then broke the silence with a final assessment. "What is most worrying, if our assessment is true, is that Francine may have been successful with her infiltration of our French Intelligence organizations, or perhaps vice versa if a double agent. Your mother consistently warned you not to trust. Sir James continues to warn us not to trust. Both have experience that cannot be ignored. Although we are new to this lethal intelligence game of cobra versus mongoose, we have the wisdom of two of the best to draw on. I'm sure that Major Mike would say the same if he were here. That's the testosterone analysis, madame."

Alexandra sat tapping her fingers on the arm of the chair, staring at nowhere and everywhere.

"I have more estrogen than testosterone, but I couldn't agree more. Your analysis and deduction confirm my *shrew* completely. I'm going to suggest that Dominique and Francine are lesbians and a couple. That's the connection I've been picking up all this time. Francine is a Russian spy or perhaps a French double agent. I don't know if she is pumping Dominique for information, excuse the pun. But my *shrew* is telling me the relationship is honest love. They just happen to be working on opposite sides."

It was Paul's turn to ponder the ramifications of this deduction. "Right, do we talk to Alder or hold back for now? He seems to trust our collective reasoning as much as anyone in his position would. If we explained our analyses and conclusions, I have no doubt he would respond seriously. However, our relationship with Tom is still young. Given that, I'm inclined to have an honest conversation with him. Thoughts, madame?"

"I agree. We should talk to Tom sooner rather than later. It's all about building trust bit by bit. But should we speak to Sir James first? I can send him a coded message requesting his assessment."

"Yes, do that. We can meet with Tom once we hear back. I'd be more comfortable with that scenario."

"I'll do that right now. I'll also text Franz and ask to meet on the pretext of a follow-up to our brief chat in the café parking lot just outside Trier and his invitation to discuss retirement options."

As Alexandra picked up her cell phone, an incoming message buzzed. "I have an email from Walter Burns, Sir James's butler. *Oh my God! Sir James is seriously ill.* Walter strongly suggests that we come as soon as we can."

"Reply that we are on our way."

Alexandra's thoughts were drawn back to the moment she received news of her mother's death. Her *shrew* had cautioned her to prepare for the news the evening before the phone call. Now, she could not get the premonition out of her mind that Sir James had already died. He had not looked well when last they met at his cottage on the coast of Dover. In addition, he had said that he had fulfilled his final promise to Maria by passing on the codes and the background information leading up to their written instructions.

She had always felt loved by her mother yet abandoned by her, left with her uncle and aunt who loved her as if she was their own but she was not. When they were killed in the car accident, she felt alone and abandoned again. She had visited with her mother who had consoled her. Thereafter, her mother had disappeared back into her work as a French Counterintelligence agent. Alexandra grew in independence but regressed into a depressive state after she was advised of her mother's death. There was a brief interlude of a few days when there was no one to help her with her sense of deep loss and regret. She loved her mother so much but hated her for all the abandoned seconds and minutes and hours and days and weeks and months and years. Then Paul appeared in her life at the funeral reception. He had buffered the blow of her mother's death. He was there when she read her mother's letter in which she had admitted to hiding their respective love letters to each other. She could never forgive her mother for keeping them apart but understood her mother's motivation. Now, Sir James was gone. She prepared herself for another loss.

Even with Paul stalwartly by her side to support her through yet another loss, she wondered when it might all end. Jo was her best friend, in fact her only good friend. She knew a lot of people but they were mostly professional acquaintances. It was just Paul who mattered now. What would she do if something happened to him? The consequences would be terminal. That thought frightened her. Collette would be her final resource to prevent her from travelling too far down that dark and desolate path with no light at the end.

CHAPTER 20

Walter opened the door before Alexandra could knock. "I saw you coming," he said with a sense of foreboding in his voice.

"How is Sir James? Where is he?"

"I am so sorry to break the news to you, madam. He died in the hospital shortly after he arrived. I called the ambulance just before I emailed you to come immediately. Know that he loved you as if he were your father. As a parent myself, I know the sincerity of his expression of adoration when he spoke of you. And he spoke each day of his love and devotion."

Silence engulfed the room. Yet there was an absence of peace of mind. The omni sense of abandonment was dominant in her emotions once again. Pain migrated from her temples to engulf her entire head, her neck, her shoulders, her entire body. Her vision became blurred. Screaming in her ears impaired her hearing. She felt nauseous. Memories of her mother leaving once again consumed her thoughts as it had done when she had been informed of her mother's death.

Walter continued, "It was very quick. It appears he had a heart attack. He was conscious only for a brief period, long enough to gasp, 'Damn, damn, I made a mistake. Tell them …' and then the last expression was 'Q'. Just before that he mentioned something about the seventh of the seven. I don't know if I heard him correctly. It didn't seem to make sense."

"Oh, Paul, he's gone," Alexandra gulped in disbelief as she fell into his supportive embrace. Confirmation of the loss exceeded the premonition she had experienced when Walter had texted her. Her mother and now Sir James were gone in a relatively short time. Her father, Philip, she had never known. Sir James she knew for only a relatively short time but seemed to know much longer. He had known of her from the time she was in her mother's womb.

"Come and sit in the sunroom," Walter invited. "I have a pot of tea on and will bring you a cup."

"Thank you, Walter. That would be wonderful," Paul replied, still holding on to Alexandra. "And how are you doing, Walter?"

"Managing, but not by much. Thank you for asking."

By the time they entered the sunroom, Paul was unable to hold back his emotions. They simply stood in each other's arms, weeping.

With tea served, Alexandra sat in her chair, her mother's chair, and Paul in his. Sir James's chair was emptier than they could have ever imagined yet occupied by the essence of his being.

Walter directed Alexandra and Paul to his desk. "Sir James was working at his desk just before the heart attack. If you look, you will see he had written 'Daur' on one line, then a series of numbers on a second line, followed by some other symbols I don't recognize."

Paul looked but could not focus. "Thank you, Walter. We'll review this later in greater detail." His attention was directed toward Alexandra.

"Yes, of course," Walter replied apologetically.

"Oh, God, he was my father in the truest sense," Alexandra spluttered. "He was the living link to my mother. My actual father didn't know I existed but Sir James did. In that way, Sir James was a surrogate, adopted father. I loved him so much for the support and comfort he had provided to my mother, and for the love and protection he extended to us."

The following moments seemed boundless and without pattern. Alexandra's thoughts raced over events of her mother's death, her reunion with Paul, the revelation of the identity of her father, and her own death duel with Thon. She cried again for a father unknown, for a marriage devoid of love, and for a life of loneliness. The pang of hollowness and the pain of abandonment eclipsed everything. Her emotions bubbled as she rubbed the amulet around her neck. It was her tangible link to Sir James and a palpable connection to her mother. In the depths of this emotional landslide, she became acutely aware that Paul needed her. That realization, confidence, complete love and commitment to a life yet to be fulfilled with her soul mate took precedence.

Paul's mind sped in a similar helter-skelter of scattered emotions interspersed with flashbacks of the recent death of Suzette, the wife he had never loved, the near death of Jean, the son he loved, and of almost losing Alexandra to a deranged assassin's obsession. His chest was tight and his breathing laboured. The tinnitus in his left ear was almost deafening. Thunderous roars accompanied a shrill high-pitched monotone. Flashbacks of Sarajevo and the other missions battled for possession of his normally rational mind. An emergent headache pounded in protest. He knew first hand that such invading memories were wolves. You cannot lock them up and hope that the haunting howls will be silenced forever. "*Du calme*," he murmured as he rubbed the ring Sir James had given him, "*du calme*." His breathing slowed, as did his heart rate. Alexandra was his *raison d'être* and she needed him at this moment. His gruesome version of Scrooge's Ghost of Christmas Past would have to wait.

"Sir James had no family, as you are aware," Walter announced. "Accordingly, I contacted his lawyer who has his Will. He will make time to see you when you are ready. Sir James shared his final wishes with me. He would like to be cremated and his ashes released to the winds here on the White Cliffs of Dover. He will fly one last mission in his beloved Mosquito against the forces of the Nazi evil which persist."

"Thank you, Walter," Paul replied. "Perhaps you could make

that appointment with the lawyer for tomorrow morning. Today, we would just like to be with Sir James here in his sunroom and in his garden, his *jardin anglais* as he referred to it when we visited."

⊰ ⊱

THE SIGN ON THE DOOR READ: CLIVE L. Bosworth, Barrister & Solicitor. Alexandra and Paul entered and were greeted by a distinguished gentleman dressed in a traditional dark blue pinstriped suit.

"Please have a seat. Sir James spoke highly of you. I am deeply honoured to meet you both and, at the same time, saddened to have to greet you on such an unhappy occasion. Sir James mentioned that each of you had recently had to deal with a personal loss. Sadly, the process of dealing with estate matters will be familiar to you."

"Thank you," Alexandra replied. "It's never easy." Politely acknowledging the lawyer's introduction was the best she could accomplish at this moment.

"Here is a copy of Sir James's Will. Please note that you have been appointed joint executors and sole beneficiaries of his estate, which is considerable. Here is a copy of the key to his safe deposit box. You will need to bring a copy of the Will with you when you go to the bank. I have prepared a letter of introduction addressed to the bank manager. Probate should be relatively quick. If you wish, I will act as the solicitor for the estate. Please do not hesitate to contact me if I can assist in any way. And again, I offer my deepest condolences to you both. Sir James was an honourable gentleman. I say that in the truest sense."

Alexandra and Paul replied, "Yes, that would be acceptable."

As they walked toward the bank, Alexandra asked Paul, "Can you open the safe deposit box and deal with the contents? The experience of discovering the contents of my mother's is still too raw for me. We'll make joint decisions but I need you to take the lead on this. I also dislike bureaucracy with a passion."

He held her hand more firmly in confirmation of her request. "Yes, ma princesse. I'll take the lead."

At the bank, they presented the letter of introduction from the solicitor, the Will and their respective credentials. The process was as officious in England as it was in Luxembourg and France. They both signed for the contents of the safe deposit box – a deed to the house and property on the cliffs of Dover, a life insurance policy and an envelope addressed to them both.

"The dreaded envelope," Alexandra warily commented as they left the bank. "Let's get it over with straightaway. There's a café. You read. I'll listen."

"My Dear Alexandra and Paul, if you are reading this letter, then I will have died.

"You are the children I never had. Alexandra, I knew of you before you were born, and held you many times thereafter. And Paul, I knew of you from the moment you met Alexandra in Montigny-lès-Metz all those years ago. Maria told me about your special relationship with Alexandra and about the toughest decision she ever had to make – to separate you. She knew you were soul mates and would eventually find each other. I promised Maria I would ensure you met and worked together. I also promised Maria I would protect you as best I could. Listen to your instincts and listen to each other, my children. You are individually blessed. Collectively, you are a *Force majeure*. Together, you can accomplish what Maria, Major Mike and I could not. Together, you can win against the neo-Nazis of the Fourth Reich and other forces of evil. This is your destiny, your mission. You can accomplish this by collectively developing your minds to a point where you neither see nor feel any barriers of time and space. At this point, the horizons will become limitless."

＃ ＃

WALTER WELCOMED THEM BACK TO THE COTTAGE. "Was your visit with the lawyer successful?"

"Yes, and thank you for your assistance, Walter," Paul replied. "For your information, Sir James has left the house and property to Alexandra and me, in addition to the contents. You have been his loyal companion all these years. What are your wishes?"

"I never wanted anything materially from Sir James. I just wanted to serve, to serve him. I have independent means so I do not want for anything."

"Alexandra and I have been talking and we would like to offer you the opportunity to stay on here and take care of the cottage. Would that be acceptable?"

"That is most gracious of you. I would be delighted to stay on and serve you both."

"We were hoping you would accept our offer – we extend it with the greatest sincerity," Alexandra said. "Thank you very much for consenting. You may remain here as long as you like."

"Then that is settled. I will prepare dinner. Please excuse me. I'll bring you a cup of tea."

CHAPTER 21

As they settled into the sunroom, Paul reflected, "Walter mentioned that the last words that Sir James uttered implied that he had made a mistake and Walter was to tell us 'Q'. But 'Q' what? Is it a Q for question? Then there are the numbers, seventh of the seven and the series of numbers. You're the mathematician, madame. What would it mean?"

"Let's examine it bit by bit and put it in the context of the source. Sir James was retired military intelligence and MI6. He was organized and disciplined. He was also compassionate. So, how would a disciplined, compassionate spy think? My mother, the mathematician, influenced him. Both were dealing primarily with the Russians and Nazis. Let's not exclude other infiltrators."

"Sir James became a practicing Druid around the time he transferred to military intelligence."

"Good point, mon colonel. Let's consider that factor in the mix. We need to bear in mind the principle of balance in numerology, like yin and yang. So, is it seven within seven, like Russian egg dolls, a connection to Russian KGB or now FSB? My mother was fascinated with the Fibonacci numbers and the resulting spiral. The seventh number would be eight. What is the seventh of eight in the spiral? Could it be the Fibonacci eight to the exponential power of seven, or seven to the exponential power of seven? Then there is the seventh day of the seventh month – July seventh. Another option could be one-seventh of one-eventh, which would equate to one forty-ninth."

"For this fraction of a seventh, we're assuming that seven is the denominator and one is the numerator," Paul suggested. "But if the numerator was equal to or greater than two, then the options would be infinite."

"Good point. I think that the probability of the latter would be low because Sir James was practical, a practical practicing Druid but practical nonetheless. As such, he may not have considered infinity to be an option. But if he did consider infinity, then we could apply our analysis to a two-dimensional matrix model because he only spoke of the same two numerals, a seventh of seven. That would propose a matrix function of seven in and seven up, or seven in and seven down, or some combination of ratio numbers thereof."

Paul stroked the stubble on his chin with his steepled fingers as he stared up at the ceiling, then out of the window at the garden before settling his attention on the immediate environment of the sunroom. He reached over to the bookshelf where he had retrieved the code books on Sir James's instructions when last he sat in the chair: 'Bring me the fifth book on the third shelf and the third book on the fifth self,' Sir James had directed him. Now, Paul reached for the seventh book on the seventh shelf. It was a book of Wiccan spells, which included invocations, blessings, healing and love spells, bindings and biddings. He flipped through the pages as Alexandra watched.

"There it is," he exclaimed.

"There's what?"

"The blessing, the incantation which he recited when he gave me my ring and the one he recited when he gave me the amulet for you. I repeated it when I placed the amulet around your neck: 'Those that guard and those that bless share, in time, life's timelessness.' It's here. This may be a window to the source of his wisdom. Next to it in the bookshelf is the *Wiccan Book of Shadows*. When we last visited, I asked him about it. He may have led us here for a purpose. You are brilliant, ma princesse. It might be the matrix of a bookshelf and a multi-dimensional matrix at that. There is the seventh book on the seventh shelf. Then there is the seventh page within the seventh book, and possibly a seventh something else within this, and so forth."

Paul's gaze was drawn to Alexandra's fingers tapping on the arm of the chair.

"You are deep in thought, madame."

"Can it be that simple?" Alexandra probed. "I would tend to agree with our analysis thus far. But it is simply simple. Sir James and my mother were simply complex. Recall her code and how Sir James explained it to us. Is the seventh of seven just dogma, pointing to something else?"

"So is the answer in the spells, in the verses of the Wiccan, or beyond? Down the rabbit hole with *Alice in Wonderland*?" Paul queried. "When we walked in his garden, he explained that the flora and fauna co-exist in peace because they depend upon each other. Even the plants that are deadly to humans survive because they benefit the others, the entire garden, the whole. Consider tomato plants growing amongst basil. The basil acts as a natural herbicide."

"It takes two to tango," Alexandra added. "His advice to us when we visited was to trust our instinct and work together. It's about balance as in numerology and in his garden. We are in the right church, so to speak, but perhaps not yet in the right pew. The answer might be in the book of spells because that was the seventh of seven. But the secret, I think, could be somewhere in the words of Wicca and the teachings and symbols of the Druids. Or perhaps another group with roots equally old and mysterious, like the Celts."

"What is your *shrew* saying?" Paul watched as Alexandra's demeanour transformed. She was present in the moment but elsewhere at the same time. Like Schrödinger's cat, she was in two places, in two worlds, at once.

"Sir James is here with us now in his chair, as is my mother. They are our guardians, just as the incantation says: 'Those that guard and those that bless share, in time, life's timelessness.' My *shrew* is telling me that the key is in this invocation and the inherent symbol. Or it could be the key to the lock, which opens the door to the answer. We need to approach it from a simple complex perspective. The answer is important but I think the process of solving the code, finding the answer, is equally if not more important. It's about process, the journey, not the end state."

"Let's talk with Jean about all the other numbers and symbols. He might be able to shed some light on a relationship," Paul suggested.

⊣ ⊢

ALEXANDRA, PAUL AND WALTER, IN ADDITION TO a few professional colleagues, were present when Sir James's ashes were released to the winds over the White Cliffs of Dover. Sir James wanted it that way, with no fanfare. Walter recited the sonnet, *High Flight*, by John McGee: "I have slipped the surly bonds of Earth."

"It was your favourite poem," Walter whispered reverently.

⊣ ⊢

THEY BADE WALTER FAREWELL. ALEXANDRA CONTACTED FRANZ and arranged to meet to renew acquaintances. She requested a personal introduction to his cousin in Geneva who was an assistant bank manager. She also emailed Jo to request a database search for neo-Nazis and Druids.

Paul emailed Dieter and Katrina at the bookshop in Munich to arrange for the purchase and potential trade of books, and an introduction to other Bavarian antiquarians. He also asked Jean to meet to talk about numbers and symbols.

Alexandra sat in her chair, her mother's chair, while Paul strolled among the trees, shrubs and flowering plants in the garden. She sensed her mother's spirit remained in the sunroom with her. Her presence had a calming influence on Alexandra who sought resolution to her conflicted mother–daughter relationship. She understood why her mother had kept them apart because of the lethal threat which Thon posed. But if she was going to be an equal and contributing partner with Paul, she would need to forgive her mother for withholding the love letters. As the aura of her mother appeared, Sir James stood beside her with a calming conciliatory smile. The three seemed to be enclosed in a haze like the ground mist that she had witnessed from the Eurail as she travelled from Amsterdam to Luxembourg en route to her mother's funeral.

Paul's meander through the English garden brought him back to the sunroom at the moment Alexandra opened her eyes to greet him. She seemed more relaxed as she beckoned him with a kiss and outstretched arms. Their embrace was tenderer than ever before and more devoted than a lifetime of affection could ever have created. Their first embrace and kiss experienced in the youthful passion of their teenage puppy love all those years ago in Montigny-lès-Metz bridged the gulf of the intervening years. They were, once again, swirling and dancing in unison like playful otters in a watery recital of a performance unfolding without a scripted finale.

He didn't have to ask if she was all right. He had detected a calming serenity in her embrace that he had not experienced before. The familiar mist passed over the White Cliffs of Dover hugging them as they hugged each other. A presence emanated from the sunroom, the garden, the cottage.

"Je t'aime, ma princesse," Paul whispered as he held her. "Know that I will be here for you forever. We will be as one."

"Je t'aime aussi, mon colonel," she replied, sealing her declaration with a long and tender kiss. "And know that I will be here beside you for eternity and every moment thereafter, in body and spirit and in soul. We became one when we first met in Montigny-lès-Metz. So, not just *my* roots are those of Charlemagne, but *our* roots are those of Charlemagne and our destiny Merovingian. In them, we will discover our strengths and unearth the truths. My mother separated us for good reason. I have forgiven her. Our struggle to find each other had a purpose. And that purpose has been moulded in the crucible of this moment. I never knew my father. Nor did I really know my mother, in retrospect. You experienced both in spirit. We knew Sir James, who was the link. My *shrew* tells me that all three will play integral roles in this endeavour on which we are about to embark."

Their first trip together on the Eurostar back to Paris had been shattered by the call from Thon to Alexandra. His threats were as clear as his assurance that she would be his penultimate victim. Collette, her kitten, as Thon called her, would be his final target. Their extermination would fulfill his master plan, to murder all previous female members of the French Resistance, the *Maquis* and their female offspring. Their deaths would be a reminder to the world that the Thousand-Year Reich was not a fantasy of the deranged Führer. Instead, it was a reality. It would assure Thon's place in history. Unfortunately for Thon, his name would vanish into obscurity.

His pseudonym, Thon, was based on an irony. Sir James had first met Maria after his Mosquito fighter had been had shot down in 1943. She had advised Sir James that there was an unknown traitor in the *Maquis*, who was turning names of Resistance fighters over to the SS Gestapo. Maria, as a teenager, had guided Sir James over the Pyrenees to safety in Spain with a friend. No one knew the name of this collaborator. Sir James referred to him as Thon. It was a contraction in the English language from two words, 'that one.' Through the actions of Alexandra and Paul, Sir James had killed the traitor, and in doing so, had condemned Thon to obscurity.

As the Eurostar sped through the French countryside again with Alexandra and Paul onboard, their mission remained the same – to deny the Fourth Reich the financial resources to achieve world domination. Thon would be turning in his grave knowing that he had not fulfilled his final mission.

CHAPTER 22

"I took from Sir James's book collection both the 1816 and 1818 volumes of the Brothers Grimm, *Deutsche Sagen* – German Legends. I don't recall seeing them in our target bookstore in Munich or on the list that Dieter gave us. The set isn't really valuable but may be a good conversation generator," Paul explained.

"Good plan. That will put the ball in their court to discuss and counter with some of their own. At this time, Tom just wants us to cultivate a relationship and see where the conversations lead. I have no doubt that Dieter is curious about us, more than likely cautious, so let's bear that in mind in all future conversations. We rightly suspect that the two people on the Eurail were foreign agents, possibly Russian, and had us under surveillance. Dieter might now do the same."

"Dieter and Katrina have replied to my email," Paul remarked. "They said they have a revised list of books in our genre. They also have a list of other clients and established antiquarians in Bavaria. Rather than emailing us the list, they want to meet. Most of their clients appear to be interested in buying or selling but may also want to trade. I'm sensing some caution on Dieter's part, similar to when he challenged me about pre-war vintage dates. I get the feeling he and his contacts are guarded and, as a result, want to proceed slowly. That's good because it suggests they have something to be wary about, like their own backgrounds and sources. Your suspicions are on target."

Alexandra nodded. "Franz just got back to me. He can't meet in Bonn right now. One of his nephews is getting married in Geneva. He wanted to know if we could meet there, at the Novotel where we stayed for the psychology conference. That's where they have reservations. He and his wife are planning to stay in Geneva for a bit of a holiday after the wedding. He'd really like to talk to me about retirement and how to move into part-time work, maybe one or two days a week."

"That's all right, madame. I'm not sure he would want to listen to us as experts on how to retire if he got an inkling of our hectic schedules these past several weeks. I was less busy when I was employed full-time at the lab."

"Got your point, partner," Alexandra chuckled. "I really liked Geneva when I was there for the conference. Maybe we could just take some time off ourselves and do the tourist thing, strolling around the lake and hiking up to the old city, just enjoying the sights. The old city on the hill has some great antique shops and cafés. We could even spend an afternoon doing nothing more than gazing at the *Jet d'Eau* fountain in the lake. There's an excellent restaurant just around the corner from the hotel, if it's still open."

"You're on, madame. Not to mix work with pleasure, but we could check out some bookstores while we strolled. That would go well with our cover of being retired antiquarians wanting to expand our collection. Given the known link between stolen Nazi gold in Swiss banks and other stolen artefacts, we might get lucky. On the return leg of the trip back to Paris, we could drop into the Munich bookstore. A bit of a vacation might give enough time for the word to get back to our Bavarian friends. It's a short distance as the Nazi crow flies."

"That's fine as long as we stop and smell the roses. I'll get back to Franz and ask if he could make hotel reservations for us for a week. That should give us enough time. Let's decide which books we want to bring with us as bait to trade, loaded with Tom's GPS tracking device. By the way, there's a Harley-Davidson dealership in Geneva."

"What are you laughing at?" Paul asked.

"Jo's email started with: *This one will cost you some serious saddle time before it gets too cold to ride.*"

"Sounds as though she got a few good hits on your Druid and Nazi research request."

"I expect you're correct as she has some attachments." Alexandra opened the first Word document. "Well, isn't this an interesting twist of events! Curiouser and curiouser. This is a major IOU from Alexandra to Jo."

"Don't keep me in suspense. What's she got for us?"

"She says there was a Druid Lodge in Zürich with affiliations to Munich and Nuremburg. It was created just before the First World War but may have closed sometime after. There's a reference to Trier, and an Order of Bards and Druids, and their goddess *Nemetona*. Jo mentioned this because Thon was from Trier."

"A coincidence?" Paul commented curiously.

"She goes on to say that Druids were active in Bavaria but primarily as a fraternity. It seems to have been a cauldron for early Nazi thought in the late 1920s and early '30s. Yet, Hitler supposedly banned this Druid Lodge after he was elected Chancellor in 1933. It went underground after that. Since the war, there has been a resurgence of interest and a growing neo-Nazi membership."

"This could very well be of interest to Tom and Helena but I think it can wait until we return. Tom wants to keep the e-traffic to a minimum."

"When we meet Franz and his wife, let's ask nonchalantly if they know anything about this connection, especially the Munich-Nuremburg-Zürich link. If they ask about my motivation, I can just say that one of my former students was from Zürich and had mentioned it. I didn't know much at the time, so I'm just interested."

"You're smiling with that mischievous grin again, madame."

"I'm just thinking I could get used to this subsidized honeymoon sleuth gig. We're still well within budget, based on our cash advance, so what else can we do to promote our white-hat, black-hat clandestine activities?"

"I'm learning to love your designing mind. Let's ponder like Pooh Bear over a pot of honey or a couple of snifters of cognac."

"Or better yet, Dom Perignon and Maurice Ravel's *Bolero* softly playing in the background," Alexandra whispered as she drew her finger over his cheek.

"*Candens es*," he replied.

Alexandra smiled. "Perhaps Marc Antony said that to Cleopatra."

CHAPTER 23

Alexandra felt her cell phone vibrate, "I might as well go back to work full-time as I got fewer emails and text messages back then, than now as a quasi-retiree. This one is from Capitaine Roland regarding a recent interview she conducted. She must mean with Rudolf. She wants me to call her on a landline and not my cell."

"Dominique. It's Alexandra. What's up?"

"Just want to bring you up-to-date with our mutual acquaintance. He is a trove of valuable intelligence about neo-Nazi activity. If only half of it is true then we have a major breakthrough. I have checked his stories out and it appears he is the most valuable informant to come along since Vasili Mitrokhin blew the lid on the history of the KGB. I can't thank you enough. We have him in a safe house and will be debriefing him for several more days. He said that the bookstore in Munich where he happened to see you is a beehive of neo-Nazi activity. I'm not sure why you and Paul were there but if you go back, you need to be very careful. Our mutual acquaintance said the neo-Nazis are an extremely suspicious tight-knit group. More importantly, they are unreservedly ruthless and will stop at nothing to get what they want, most notably silence. They have stockpiles of firearms and explosives, and connections in the Middle East. He confirmed they were involved in the recent bombing of the synagogues in the U.S."

"Thanks," Alexandra acknowledged. "It's reinforcement of intelligence we already suspected."

Capitaine Roland continued, "In addition to the Middle East, they have renewed relations in North Africa, which Field Marshal Erwin Rommel and his successors had cultivated when they commanded the Afrika Korps. Nazi spies attached to SS Intelligence Units had been inserted as early as 1937, four years before Rommel's Panzer tanks rolled onto the desert. Many of these spies remained after the Nazis were defeated and pushed out of North Africa in 1943. These spies were augmented in the latter months of the war when Admiral Dönitz was preparing to sign the surrender treaty. Still others were inserted as a third wave by the hierarchy of Fourth Reich during the Cold War. Clearly, the vision of the Thousand-Year Reich was not defeated in 1945. On a positive note, French, British and American Intelligence services were active in North Africa in the wake of Allied military victories and remained aware of Fourth Reich Intelligence activities. As an added note, the Nazis buried caches of supplies in advance of Rommel's invasion. They contained fuel, food, water and a considerable amount of gold. Unfortunately, the winds have altered the topography of the sand dunes and their whereabouts remain unknown."

"Thanks for the intel, Dominique. I'll discuss it with Paul. Next time you speak to our mutual acquaintance, can you ask him about any links between neo-Nazis and Druids in Munich or Nuremburg and Zürich? I'll explain later. One last question. Have you spoken with Commandant Benoit Parent about this, or anyone else?"

"Benoit has been with me during the interviews. Francine Myette from French Intelligence is also aware. Why do you ask?"

Alexandra took an anxious breath before responding. "My mother used to always remind me to be careful, Dominique. So, I pass on to you that need for caution."

"Thanks for the concern. I'll be in contact with more updates. Take care and say hi to Paul for me."

Alexandra hung up and stared at Paul with a gaunt expression and wide eyes.

"Oh my God!" she exclaimed. "Oh my God! Francine is in the intelligence circle."

After a moment of somber reflection, Paul said, "That raises the stakes considerably. I think we might need to meet face-to-face with Tom. He said he was going to Interpol in Lyon. He might be available to meet in Geneva by the time we arrive. How about sending an email to the service manager in the Harley dealership? Say that your bike has broken down and you need a replacement clutch cable delivered by the service rep. Onsite consultation is required on its installment and proper use."

CHAPTER 24

"Franz just texted me back. He and his wife are running a bit late with the pre-wedding family activities. He wants to know if we would like to meet them at the restaurant on rue des Pâquis just around the corner from the hotel. He has made reservations for seven. His cousin Karl, the assistant bank manager, will be with them."

"Let's leave shortly so we can arrive before them. That way, we can adjust the seating. You sit beside Karl. That will let you cast him under your mystical spell, as Franz described your influence when we first met at the coffee shop near Trier. You can draw him into your sphere with some binding incantations."

"Me, influence others?" Alexandra jokingly responded with the innocence of a scheming little schoolgirl.

Paul just smiled and returned her rascally gaze. "Ha! Me, influence others? she asks." Paul laughed. "Yes, madame, I speak from experience. I am a willing recipient of your spells."

As they walked to the restaurant, they lamented the absence of such good-humoured loving exchanges in their previous marriages.

They had barely started to sip their aperitif when Franz arrived with his wife and cousin.

"Alexandra, it's good to see you again. You remember my wife, Anna? This is my cousin, Karl. And Paul, nice to see you again. Can I interest you in a BMW rather than a Harley, or would that negatively affect your relationship with Alexandra?"

"Ah, the Harley wannabes never give up. As JFK so eloquently commented when he introduced Jackie on his first visit to Moscow, 'I'm with her.'" Paul continued to smile at Franz, who introduced him to Anna and Karl.

"Come and sit beside me, Karl," Alexandra said cordially. "Franz tells me you are an assistant bank manager here in Geneva. Banking is a profession that has always intrigued me. I've never really been good with numbers and finances beyond balancing my chequebook. Why is it that Switzerland is a banking center of choice for so many non-Swiss investors?"

While Alexandra asked Karl about non-resident depositors, Paul kept Franz and Anna entertained with stories of interesting cases he had worked on at the lab. Without divulging any details, Paul mentioned that Jean had been injured recently. He asked Franz but especially Anna for advice on trauma consulting. This discussion kept Franz and Anna talking exclusively to him. When Alexandra re-joined the larger conversation, Paul adopted the position of second fiddle in the quintet. After dessert with schnapps, they bid Karl, Franz and Anna a good evening, and returned to the hotel.

"Okay, give me the scoop on Karl and Nazi gold and other suspicious deposits."

Alexandra began, "Franz had mentioned to me a while back that for years Karl has been emotionally torn between his loyalty to the banking code of ethics, which requires complete confidentiality, and his personal ethos which deplores all that ever was Nazi and all that is today neo-Nazi. This was evident in my conversation with Karl this evening. Initially, he just talked about generic banking. Then when I asked him about non-Swiss resident deposits, he became quiet and admitted that his anxiety has increased over the years to the point where he has taken some stress leave. He hasn't seen a psychologist or clinical counsellor because he doesn't feel comfortable discussing the details of such sensitive topics, especially with any professional from Geneva or other locations in Switzerland. German is the language of education and culture in virtually all of Switzerland. He did say that for many traditional Swiss with German ancestry, loyalty remains with the Fatherland.

He alluded to the fact that some sizeable sums have recently been transferred to the branch of a foreign bank here in Geneva. He knows what is going on and this is causing him increased stress once again."

"Where do we go from here? What's your *shrew* telling you?"

"I put on my psychologist's hat and, as you suggested, I cast my spell of compassion. I offered to meet him for breakfast to continue our informal counselling session. He very much appreciated my invitation. My *shrew* tells me he was immensely relieved just to talk to someone he could trust in a relaxed yet confidential atmosphere. I expect he will disclose much more tomorrow."

"Do you want me to join you?"

"As much as I love you and want you with me all the time, I think not. It's a trust issue and I have gained his trust."

"Understood. Call me when you've finished."

After a contemplative pause, Paul reflected, "This was a good day at the office, madame. Would you like a nightcap?"

"Oh yes! We'll put it on my tab as a business expense."

"We worked well together this evening for our second round in the ring as a tag-team. Sir James saw it and I am now confident in our ability to succeed in this business of sleuthing."

Alexandra smiled over the first sip from her snifter of cognac. "After our meeting with Dominique, you mentioned that French women are just perfect. So, you think I am not just beautiful but secretly mysterious."

"You cultivate mystery, ma princesse, and I find that wonderfully alluring. And I love you all the more for it."

Alexandra could not remember when André had ever complimented her in any manner close to these words. She wrapped her arms around Paul's waist, leaned forward until the tip of her nose touched his, and whispered as she gazed into his brown eyes, "You may never know how much I love you at this moment."

"If it's anything like the love I feel for you, then perhaps I do. Words cannot describe my feelings. Actions speak louder than words."

"Yes, but keep the words coming, forever. We have a lifetime to make up. I hurt so much inside just thinking about what we missed, what we could have had if only...."

Their kiss ended the poetry of Milton's *Paradise Lost* and replaced it with the sensuous affirmation of *Paradise Regained*, never to be set asunder.

꜒ ꜓

PAUL'S PHONE BUZZED WITH AN INCOMING MESSAGE: "Meet me in the lobby."

"I think from your subdued smile that Karl was forthcoming at breakfast, perhaps in ways you weren't expecting."

"Let's go for a stroll along the lake. You won't believe what he revealed."

"I'm all ears, madame."

"Last evening, Karl mentioned that he was experiencing considerable stress because he had a pretty good idea where previous funds had been transferred. He is confident that the latest transfer of money from banks in Zürich and Geneva was used to finance the recent attacks on the synagogues in the U.S. That revelation has left him feeling tremendous remorse. He wants out, or at least he wants to be able to prevent further destruction and death. His banking code of ethics has now taken a back seat to his integrity – his desire to do what is right and not just follow policy. But he is convinced there is someone else pulling the strings of the neo-Nazis."

"Does he know who?"

"No, and that is worrying. He is convinced his manager knows and may be involved somehow."

"Is he fearful, for his own safety or life or for his family?"

"Yes, and he knows he must tread carefully. He is really upset that the most recent releases of bearer bonds that Tom mentioned are being used to plan a series of Islamic terrorist attacks across Europe, Southeast Asia and North America, most to be funded by the proceeds of stolen Nazi funds. Switzerland may not be immune from future attacks. The thought of his family being targets and victims drove a dagger deep into his soul. When he mentioned this, his eyes welled up."

"What did you say to keep him talking? To console him?"

"I merely said that from my work as a forensic psychologist, I knew someone at Interpol who was completely trustworthy. He wants to meet this person as soon as possible because he believes the attacks are imminent. He can't bear the thought of doing nothing. He remembers too well the stories his parents told him about apathetic citizens who turned a blind eye while the Nazis systematically exterminated Jews and Gypsies and other undesirables in concentration camps."

"There's no lingering doubt now. Time to send the Harley service manager an email explaining that the clutch cable is broken. Delivery of a replacement and onsite installment is needed."

CHAPTER 25

Tom's text to Alexandra read: "Just leaving Lyon. Should be there in time for lunch. Meet at the Café Restaurant next door to Le Saint–Gervais on rue des Corps-Saints."

"He seems more cautious than usual," Alexandra suggested to Paul. "I think other forces are at play, some coming from his organization and others external. None is in his orbit of influence." She paused for a moment. "I still trust him and remain confident that he would not knowingly put us in danger's way. The operative word is knowingly."

Her concern caused Paul to seek confirmation or clarification. "You said you still trust him. An interesting expression. Why would you not? Where is that feeling coming from?"

She drew her eyebrows together and looked upward searching for an explanation, considering the pragmatic nature of his question.

"I trust Tom because of his close connection with Major Mike whom my mother and Sir James trusted without any doubt. Based on that relationship, my *shrew* is telling me he is not a threat. His integrity is solid. The source of the threat is elsewhere."

"Right," Paul responded with a terse nod. "I ask not because I don't believe you. I'm trying to understand your intuitive reasoning."

"If you find out, let me know," she jested with a quizzical twist of her lips, which accentuated the humour.

"The restaurant Tom mentioned isn't far from the train station, about a twenty-minute walk from here," Paul confirmed.

"Dominique is calling. Damn, we need to retire completely."

"Alexandra, I just want to update you on our mutual friend.

2

Tomorrow, he will be taking us to a house in Moulin-lès-Metz where his father used to live. Apparently, his father buried some stolen gold and jewellery, in addition to documents. A map will identify the whereabouts of other significant caches. The address is at the end of Chemin des Grandes Vignes. Paul might remember it as it's very close to Montigny-lès-Metz where he lived. Commandant Parent will be with us. I'll call you back and let you know what we find."

"Take care, Dominique. Keep your radar up," Alexandra replied.

"One last point, Alexandra," Dominique added. "Our mutual friend did confirm a relationship between Druid lodges in Munich and Zürich. He'll explain more on our trip to Moulin-lès-Metz. He emphasized the need for great caution because the association between this mysterious Swiss lodge and the Fourth Reich is very close. The membership demands adherence to a vow of silence, a vow of invincibility. Those who do not comply have their affiliation revoked, permanently." Dominique's blunt pause was all the emphasis Alexandra needed to understand the finality of the terminology. "I'll call after we leave Moulin-lès-Metz. And you take care, also."

"You're rubbing your amulet. What's going on?" Paul enquired.

Alexandra relayed Dominique's communiqué. "We need to be vigilant. Something's not right and I can't focus any further now. That's worrying. First Tom, now Dominique. My sense is that we only chat with Tom about the Zürich-Druid connection, Karl's information regarding stolen gold and deposits of other securities in Swiss banks, and Dominique's trip to Moulin-lès-Metz with Rudolf. I don't want to mention Karl's name to Tom for now. Let's just say we need to confirm the source. Also, I'm not yet comfortable talking to Tom about our suspicions concerning Francine. Something is just not right. I detect imminent danger, perhaps not directed towards us. Something is going to happen and it will have a major impact. Oh, I wish that Sir James was still here."

"I'll support you. You take the lead in the discussion with Tom. If he asks me for my opinion, which he usually does, I'll simply say that I completely agree with your assessment. And Sir James is here. He is telling us to proceed slowly and warily, and not be too willing to trust others completely."

⊣⊢

AFTER BRIEFING TOM ON THE DRUID-ZÜRICH LINK, banking intelligence and Dominique's update regarding Rudolf, Paul and Alexandra suggested their next step would be to rendezvous with Helena LeDuc to pick up the bait books with the GPS tracking devices. They would then return to Munich to meet Dieter at his bookstore. If they weren't able to sell the bait books, they would leave one of them on consignment as a sign of good faith and an investment in a maturing relationship.

"Well done," Tom acknowledged. He again reminded them that their sole purpose was to gather intelligence and report back only to him. They would await further instructions before contacting Dieter Bayer after this next visit. Tom explained he didn't want Dieter or any of his antiquarian associates to become suspicious. "Building relationships in this New World Order takes many slow baby steps."

Tom would contact Helena LeDuc about the bait books and ask her to set up a time and place for the handover.

"You've mentioned repeatedly to report only to you. Is there anything we need to know?" Alexandra enquired, openly revealing her cautiousness. Her *shrew* was signalling a higher level of wariness.

"Just be vigilant," Tom replied. "There are ears and eyes we don't know about."

Alexandra had never seen him not smile. Even at the hospital after she had been abducted and almost killed, he managed to reassure her with his customary slim smile that all was well.

⚐ ⚑

"Bonjour, c'est Aulne." – *Hello, this is Aulne.*

"J'écoute" – *I'm listening.*

"Я буду на связи. Завтра они поедут в Мулен-ле-Мец." – *I have been in contact. They will be going to Moulin-lès-Metz tomorrow.*

"Да. Принято." – *Yes. Acknowledged.*

CHAPTER 26

"How well do you know them and what they have been up to, Benoit? How much do you trust them?" The Commissionaire de police, Brigitte Poulin, asked tersely. The nature of the betrayal prompted her intensity.

Benoit absorbed the current of every inflection uttered. The Commissionaire's *bête noire* was the thread of suspicion that had been gnawing at him since his recent promotion and subsequent briefing. But today, the stark reality struck at his core. Benoit was all too familiar with the Commissionaire's rapier mind and reputation for relentless pursuit of duplicity and betrayal while doggedly supporting the faithful.

"I've known Dr. Bernard for years and trust him completely. You've read his file. I trust Dr. Alexandra Belliveau to the same high level. Although I haven't known Dr. Belliveau for as long, I'm familiar with her work and she comes with impeccable credentials and references. She is unreservedly trustworthy. I'd put my life on the line for them."

"Dominique did."

"Perhaps a poorly chosen expression at this time," Benoit acknowledged. "But I stand by my commitment to them both."

"I can sense a closer relationship, Benoit. Talk to me."

"As you well know, Commissionaire, we have suspected a leak, more likely a Russian mole, not necessarily in our ranks but infiltrating our bastions. Could be American. Perhaps Tom Hunt, or someone in his organization. I'm not excluding Interpol. I became aware that Tom was recruiting Alexandra and Paul to become confidential informants for him and the CIA. I got to them first. They assured me they would keep me informed of Tom's activities, and they have done so consistently. Alexandra and Paul are steadfastly loyal to the Republic of France, first, last and always. That's the relationship you may be referring to. So, when I say I'm completely confident in both, I mean just that. I say from firsthand experience that they are devoted to our cause."

"That was a gutsy move on your part to get them to commit to us. Bring them in as soon as possible. When they arrive, put them in separate rooms. We'll interview them individually first, then together. Don't mention anything until they are together. I want to see their collective reaction."

"With all due respect, Commissionaire, they're not suspects. They're on our side and if you want to invest in a more formal working relationship with them, which I strongly suggest you do, you shouldn't treat them as suspects. We treat them as colleagues, as the professionals they are. We meet them together in my office, not in the interview room. That would set the wrong tone."

"This will not be a career-enhancing move for either of us, Benoit, if you're wrong or if anything more goes sideways."

Benoit knew that the Commissionaire did not tolerate human foibles or weak arguments. Her default mode was to hold everyone immediately accountable for their actions. Benoit had stood his ground before with Brigitte and would do so again.

"I'm not wrong and I place my reputation and my career on the line for them," Benoit restated.

A silence settled in the room as the Commissionaire tapped her fingers on the table and took a series of slow deep breaths. "As you wish. Call them in. We'll meet in your office all together. But we brief them as planned with no deviation from the script, for now. This is on a need-to-know basis. Is that understood?"

"Understood." The ramifications of the Commissionaire's guarded approval were abundantly clear. Benoit was confident in his unquestioning defence of both Alexandra and Paul.

"By the way, I admire your courage, Benoit. This organization is inhabited by too many wimps who lack integrity," the Commissionaire announced.

Any acknowledgement by Benoit would have been inappropriate. Instead, he merely picked up his cell phone and speed-dialled as he left the office.

"Alexandra, this is Commandant Parent. Where are you?"

"On the Eurail en route to Paris. We should be there in about a half hour."

"Is Dr. Bernard with you?"

"Yes, he is. Why do you ask?"

"Can you come to my office as soon as you arrive? I'll explain when you get here."

"Yes, certainly."

Alexandra put her cell phone back in her pocket.

"Who was that?"

"Commandant Parent. He sounded very formal. He asked us to meet him in his office as soon as we arrive. I think it has something to do with Rudolf."

"Why would he be calling and not Dominique?" Paul queried.

"Good question. Not sure. But we'll soon find out." She was as curious as Paul regarding Commandant Parent's request, more like a dictate. Her *shrew* signalled that she needed to remain on high alert.

⌐ ¬

"ALEXANDRA, PAUL, THANK YOU FOR COMING AT such short notice." Commandant Parent extended his hand in a semi-formal fashion. "You know Commissionaire Poulin." He directed them to a round meeting table adjacent to his desk.

"You sounded a bit distant when you called, Benoit," Alexandra responded, noting his stoic expression and reserved posture.

Commissionaire Poulin was equally reserved as she stared at Benoit as if he had called the meeting on her insistence.

Benoit paused briefly while his eyes darted from Alexandra to Paul and back again. His temporary silence was not an indication of calm. "There's no easy way to break this news to you. Dominique and Rudolf are dead."

Alexandra and Paul gasped as they stared at Benoit, the Commissionaire and each other. "How? Where? What happened?" Alexandra asked in rapid succession.

Benoit exchanged a terse nod with the Commissionaire then provided a formal detailed summary of what had happened. "As you are aware, Rudolf was taking Dominique to a house in Moulin-lès-Metz where his father had lived briefly in the 1960s. Dominique, Rudolf and another agent were in one vehicle. I was following in another. As they turned left off rue de Moulin on to Chemin des Grandes Vignes, over what had been the railway tracks, multiple shots rang out from behind a reinforced concrete fence of the first house on the right. It was over by the time I had exited of my vehicle. The assassin escaped over a brick wall into the compound of what had been the old French army wine factory, now a storage facility for the Ministry of Cultural Heritage."

"But how?" Alexandra exclaimed in disbelief.

"We have reason to believe that the assassin and others behind this attack somehow had prior knowledge and, as a result, were waiting for Dominique and Rudolf," Benoit replied. "Although the residents of the house were at work, the shooter would not have had time to set up and just wait. Every detail had been expertly planned and executed. The media are aware of the shooting but have only been told that the names of the deceased are being withheld pending notification of the next of kin."

In a deliberately disciplined response, Alexandra adopted the professional mode she had done so many times before when confronted with violent deaths and murder. The only difference was her knowledge of the victims. She had developed a personal and professional relationship with Dominique. *Had I not warned Dominique sufficiently?* she wondered. But, in the company of Commandant Parent and the Commissionaire, now was not the time to question herself, to second-guess. She would talk with Paul who was the only person with whom she could share her thoughts, feelings and senses.

Commissionaire Poulin took control of the conversation. Her tone had a hard edge. "Right now, we need to debrief you both on all the events from your first encounter with Rudolf to your final contact with Dominique. In particular, we need to know if you spoke with anyone else about this case. Dominique kept excellent case notes and Benoit had been with her in most of the interviews with Rudolf. But we need to find the leak, and fast. That is our immediate priority."

"Ironic," Paul uttered quietly as he shook his head from side to side.

"Explain," Benoit queried, not challenging the motivation of his statement but requesting clarification for the benefit of Commissionaire Poulin who was not as familiar with Paul's means of communicating. His expressions were as much a prompt for his own inquisitive mind as for the benefit of others in his team.

"I know the house you described where the shooter was hiding. The Nazi SS commandant for the Moselle region occupied it during the war." After a pause, Paul exclaimed with a sigh of resignation, "The war isn't over. The Nazis have not been defeated. The Fourth Reich continues to rule. Perhaps the myth of the Thousand-Year Reich is not a myth."

Alexandra and Paul described the events from when they first sighted Rudolf in Munich to the final phone conversation Alexandra had with Dominique, including the brief confirmation regarding the

Druid-Munich-Zürich connection and Rudolf's caution to them. They also described their communiqués with Tom Hunt, which brought an immediate yet subtle reaction from both Benoit and the Commissionaire. An apprehensive silence filled the room.

"I get the impression that you may not be telling us everything, Alexandra," Benoit commented. "Now is not the time to hold back. Even your slightest suspicions or feelings could hold a clue."

Alexandra glanced at Paul who deliberately nodded in response. She looked at Benoit and cautiously affirmed, "We have a concern. Both Paul and I have been uncomfortable with Francine Myette since we first met at the Thon briefing that Dominique held. We get the feeling that Francine is a foreign agent, more than likely a Kalashnikov. Also, I have a feeling that Francine and Dominique were in an intimate relationship. There would have been some pillow talk if we are correct."

Commissionaire Poulin and Benoit excused themselves for a moment and left Alexandra and Paul in the office. They went to an adjacent room where they were met by a professional, unassuming yet commanding female figure.

The Commissionaire needed clarity. "Events have changed, madame. What is your direction, given the extent of their knowledge regarding Francine, and the relationship between Francine and Dominique?"

All three silently stared at the monitor tracking Alexandra and Paul.

"As you previously described, they are the best," the woman confirmed in a soft but deliberate tone. "Bring them up to speed on Francine but caution them about keeping all details completely confidential. Remind them this has a Thon threat level. Adjourn this meeting and request that they come back tomorrow morning at which time we will invite them into the fold."

"Will do, madame," Commissionaire Poulin replied without

hesitation. "Continue to take the lead, Benoit, as they're your people."

They returned to Benoit's office and again sat across the table from Alexandra and Paul.

Benoit re-engaged. "Individually, you are the best. Together, you are a superior team. You know that what I am about to tell you demands the highest security clearance. As a benchmark, multiply the Thon threat level exponentially. Any questions?"

Alexandra and Paul sensed the seriousness of the pending communication. They replied in unison, "Understood."

"You are correct in both your assessments. Francine Myette is a Russian agent. We have known this for over a decade. She was trained by the KGB and stayed with that organization until it was dissolved. She then transferred to the new Russian spy agency, the FSB. Dominique was aware of her background and courted her in a personal relationship. Francine was the third person in the car with Dominique and Rudolf. She survived with serious but non-life-threatening wounds. We will report that the assassin also killed her."

"Where is Francine now?" Alexandra asked, still reeling in disbelief from the news Benoit had passed along.

"I'll get to that. After the shooting, Francine was distraught about Dominique's death. She felt she had been set up by her own people and betrayed because she had also been an intended victim. After the ambush at Moulin-lès-Metz, Francine approached me and came clean regarding her FSB and KGB background. She reassured me that, although she had been in constant contact with her Russian handler, she had not disclosed any details about Rudolf or the trip to Moulin-lès-Metz. Her Russian handler did mention that the word was out about an ex-neo-Nazi who had defected. Rudolf's name was not mentioned though. Francine felt that her handler was hedging so she became suspicious. Like the West, the Russians want to get their hands on the stolen Nazi gold to fund Islamic terrorism against the West as surrogate fighters. Your enemy's enemy is your friend. The Cold War is far from over as you rightly surmised, Paul. In response to your question, Alexandra, Francine has been moved to a safe house."

"So, if Francine wasn't the leak, who was?" Paul asked somberly.

"We suspect the leak in the intelligence that led to this incident may be with Tom Hunt. We don't believe Tom has gone rogue but someone close to him in the CIA or Interpol is the Russian mole. We picked up some e-traffic just as you were leaving CIA headquarters in Virginia and again just before Dominique, Rudolf and Francine left for Moulin-lès-Metz. There may be another internal leak, but we haven't been able to identify it."

"One final question for clarification, Benoit," Alexandra asked. "Did Dominique leave any notes about connections between Druids, Zürich and neo-Nazis?"

"No notes, but Francine did say that Rudolf had been recruited into the Druids by the Munich Lodge. It is a beehive of neo-Nazi activities. So, you need to be on highest alert if you find you have rubbed shoulders with any of them. Our direction to you is to avoid them at all costs at this time. Instead, just report back. Only present yourselves to Dieter and Katrina as recent retirees, antiquarians and newlyweds. Nothing more. Carry on working with Tom Hunt but say nothing to him about our meeting today. And keep in close contact with me through our normal channels. Any questions?"

"No questions, Benoit," Paul replied. Alexandra nodded in concurrence.

"One last point, well two points," Benoit added. "Alexandra, don't ask Jo to query any topics. And Paul, don't ask Jean to conduct any inquiries. Until we know for certain, we must assume that all online queries you make, either directly or through others, are being monitored. Use non-e-traffic when communicating with me. If the leak is in the CIA, the Russians may know of your association with Tom at least. The good news is that the probability of the Russians telling the neo-Nazis anything is infinitely small because the Battle of Stalingrad is still too raw. Nazis aren't necessarily anti-Communist but ardent Communists are certainly fervent anti-Nazi. Finally, beyond the policing connection of your respective pre-retirement careers, your association with me would not be suspected so do not alter your normal routine with me."

"Can we meet tomorrow morning here in Benoit's office?" Commissionaire Poulin asked. "There is another matter we must discuss. But first, I need to attend another meeting now."

"Yes, certainly," Alexandra confirmed.

Alexandra muttered to Paul as they left the police department. "My *shrew* was warning me, more like yelling at me, that something was going to happen, and it did. Why didn't I warn Dominique more strongly?"

"Don't beat yourself up. Each time you spoke, you encouraged her to be careful. You had no more details to pass on. Assassins by definition are nasty, ruthless people. Francine might have been the prime target and Dominique and Rudolf just collateral damage. Or Rudolf was the primary target and Dominique and Francine the collateral damage. Or some combination thereof. We don't know at this juncture. We don't even know if this is a Thon-related matter, a Nazi related initiative, or an old KGB or new FSB Moscow factor. We do know that Thon wanted you dead as a direct result of your mother's association with the French resistance, the *Maquis*, and believe the Russians wanted to keep you alive because they wanted your mother's cryptic code."

Alexandra nodded in frustration of too many unknowns.

"You're right. We don't know. But I will not rest until I find out. Retirement isn't even on the back burner."

Paul echoed her commitment. "We will become more proficient hunters and gathers of intelligence."

CHAPTER 27

"Good morning, Colonel."

Paul recognized the voice but it seemed out of place in Benoit's office. As he scanned the room to confirm the source, he found himself looking at General Daan Segers. Out of habit, he replied, "General." Still perplexed by the association of the person with the environment, he exclaimed, "I'm surprised to see you here. It's been a long time since we served together with the United Nations Protection Force in Sarajevo. It would have been 1992 or '93. What brings you to Paris? We were expecting to meet Commandant Parent."

"Commandant Parent will be a few minutes late. An urgent matter has delayed him so he asked me to welcome you. And this must be Dr. Belliveau."

"Yes, it is. Please excuse my manners. Alexandra, this is General Segers. Sir, my partner, Alexandra. The General and I served together in Sarajevo with UNPROFOR. He was our senior military intelligence officer."

"Call me Daan, Dr. Belliveau. And the same for you, Paul."

"Only if you call me Alexandra," She responded.

"Agreed. Please have a seat." Daan gestured to Paul and Alexandra to join him at the meeting table.

"I thought you had retired from the Belgian Army and were living in Brussels. What brings you to Paris and to Benoit's office?" asked Paul.

"You are correct. I am retired from the military and teaching part-time at the university in Leuven. I'm also engaged part-time in intelligence activities elsewhere. Why am I here? Allow me to explain."

"Please do," Paul requested as he reached over and touched Alexandra's hand under the table to reassure her that Daan was one of the white-hatted good guys and could be trusted. She returned the tactile communiqué reservedly.

"You have been a busy man since Bosnia," Daan continued. "I've been following your career and exploits. I will get directly to the point. Yesterday, Benoit briefed you and Alexandra on the fatal shooting of Capitaine Dominique Roland and Rudolf Heydrich in Moulin-lès-Metz. Allow me to put this in context. I will then present you and Alexandra with a proposal."

"Why do I get the feeling that you will not be offering us a share in a retirement chalet in Liechtenstein?" Alexandra interjected in a jocular tone.

"Close!" Daan replied. "Not too far off the mark. How about a chance to travel to holiday resorts, even Liechtenstein?"

Paul knew Daan's leadership style of proposing missions as just a ride in the park. He sat back and awaited his marching orders, only this time he had the choice to decline. He suspected otherwise, that he would be working with Daan once again.

"As a bit of background information, the European Union evolved from the European Economic Community. Its purpose was to promote peace by eliminating barriers to mutually beneficial trade among its initial six-member states. This community would be an antidote to the nationalism that had manifested itself in continental wars for centuries. It has worked if the absence of war since 1945 on the continent is a measure of success. But from its inception, factions, both internal and external to Europe, have wanted to destroy the EU because these groups benefit from conflict and war, not from peace and prosperity. To counter these threats, the European Union Intelligence Unit was created."

Daan paused to take a sounding from his new and renewed

colleagues. He smiled at Alexandra and Paul who reciprocated, signalling understanding, acceptance, and consent to continue.

"I head this select group, which includes agents from the initial six EU members. Our direction comes from Brussels. I will explain later why just the initial six members. The EUI Unit has a mandate to gather intelligence only on those who pose a threat to the continued successful existence of the European Union, with an emphasis on peaceful co-existence. Over the past decade, the threat level has increased exponentially."

"Who handles the counterthreat component?" Paul asked. "You know better than I do that intelligence without a means to act is of little value."

"You are as astute as ever, Paul. Enforcement in the EU is undertaken by the respective national police organizations. External threats are handled by security and intelligence organizations within the respective member states."

"And…" Paul said. Daan's introductions invariably had a loaded question.

"And I would like to invite you and Alexandra to join the European Union Intelligence Unit."

"I get the feeling the implications are as serious as any we faced in Sarajevo, Daan," Paul countered.

"An astute observation, Paul. I would not make this proposal if I weren't completely confident in your individual and collective ability to work with me in this environment that sometimes can be vague. The first rule remains the same as in Sarajevo. Nothing is what it appears to be. Truths are laced with deception in the conventions of politeness. Success will be a function of flexibility, finding a balance between too many rules of engagement and too few."

"And our relationship with Tom Hunt?" Alexandra enquired.

"I'm aware of your operational association with Tom. I trust him, personally. Although not a member of the European Union Intelligence Unit, we are working towards the same end. The difference is that the U.S. focus is ultimately the U.S. The EUI Unit is regional. The similarity in approach is in identifying and eliminating external threats before they arrive on our respective shores. There is an unofficial mutual aid protocol in place with the United States."

"May I be so bold as to conclude that somehow there is a formal connection to Benoit? Else, why would we be meeting in his office" Alexandra probed. She responded to her own supposition. The relationship had to be formal between Benoit and Daan, and beyond simply collegial. From the first moment she met Benoit, her intuition confirmed that he was a rising star within the Police nationale. Clearly, Daan was cut from the same exemplary cloth.

"You are correct. Allow me to explain why I am here in Commandant Parent's office. Benoit is our French police liaison officer. His superior, Commissionaire Poulin, is the only other person in the department who is aware of the Memorandum of Understanding between the European Union Intelligence Unit and the Police nationale, in addition to the Directeur des Services Actifs. Capitaine Dominique Roland had been working with Benoit because of the neo-Nazi link and a terrorist threat. Rudolf's information reinforced and added to our known and suspected intelligence database. Alexandra, the work that your mother had been involved in led to the conclusion, decades ago, that neo-Nazism was and remains the first of two high priority threats to the political and economic stability of the European Union."

"And the second priority threat?" Paul pressed.

"Terrorism, currently *Al Qaeda,*" Daan confirmed. "There are others, as there was more than one intervening factor behind the conflict in the former Republic of Yugoslavia. No longer do we have squadrons of tanks or battalions of uniformed infantry amassed on battlefields, supported by regiments of artillery waging open war. Instead, there is a growing number of virtually unseen terrorists, most masquerading as lone wolves, or small partnerships holding various populations hostage. Both have political and economic disruption as their goal."

Daan paused and looked at Paul and Alexandra. He sensed that they were intrigued by the concept of an intelligence gathering organization within the European Union but they would not accept his invitation without considerable thought. That was one of the fundamental characteristics of a successful EUI Unit agent. He would have been disappointed otherwise.

"Alexandra and I need to think about your proposal, Daan. Although I would thoroughly enjoy working with you again, engagement with the EUI Unit does not come without inherent long-term commitments fraught with risk. We are seeking a retirement lifestyle that is as risk-free as possible. I'm sure that you can appreciate our perspective."

"You are correct, Paul. There are risks. Dominique was aware, although she was on the enforcement side of the equation, not on intelligence gathering. As Benoit explained, there is an intelligence leak. We suspect that it is associated with Tom, either CIA or Interpol. So, take all the time you need. When you have decided, let Commandant Parent know."

⊰ ⊱

"THOUGHTS, PARTNER?" PAUL POSED AS THEY LEFT the police headquarters building.

"I need time. I'm still processing the murders of Dominique and Rudolf, and the Francine connection. But there is something else gnawing at me. Something to do with Commissionaire Poulin."

Paul gave her an inquisitive look. Although their working relationship had been relatively brief, he had learned not to interrupt her intuitive thought processes. When her *shrew* suggested that she take the time to reflect on her reservations, interrupting that thought progression would bring about dire consequences. Unless she specifically asked for input, he could best help her by not asking probing questions but instead by supporting her in sentinel silence. Just be there.

"I can't place it. Perhaps it's just that this is a formal step up from merely keeping Benoit informed regarding our work with Tom. We have been correct in all our assessments thus far because we have worked together as Sir James directed us to do." She looked at Paul. Her request was inherent in her extended stare.

"I share your feelings, madame. I suggest we go back to Luxembourg to the sanctuary of our home. We can visit Father Luke. Without divulging anything, we could seek his blessing. He seems to hold the wisdom of all those whose photos adorn the walls of his office in the Priest's House."

"My sentiments exactly, mon colonel. We have much to ponder like Pooh Bear over a pot of honey, or better yet, cognac." I think best when I walk. We can discuss the pros and cons of Daan's proposal as we stroll along the cobblestone lanes of the old city this evening. Do you get the feeling that we are being employed as agents for French and American intelligence, a bit like Helena LeDuc was with the Canadian Security and Intelligence Service?"

"Yes, and it's cutting into our retirement plans," Paul replied, wistfully yearning for a retirement life free of constraints and responsibilities. *If we do accept Daan's offer, at least we will be working together, not heading off to separate jobs lamenting the fact that we are not together,* he thought.

"We need to figure out what we want to do and place parameters on these precious moments together. We have been apart far too long due to circumstance beyond our control. Any decision we now make will be wholly ours to make."

"What do you think of the idea of talking to Helena about how she controlled her CSIS handler?" Paul queried.

"Given these circumstances, perhaps not now because she might become suspicious," Alexandra conjectured. "We wouldn't want her talking to Tom before we can figure out where we fit into this kaleidoscope, if we decide to continue to work with Tom, and/ or Daan and Benoit."

Paul continued to gaze at nothing while his wrinkled brow reflected the complexity of his thoughts. "Regardless, we need to go back to Munich to see Dieter about the books. We owe Tom that much. If we decide to take Daan up on his offer, this ongoing intelligence could be valuable. As Daan outlined, the Fourth Reich is an internal threat to the political and economic stability of the EU."

"I'm really bothered by the monstrosity of the betrayal, as Commissionaire Poulin described the intelligence leak," Alexandra confessed. "The source of the leak causes me grave concern. The consequences could be worse than the Thon scenario when we didn't even know Thon's gender, let alone any other tangible attributes of his character beyond his sheer elusiveness. With Thon, it was just one threat and one target, me. In this case, the magnitude of the Russian threat, if it is FSB initiated or even former KGB, is much greater. Do we really want to go there? Or are we already in the thick of it? Is it too late to withdraw?"

"As your mother explained in her letter, just being her daughter has placed you in the thick of it and I've been with you since her funeral."

"Being my mother's daughter has created an everlasting link. It may be too late to withdraw. We also need to think about the impact on Collette and Jean."

"So, what is your *shrew* telling you, madame?"

"There are too many factors to consider to make a decision right now. Daan's proposal has far-reaching implications, far more than our relationship with Tom. I need some downtime. Perhaps dinner at the Café Kaempff-Kohler and a walk through the old city will help clear the conundrum."

CHAPTER 28

The alluring aroma of freshly brewed Colombian coffee greeted Paul as he wandered into the kitchen. "You're up early, ma princesse."

"I couldn't sleep. I've been awake since 2:00 a.m. Too much stuff to consider."

"I didn't sleep much better. Is your *shrew* any clearer now?"

"I don't feel any ominous signals. Instead, just a need to be cautious, especially when so much is coming at us at once. I'm drawn to follow in my mother's footsteps. I hear her voice with all the caveats and encouragements, and the wise counsel of Sir James. They are drawing me to consider Daan's offer. But if we proceed, I'm concerned the association with him may trigger your ghost from Sarajevo to rise up. Your wellbeing, Paul, will always be paramount in any of my decisions."

"I was thinking the same thing. I was also reflecting on the judicious advice Sir James gave. When Daan greeted us in Benoit's office, the sound of his voice took me back to Bosnia because that was where we met and worked. I don't think I ever told you about two incidents that I experienced. The first was in Sarajevo. Some Muslim children had been playing in a courtyard when mortars hit them. Limbs and other body parts were strewn everywhere. We found out later the Muslims had targeted their own children purposely. They blamed it on the Serbs in an attempt to garner media sympathy."

"How did they get away with it?"

"The first casualty of war is the truth, madame."

Alexandra stared in disbelief. "How could anything be worse than that? And the second experience was…?"

"The second was just outside Sarajevo when we came across a war crimes scene. A little girl was lying face down in a ditch. She was perhaps five or six. It was difficult to judge her age. Her little emaciated arms had been tied behind her back with barbed wire that had ripped into her wrists. Blood was oozing out of a bullet wound in the back of her head onto her pale blue dress. Some irregular militia soldiers were standing close by laughing. The body was still warm. We knew they were responsible."

Alexandra raised her hand and covered her mouth as she gasped in disbelief. "And I thought some of the crime scenes I visited were awful."

Paul sighed. "On a positive note, these memories didn't haunt me when I heard Daan's voice in Benoit's office. Sometimes the tightness in my chest, the gnawing headaches and the screaming tinnitus overwhelm me. But not this time. I think that, for the most part, I have been able to manage my haunting version of Charles Dickens's Ghost of Christmas Past."

Alexandra continued to gaze at Paul, supporting him in the silence that followed. "Thank you for sharing those stories with me."

"Rest assured, ma princesse, I'd never do anything that would come between us being happy together. Never is a very long time, but when I say never, I mean never. I love you too much. We have less than a full lifetime to make up for, less a lifetime of experiences."

"We are sleuth partners and life partners," Alexandra whispered as she tenderly held him in her embrace and kissed him warmly. She felt his pulse increase slightly but not near as disturbing as it had been on those other occasions when those memories had temporarily robbed him of his soul and sanity.

Paul reciprocated. "Sir James assured us that together we would be successful in carrying on the battle he and Maria and Major

Mike had started. So, I'm comfortable if we decide to work with Daan. But it's a matter of balance between playtime and work, with the emphasis on playtime. Perhaps a visit with Father Luke might clear up any lingering doubts. I'm up for a morning stroll. How about you?"

⚑ ⚐

"Good morning, my children," Father Luke greeted his parishioners as they were about to knock on the back door of the Priest's House. "I'm always pleased to see my newest members of the congregation. And to what do I owe the honour of your visit?"

"Just a social call if you have a few minutes," Alexandra replied.

"I certainly do have the time. Please, come in." As he led them into his study, a poised, confident yet reserved gentleman in his early fifties met them. His stature and lean athletic physique commanded immediate respect. There was no weakness in his appearance, instead, nobility and chivalry, courtliness and intelligence.

"Alexandra and Paul, I would like to introduce you to Matthieu Richard, one of my parishioners who is currently living in Dieppe. Matthieu grew up in Luxembourg. He was and remains a loyal member of the congregation. You will recall, Alexandra, my reference to Matthieu the morning after your mother's funeral that Madame Deschaume had fallen to her death. I said that a parishioner had called me. It was Matthieu."

"I'm very pleased to meet the enigmatic parishioner." Alexandra extended her hand, as she looked into his inquisitive eyes. Her *shrew* was in full force as she conducted an initial psychological profile. She detected a residue of faith and trust that overshadowed his self-assured persona.

"I especially thank you, Matthieu, for your discretion so we can speak openly," Paul said as he shook his hand. He seemed to be looking at a double of Father Luke. There was a strong resemblance in stature and character, and command presence. Their genealogy could easily have been traced to similar gladiator roots. But it was more than that. Something was very familiar.

"Might I conclude that you were aware of the circumstances surrounding her death, and you are aware of what ensued?" Paul enquired.

"Yes, very much aware. Father Luke told me about how you dealt with the perpetrator. You have quite a reputation. And Paul, I understand that we have a mutual acquaintance from the Former Republic of Yugoslavia, General Daan Segers. Perhaps serendipitously, Daan and I were chatting last evening."

Paul looked at Alexandra who had been glancing back and forth between Father Luke and Matthieu. "It is a small world. Would I be correct in suggesting that you and Daan share an interest in the information-gathering profession?"

"Your assumption is correct," Matthieu replied with a nod, perhaps reserved for close friends or brothers in arms.

"You were in Sarajevo also, in Tito's palace, if I recall correctly. That's where we met briefly," Paul speculated, seeking to place Matthieu's face.

"Correct again, Colonel. You have an excellent memory of that very brief encounter. We never met formally. I tried my best to stay on the periphery. I guess I wasn't successful in just being a fly on the wall or you have a particularly sharp memory."

"Is it more than serendipitous that you and Father Luke look very much alike?" Alexandra commented nonchalantly, although there was nothing unpremeditated about any enquiries that her forensic psychological mind made.

It was Matthieu and Father Luke's turn to exchange glances. Father Luke broke the awkward silence. "Correct, Alexandra. We are half-brothers. We have the same mother who was the house-keeper for a previous priest. But we can talk about that later."

"I can now understand why Daan extended an invitation to re-establish relationships, Paul. Perhaps our paths may cross again in the near future, but for now, I must excuse myself," Matthieu announced.

"*Jusque à plus tard, mon frère* – until later, my brother," Father Luke replied with a voice as sincere as his double handshake. Matthieu departed through the front door.

"And my children, you dropped by for a visit. How can I help you?" Father Luke enquired.

"Just happy to take every opportunity to see you, Father, and to benefit from your benedictions," Alexandra replied. "We must be off ourselves. Thank you for the introduction to Matthieu, your parishioner from Dieppe." She sensed an odd connection to her mother's spirit. *Had Matthieu met Maman at some juncture, perhaps through Father Luke*? she wondered. Her warm feelings toward Matthieu increased. She hoped that they would cross paths again.

As they left Father Luke's office, he directed them to the front door, not to the kitchen and the back door, as had been the practice. It was a gesture of an elevated personal stature because only important visitors such as the bishop or mayor used the front door, and now Matthieu. Regular parishioners always used the back door.

"Curiouser and curiouser has become my favourite expression since becoming more involved in my mother's world," Alexandra commented with amusement. "So Matthieu and Father Luke are half-brothers, and Father Luke has a strong resemblance to a previous priest whose photo hangs on the wall of the parish pantheon with his predecessors."

"And?" Paul queried. He sensed that Alexandra had successfully resolved her reservation and was once again at peace with her *shrew*, herself.

"And my *shrew* isn't throwing up any caveats, but there's more here than meets the eye, mon colonel."

"And there is more to Father Luke than just being a humble parish priest, je pense. He has *ruse de guerre* – a shrewdness born from the haunting experiences of the war, known but not spoken. Your mother referenced that in her letter to you left in her safe deposit box. In addition, he exhibits the charm and wisdom of those more aligned with the world of espionage than a man of the cloth whose mission is guided by the scriptures," Paul suggested.

"I agree. He was more to my mother and her work and has been more to us than simply the modest shepherd of his parish flock. If you look at his hazel eyes, which by the way are a replica of Matthieu's, you will notice that his subtle glances are less than neutral. When in his office, his communiqués seem to be steeped in intrigue which is somehow connected to that pantheon of portraits on the office walls. I can only surmise there's more to this story, his story. Perhaps more than his bishop may even be aware of."

Paul speculated, "We do live in an intriguing world of double entendre, perhaps even multiple intertwined entendre."

"So, how do you propose we respond to Daan's invitation to join the European Union Intelligence Unit?" Alexandra probed with a confident voice and a self-assured smile.

Paul replied, "From our time in Sarajevo, I knew more about Matthieu by reputation than actually knowing him. He had a stellar reputation for thoroughness and integrity, as did Daan. They were the best in the intelligence field. I don't remember Matthieu being military. I thought he was simply attached to the intelligence section as a resource, just a fly on the wall as he described himself. Although he didn't say outright that he was part of Daan's EUI Unit, I bet that he is. More than likely, that was his role in 1993 when our trajectories intersected. His mission in Sarajevo was simple: to gather intelligence. The consequences today, as in Sarajevo, are not simple."

"Why would Daan have chatted with him last evening, after our meeting in Benoit's office with Daan, if there wasn't another motive, a stronger connection?" Alexandra reflected.

"Good question, madame. If Matthieu is any indication of the calibre of colleagues we might be working with, I'm more confident and certainly less wary of accepting Daan's invitation to join the EUI Unit."

"I agree," Alexandra responded. "We just need to mesh the playtime with the work commitments."

"*D'accord* – OK," Paul nodded. "But we must stop saying that we need to retire because each time we do, we are drawn further into the intoxicating vortex of your mother's world of counterintelligence intrigue."

CHAPTER 29

As they walked across the viaduct to the old city behind the ramparts, which provided a visual but perhaps not a visceral sense of security, the familiar voice of Walter Burns, Sir James's butler, hailed them from behind.

"Keep walking and don't look back at me," Walter announced. "I have news about Sir James. He did not die of a heart attack brought about as a result of natural causes."

"But you said it was a massive heart attack," Alexandra countered.

"Let me explain. Just keep walking at the same pace. I was not just his butler. As Sir James told you, I was his sergeant in military intelligence during the war. When he transferred to MI6, I joined MI5. Sir James wasn't just another analyst in Her Majesty's Secret Service but a senior officer with extraordinary espionage and counterintelligence skills. Others wanted what he knew, especially the Russians. I was still in the employment of the Service, as were others, to watch over him in his retirement. Last week, someone came to the cottage enquiring if the property and contents would be sold. I said no and did not reveal who the new owners were. The next day, while I was out shopping, someone entered the cottage. Surveillance cameras caught him carefully rummaging through the contents, paying deliberate attention to bookshelves and papers. He has since been identified as a Russian agent. He did not appear to have found what he was looking for. As Sir James reminded you many times, be very careful and guard whatever it was he entrusted to you."

As Walter brushed by Paul, he handed him a business card. "Here is contact information you can use to get hold of me. Do not use public phones or email. You can also contact me through your spiritual shepherd who has an extended congregation as part of his local parish."

As they left the viaduct, Walter got into the front seat of a car that had just pulled up alongside him. The car veered left into the tunnel, as Alexandra and Paul turned right and entered the gates to the ancient city.

"Let's go to the bank and drop off a few additional valuables in our own safe deposit box, madame."

"We may require a larger box," she murmured. "Faith and trust are forged in tradition like the ancient parapets that encircled our home." The surveillance cameras in both apartments would provide another ring of defence.

⊰ ⊱

"Daan asked to meet us tomorrow afternoon if possible, in Benoit's office," Paul announced. "No peace for the semi-retired."

"Confirmed, mon colonel. We can update him on our conversation with Walter and our intention to visit the bookstore in Munich. We can also pick up the bait books from Helena. I'll call Collette and mention that we'll be dropping by tomorrow evening for a visit. Coffee with Jo has to fit in the schedule too. Those conducting the retirement seminar didn't cover this aspect of scheduling retirement time. Or, if they did, I must have slept through that lecture."

"We have a bigger issue," Paul proposed. "Do we tell Daan about the books Sir James gave us and, more importantly, Maria's codes? And if so, when? We haven't told Tom. And in retrospect, that was a good decision not to, because of the suspected leak somewhere in Tom's world."

Alexandra mulled over all the factors. "You've known Daan since Sarajevo. You indicated he was trustworthy. The stakes have been raised with the suspicious death of Sir James, and with Walter's warning about guarding the code books. My mother, Sir James and Tom all reminded us to be vigilant because of ominous consequences. We have both lived our lives on the periphery of this world we are about to enter. I get the feeling that the work Daan is involved in is more serious and the European Union Intelligence Unit is far more professional than just being informants for Tom. I don't think there are options. We are in the thick of it whether we like it or not."

Paul nodded. "Can we back out at this point and merely say, thanks but no thanks? You're correct. There are no options. We're in."

CHAPTER 30

"Welcome to the EU Intelligence Unit," Daan announced as he greeted his latest recruits. "And you have met Matthieu."

"We meet again," Matthieu smiled. "This time I will not be a fly on the wall."

Alexandra and Paul shook hands with Father Luke's not-so-mysterious parishioner.

"As you have probably surmised, Matthieu is a member of our team," Daan confirmed. "In the fullness of time, you will meet others and come to depend on them as they depend on you. The purpose of this afternoon's meeting is to formally welcome you, brief you on our operations and take care of some administration such as issuing you with identification documentation and addressing other security issues. First, I need to know what you have been up to with Tom."

"Okay, but before we brief you on our work to date with Tom, we need to tell you about a conversation we had with Sir James's butler, Walter Burns," Paul announced.

Paul recognized Daan's expressionless response to yet another briefing from an old colleague.

"You haven't lost your talent for making a thorough situation report," Daan commented. "This news regarding Sir James muddies the waters a bit but doesn't change the objective. And your work with Tom?"

"Consistent with our latest update to Benoit Parent, our focus has been on gaining the confidence of a bookstore owner in Munich, who has links to the Fourth Reich," Alexandra added. "Our intention was to go to Munich, perhaps tomorrow."

Glancing at Matthieu, Daan paused for a moment. "All right, continue with your plan to proceed to Munich for your meeting with Dieter and Katrina. I want Matthieu to go with you to Munich and act as your backup. Please provide him with your itinerary."

"Let me know what your agenda is while in Paris, so we can coordinate," Matthieu asked. "We'll travel on the same train and stay in the same hotel. I'll arrive at the bookstore before you."

"When we first met, Alexandra, you asked light-heartedly if associating with me would involve a holiday to Liechtenstein. You weren't too far off the mark," Daan chuckled.

"After Munich, the three of you are to go to the Principality Grande Hotel in Liechtenstein. There you will stay for a week and receive formal briefings on the EUI Unit and training on intelligence gathering. I'm aware that you received a briefing from the CIA, arranged by Tom. You'll find this week's information has greater emphasis on personal security. While you're in Munich, I'll have our internal security team sweep your homes in Luxembourg. I'll need your keys and security surveillance codes."

"Question, Daan," Alexandra responded. "We have a working relationship with Tom. We all know there is a security leak somewhere within his network. It could be CIA or Interpol. You speak of muddied waters. Our relationship with Tom exists. He is not aware of the antiquarian books that Sir James gave us. What do we tell Tom and when?"

"Soon," Daan replied. "But we need to be careful, because of the leak somewhere in Tom's network. We don't believe that Tom is a double agent. It looks more like Interpol with a strong connection to Virginia. It could be more than one Russian agent. Because we don't yet know for certain, we need to be guarded. That is the main reason why Matthieu will be your backup. The neo-Nazis are on edge with the killing of Rudolf. Not surprisingly, they're suspicious of anyone. They are very close-mouthed at this time. This imposition of increased silence is telling, perhaps even intelligence. So, just talk to Dieter and Katrina about the books you have brought them and which books you might like to purchase. It's imperative you do not talk or enquire about anything else. If you feel uncomfortable about the engagement with Dieter, back out immediately. Understood?"

Alexandra and Paul nodded.

"As Daan has indicated, I'll be in the bookstore. If I get any indication of an increased threat, I'll ask Dieter about Hans Christian Andersen books. That will be your signal to back out immediately," Matthieu added.

"We have the cart before the horse on this one," Daan suggested. "Ideally, you would not be involved in any case without first receiving our full briefing and training, about how to go black – identify surveillance of your movement and disappear out of sight of those tailing you. But you have some experience and Matthieu will be with you."

Alexandra and Paul exchanged glances without saying anything. Their communication did not go unnoticed by Daan and Matthieu.

"Something you want to mention?" Daan asked.

"The surveillance has already begun. In fact, I believe it started before Thon. We suspect that after our previous meeting with Sir James, a couple, possibly Russian, on the Eurostar had us under surveillance."

"Thanks," Daan responded. "That is why Matthieu will be with you, to look out for any watchers among other things. Any other concerns?"

"None," Paul responded. "We are good to go."

"Be vigilant and, above all, be safe," Daan replied.

His newest recruits nodded.

With Matthieu providing backup, Daan was more confident and less concerned for their safety. In addition, Paul had a proven track record of sage decisions while under fire. Coupled with Alexandra's uncanny ability to read the tea leaves, so to speak, the probability of mission success was high. Notwithstanding such positive variables, there had been other missions where confidence level had been elevated but success denied and the lives of qualified agents lost. That was why statistical probability could be guaranteed only to the 99.98 percent level. Every intervening variable operating in the environment could not be assured. Daan knew from personal experience that the greatest sin of any commander was arrogance, manifested in over confidence.

⚐ ⚑

"Bonjour, c'est Aulne." – Hello, this is Aulne.

"J'écoute." – I'm listening.

"Ты нашёл это?" – Did you find it?

"Нет. Хотя, это, скорее всего, всё ещё у них." – No. They may still have it though.

CHAPTER 31

"Maman, Paul, great to see you both. It's been forever since you came to visit. How long will you be here?" Collette asked.

"We had a meeting with one of Paul's old friends from Leuven who happened to be in Paris for the day. We'll leave tomorrow. And where is Jean?"

"Oh, he's out walking MV. He should be back shortly. Neither of us realized how energetic Bichon Frise puppies are and how much attention they need or actually demand when we get home. We were visiting Jo the other day and MV dug up one of her indoor plants."

"Oh dear. How did Jo react? It may be another IOU from Alexandra to Jo."

"Any other puppy would have received a life sentence or have been condemned to the jaws of the guillotine. Speaking of 24601, here are Jean Valjean and his prisoner escort now."

As they sat down to dinner, Collette stared at a bright gold wedding band on her mother's finger. "Ah, Maman, is that what I think it is? What's going on?"

Immediately on the heels of Collette's query, Jean pointed to his father's ring with an equally enquiring smile.

"Let me explain," Alexandra announced. "This is between the four of us and no one else, not even to be shared with Jo yet. Understood?"

"We understand," Collette acknowledged. *Not to be shared with Jo. That is secret beyond all secrets,* she surmised.

"As you are aware, Paul and I are working part-time with some interesting people, doing interesting things, in interesting places.

As part of our ruse, we are presenting ourselves as a married couple. We have the cart before the horse because of the urgency of the case. In fact, we're planning to get married just before Christmas. This news must be kept secret for the same reason, especially from Jo because, as you know, she tends to get very excited. Understood?"

"Okay, Maman," Collette giggled. "You are full of surprises. Will we be invited to the wedding?" she jested.

"Of course, dear."

"Papa, interesting insignia on the ring. Do you know anything about it?"

"It belonged to Alexandra's papa. I'm not sure. Why do you ask?"

"If it is what I think it is, it looks like old Celtic or Druid. It might even be old Runic and could date back to the time when France was Gaul. In Runes, 'F' is similar to old Anglo Saxon 'f' for feoh which is a symbol for cattle and, accordingly, wealth and affluence. Cattle were the source of wealth. A class of elite males wore it because of their prosperity. It held considerable power and influence. When Caesar's legions invaded, the group went underground and became a secret society, a bit like the Knights Templar after King Philip IV of France ordered their massacre on Friday 13th October 1307. There would have been less than ten, perhaps just a half dozen members at its pinnacle then."

"Interesting, mon fils. I would never have guessed."

Jean continued, "If I remember correctly, the rings were passed down from father to son who took over the family fortune after being groomed for the governance role. Rumour has it that this clandestine group still exists but on a much wider scale and wields considerable global economic clout. Their political influence is considerable, with tentacles in virtually all political arenas. The

Italian mafia is a minor player in comparison. They are definitely not a group to mess with."

"Did this group have a name, Jean?" Alexandra asked. "I'm intrigued as to why or how my father was involved."

"There is no written record from their inception, probably because they were so secretive. But there are some references from the mid-seventeenth century to *Quer,* which is old French for what we might translate today as a choir, as in church choir. It could be connected to *Gaultier*, a Nazi word for district leader. It could just be a coincidence though because the Nazi Gaultiers were not nice people. Just thugs and bullies who had no monetary influence. I'll do some more reading."

"I had no idea," Alexandra commented. "Ma maman just said it belonged to my father. It's the only physical connection I have to him. I seem to be learning more about ma maman since her death than I knew before."

"How do you know this, Jean?" Collette asked.

"When I was studying computer programming language, I also studied linguistics, the history of other languages, English, German, early Nordic of Jutes and Angles, French, Latin, and some Sanskrit. That reminds me, Papa, and I am sorry for not getting back to you sooner. It's just been so busy at work."

"What's that, mon fils?"

"The symbols and numbers you sent me that Sir James had been working on just before he died. The origin of the symbols is Runic and possibly Celtic. And they are symbols and not phonetic alphabetic script, although there is a connection between symbols and sounds. They could be linked. Now that I've seen your ring, I'll research further."

Paul gazed at Alexandra. She shrugged her shoulders and raised her eyebrows in astonishment. She whispered, "I had no idea."

"One last thing, Papa. It would be a very interesting

conversation if someone recognized the ring and gave you some furtive expression of acknowledgement, like clanship. If that ever happens, I'd be pretty cautious. These secret societies have a reputation for being particularly ruthless toward outsiders or possible confederates."

Alexandra leaned over and said, "A bit like our new acquaintances in Munich. Rudolf cautioned us in the same way."

"I was thinking the same thing," Paul said. "I wonder."

"We need to put this on the agenda as another conversation to have with our new business partners, mon colonel."

"I can't ask you to do any research for me, mon fils. In fact, I've been told *not* to ask you for security reasons."

"Understood, Papa. I've received direction from my superiors not to conduct any electronic enquiries for you. Something's going on at a very high level. What I can do is let it be known that I am conducting research for an academic paper that I plan to publish."

"Okay, let me know if you come up with any new information, Jean. We'll be going into black-hat country tomorrow. Be careful, won't you?"

"Yes, I know. Life with Papa and now life with Papa and Alexandra has implications. If I come up with anything that has ill-omened overtones, I'll email and mention that I'm thinking of joining a local choir. And you be careful too. We don't want anything to get in the way of wedding plans."

Wedding plans. Alexandra pondered the reality of those words. It both excited and frightened her. She never imagined she would be using that expression again. For Collette's wedding, of course, but not her own. A warmth rose from her inner soul to her face. A smile on her lips embraced her eyes. If only her mother could be here.

Her engagement and marriage to André had happened without fanfare. He didn't want a traditional wedding with bridesmaids and guests. He thought it was too expensive. Only Jo attended as her maid of honour with a best man whose name Alexandra had forgotten many years ago.

Yet, she thought, *I was a bright, intelligent individual, a forensic psychologist who solved cold cases which teams of seasoned police investigators could not. How could I have made such an ill-informed personal decision? In retrospect, that one horrible decision affected all the decisions made afterwards regarding platonic relationships. I merely walked away from friends and kept colleagues at a professional distance. That was why I had become a workaholic living in temporary accommodation out of a bag. I was my mother's daughter, living the transient life I so hated about ma maman. Collette would be justified in hating me. There was just Jo, and the fleeting memory of my teenage love with whom, in my fantasy world, I would discuss wedding plans. I would have to speak to Jo about her misgivings, my dearth of self-confidence and growing anxiety and trepidation to recite the two words, I do. Perhaps Paul and I could just wear the wedding bands which we have already informally exchanged. Another option would be to step back from this impending decision. How could I be so much in love but so fearful of being in love and of being loved?*

Her *shrew* spoke to her but she could not understand the communiqué. She needed to calm down, to withdraw in order to regain focus. Love would have to wait. Her world, their world, was on the cusp of turbulence.

"What's the matter?" Paul asked. "You are flushed."

She looked at him with a blank stare as if confused. Her hand had grasped the amulet around her neck so tightly her fingers were white, her palm wet with perspiration.

"What's the matter?" Paul repeated.

"Something has happened. I don't know what," she gasped.

CHAPTER 32

"Helena, how is Frankfurt University life treating you?" Alexandra asked. "Are these the bait books with the GPS devices installed?"

"If it was just university life, with no interruptions, I'd be quite happy with the thought of being a perpetual student. But, as you can appreciate, life gets in the way. Something has come up which has huge implications for us all."

"What are you saying? I have a feeling something bad has happened." Alexandra replied to her ominous communiqué.

"Bad is an understatement, Alexandra. Tom is dead. He was poisoned. Needless to say, his death is being kept secret. INTERPOL has been advised that another senior American police representative will replace him. When I have more details, I'll share as much as I can. But for now, you need to stand down from all operations. GPS tracking devices have *not* been inserted in the spines of these books."

"Poisoned? How? Where?" Alexandra gulped. She stared at Paul whose stunned expression mirrored her own.

"All indications point to the FSB with links to the old guard of the KGB. Tom was very good at what he did which meant that he had ran afoul of some of his KGB counterparts over the years. As you can appreciate, they have long memories. One of these KGB agents caught up with him and settled an old score. The Cold War isn't over. Instead, it has just taken on yet another guise."

"All right, we stand down," Paul confirmed. "But we would appreciate a bit more direction. Clarification. What can you provide us with now? Appreciate our position, being left out in the cold... of the Cold War."

"Fair enough, Paul. We've suspected a leak for quite a while. Recently, a Russian operative defected and identified his contacts in INTERPOL and the CIA. They've been picked up. The defector has come clean on what information he had passed along to Moscow. The Russians knew that Tom's code word was Alder. They used the French translation, Aulne, to confuse our communications to and from Tom. The implications of that intelligence are currently being analyzed for any broader implications."

"Have our connections with Tom been compromised?" Alexandra pressed. Her heart was pounding in response to the news. Her mouth dried as her palms perspired.

"No. Your identities were not mentioned, and our interrogators did ask the defector specifically," Helena replied with confidence. "However, like our operatives, Russian spies do not know what other operatives do or what their missions are. Neither of you came up on his radar screen because, we suspect, your association with Tom was too recent."

"Thanks for that confirmation. Can we safely conclude that 'stand down' doesn't mean go into hiding?" Paul responded. "Or does it?"

"If you were in any danger, I would have contacted you immediately. Tom would have done that. Rest assured, I will do the same if something comes up," Helena confirmed.

"Thanks, Helena. We're glad to know that," Alexandra replied. Her concern calmed and her composure returned.

"I understand this news is shocking, especially for you because of the relationship you had developed with Tom on the Thon case."

"What else do you know that might overlap with the Fourth Reich?" Alexandra followed up. "We are on our way to see Dieter."

"We are confident the Russians have not passed any information along to the Fourth Reich. Nonetheless, the neo-Nazis are skittish and on high alert regarding any infiltration, particularly with the death of Rudolf. We have no indications you are under any suspicion or threat. For now, you are to return to your lives as recent retirees. I'll be in contact through the parts manager at the Harley-Davidson dealership. We suspect another player but have no information. It's just an unconfirmed lead. I know that this news comes as a bit of a shock to you. As Tom would say, welcome to the New World Order."

"Comes as a bit of a shock is an understatement, Helena," Alexandra reiterated with a sigh of resignation.

As they left, Alexandra said to Paul, "Tom poisoned, Sir James poisoned, in addition to all of Thon's poisoned victims. Time to re-evaluate our retirement plans."

Paul was silent.

Alexandra quietly prompted, "Thoughts, partner?"

"Tom reminded us on numerous occasions that we are living in a new world with new world rules. There is still the rule of law. It's just that the rules have changed as have the means of enforcement of the law."

Alexandra nodded. "I'm with you."

"Sir James talked about the same thing on our final walk in his garden. He said that in 1939, a formal declaration of war changed the rules of war. War exposed him to the insanity of hell, the insanity of Nazi concentration camps. I experienced the same insanity, the deliberate murder of innocent children in Sarajevo, although there never was a formal declaration of war in the former Republic of Yugoslavia. A declaration of war, whether formal or informal, brings with it a righteous obligation to kill. The unofficial Cold War between the East and the West has morphed into new battlegrounds, battle spaces with evolving rules. Sir James's murder and Tom's murder reinforce this reality. There is a New World Order with new often un-codified rules of engagement."

"I agree completely," Alexandra confirmed.

"Are we in unison, ma princesse?"

"We are. The new world order requires different rules of engagement for the white hats."

"Okay, I'll contact Daan."

Red sky at night, sailor's delight. Red sky in the morning, sailor's warning. It wasn't a nautical verse Alexandra had muttered. Red referred to Russia. All but one would rise on the flood tide. It became readily apparent that Tom would not rise. The premonition linked aftershocks to a single shift of two tectonic plates – East and West, communism and democracy. Those within the trajectory of Alexandra's orbit would be affected. Tom's demise had altered that course, their course.

CHAPTER 33

"There's a fine line between intelligence gathering and operational enforcement," Daan explained. "Mission success is often due to coincidence. The work you will be doing with us will cross these lines. Your mission will remain intelligence gathering but you must be prepared for the consequences of both. Always remember that in our business, information is a currency based on the gold standard. Intelligence is that gold standard."

"Understood, Daan," Paul calmly confirmed.

Noting a subtle hesitation in Paul's and Alexandra's expressions, Daan posed the unspoken question. "Given what has happened to Tom, I need to know if you are still committed to the EUI Unit. If not, then now is the time to step away. I will understand if you do. If you want to stay, then we proceed with the training and there is no better place than Liechtenstein for careful consideration."

A measured pause followed as Paul and Alexandra looked at each other for confirmation. Paul returned his attention to Daan. "We've talked it over and remain committed."

"You realize you will be crossing the Rubicon?" Daan asked. "This is the point of no return."

"You promised Alexandra a holiday in Liechtenstein and I'm holding you to your word," Paul grinned.

"Thank you for your confidence in our evolving relationship and your commitment to the objectives of the EUI Unit," Daan replied with a smile. He held out his hand in a gesture of friendship and loyalty, as a professional pledge to the honour of comrades in arms.

"We still have the books we were going to use as bait, but with no tracking devices," Alexandra advised. "What do you want us to do?"

"The concept of the Antiquarian Book Collectors Club remains viable and you have already started to develop a relationship with the bookstore owners in Munich. So, let's proceed as planned. If you give me the books, I'll have our technicians implant our GPS chips right now. We'll have Matthieu and the back-up team accompany you to Munich. You drop them off and then go to the hotel in Liechtenstein. The team will be with you all the way. If you are being followed, we'll know immediately and the team will take evasive action. If you aren't being followed, we'll conclude that the neo-Nazis are not on to our ploy. Either way, we'll see you in Liechtenstein."

≒ ⊫

"WELCOME TO THE PRINCIPALITY GRANDE HOTEL," DAAN greeted his guests. "Matthieu tells me that your visit with Dieter and Katrina in Munich went without a hitch. Your passage to Liechtenstein also went without any incident. Well done. What are your individual assessments?"

"I didn't get any indication that Dieter or his wife were suspicious," Alexandra replied. "They were cautious, yes, and that's understandable given the circumstances. But not suspicious."

"Your assessment, Paul?"

"I agree with Alexandra. It was comforting to see Matthieu there. I couldn't readily identify your back-up team."

"We'll introduce them to you shortly. You'll get to know them better this week as they'll train you on surveillance techniques."

"Looking forward to being trained by the best," Paul replied confidently. *I would not have expected anything less than perfection with Daan at the helm,* he presumed.

"I mentioned I was going to have our counter-surveillance team conduct a sweep of your homes in Luxembourg. They reported back that your place, Paul, was clean of any bugs. This was not the case for Alexandra's apartment. They found a bug in a large plant pot in the living room. Our people left it there, intact, for two reasons. First, you are both living in Paul's place. Second, we'll use the bug to provide false information to its owners who, we suspect, are Russian. We'll be able to confirm this as soon as we provide you with a script to use every time you enter Alexandra's apartment. Eventually, we'll disable it. The owners of the bug will think it had simply gone offline. The good news is we can safely conclude that it isn't Fourth Reich because they don't work at this level of technological sophistication. We have also eliminated other players such as the Chinese."

"I thought there was something odd about it," Alexandra reflected. "The gift card said it was from Josephine. I concluded it was from Jo, but the name was wrong. It should have said Jo. Damn. Missed another one. I need to keep the radar up 24/7, even when relaxing at home."

"A second level of surveillance cameras has been installed in your homes," Daan continued. "You'll be briefed this week on how to activate and deactivate them when you are there. Know you will not be able to deactivate external cameras that provide constant coverage."

"Thanks, Daan, that's reassuring. Like Sarajevo, it's comforting to know we have 360-degree perimeter security."

"Here's a copy of our agenda for the week. It's comprehensive but informal, tailored to your level of sophistication. I'll start off briefing you on the genesis of the European Union Intelligence Unit and where we are today. I will introduce you to our superior from the EU Commission in Brussels. Matthieu will reacquaint you with a few folks whom you already know and a few more you will get to know and come to depend on."

"Before we get underway, we would appreciate clarification of our status with Tom's colleague, Helena, and her employer," Paul asked.

"It's on the top of my list," Daan replied. "The CIA uses people and organizations, some of which are false. In that way, they can deny contact with no audit trail should a problem occur. The EUI Unit doesn't work that way. All our people are members of the European Union. We create relationships but not as you had with Tom. As of now, you sever all relationships with the CIA. It's less of an issue but perhaps an opportune time with Tom's death. You will contact Helena and explain that to her, although she may pop up on our radar screen from time to time. You will find the EUI Unit to be far more professional. Any other questions?"

"Just one," Alexandra replied, "or just one for now. Thon poisoned his victims. Sir James was poisoned. Tom was poisoned. There seems to be a pattern."

"Poisoning is a common method of dealing with adversaries," Daan replied. "It is both the best and the worst method of murdering someone. Best because it is the most difficult to trace – such as a nerve agent. It can be the worst because it is virtually impossible to hide, like cyanide which gives off a bitter almond smell but it's not always detectable. We can go back to Socrates drinking hemlock and beyond. Thon's method was effective for his day. The poison used to kill Sir James and Tom is far more advanced, sophisticated. In the spyosphere, death by poisoning can be the best revenge. As I mentioned before, there's a difference between intelligence and evidence. With Thon, intelligence became evidence that confirmed his MO. With Sir James and Tom, it is currently viewed as intelligence that is being analyzed. It now begs the question: Who tends to use those poisons more often? Having said that, I commend you on your observations, Alexandra."

Matthieu added, "Half our work deals with intelligence – what you will be doing as hunters and gatherers. The other half is for colleagues to analyze. You bring great experience to that table. Thus, your acumen will always be sought after. The line gets a bit blurry at times. To be effective at this job, you need to navigate both. Sometimes you come across dogs that don't bark or what appears to be a non-event. It's as important to ask why they are non-events as much as why they are events. In that regard, patterns in non-events are intelligence as much as patterns in events. If the dogs aren't barking, you have to ask yourself why. If poison as a modus operandi, why or why not?"

By mid-morning coffee break, Daan had completed a thorough briefing with military precision. "Any questions or observations before I introduce you to our superior from the European Union Commission in Brussels?"

"Alexandra can speak for herself but I can say that I am honoured to be associated with this select group of professionals, and with you once again, Daan."

"I agree with Paul completely," Alexandra added. "I'm feeling very comfortable – in fact more so than working with Tom."

An elegant, unassuming lady entered the room. *She could have been Madame Simone Deschaume, her mother's Maquis colleague from Normandy, in her younger years. She may be petite but she conveys a commanding presence*, Alexandra reflected.

"Alexandra and Paul, I am honoured to introduce you to the head of the European Union Intelligence Unit, Yolina Lambert. Yolina founded the EUI Unit and authorizes all missions and budgets."

"Thank you, Daan. I am very pleased to meet you both in person. I have followed your distinguished careers and am deeply honoured to welcome you to our organization." With that brief welcome, she shook hands with a double clasp accompanied with a warm, inclusive smile. "We will get to know each other better but for now, I will not interrupt your briefing."

"Over to you, Matthieu," Daan advised. "They're all yours."

CHAPTER 34

"Thanks, Daan." Matthieu began with the familiarity of the known. "You may have already suspected some of what I am about to tell you. Other details may cause you to raise your eyebrows a little. Let's start with some history. During the Second World War, there were some in the Vatican who sided with the Nazis and aided in the movement of high-ranking SS and other senior Nazis to South America in return for major deposits of stolen Nazi gold to bolster the coffers of the Vatican bank. But not all in the Roman Catholic community were onside with that element in Rome. Some parish priests sided with the Allies. The priest in the l'Église du Sacré-Cœur in Luxembourg, Father John, was one of them."

"That brings back recollections," Alexandra reflected. "Thinking back, my mother alluded to a connection but never filled in the details."

"Just as a side, let me enlighten you on a related variable. When we met in Father Luke's office last week, he mentioned we are half-brothers. That is almost true. Father Luke said we have the same mother who came to work in the Priest's House with a dark cloud over her head because she was a single parent. Father Luke was her child. That priest, Father John, in addition to working with the Allies to smuggle downed Allied aircrew back to England, was not exactly celibate. I was born into the parish house a few years later. Father Luke and I are full brothers. We have the same mother and father."

"The resemblance to the photograph," Alexandra commented with an acknowledging smile.

"You will make a good intelligence gatherer, Alexandra. Father

John also worked with Maria, your mother, when she was in Normandy in 1944 and 1945, and briefly after the war. Father John also knew Major Mike Murphy and Sir James. Father John retired early because of illness and was replaced temporarily while Father Luke was completing missionary work abroad. Just before Father John died, he summoned Father Luke and me to his bedside. He revealed his sins and his work with the Allies. Although I am a few years younger than my brother, I was old enough to understand the implications. Father Luke took up Father John's cause of assisting parishioners in other than purely traditional parish ways. Father Luke was ultimately appointed as the parish priest at l'Église du Sacré-Cœur. Suffice it to say there were others of a similar philosophical persuasion in the hierarchy of the Catholic Church who worked in clandestine ways to support this league. Their association was no different from other quasi-secret associations which have far-reaching tentacles in the world of commerce and governance. I stayed in close contact with my brother as I pursued a career in intelligence. That's where I met Daan."

"It's a small world," Paul murmured. "Why don't we take a break while Alexandra and I process what we have learned thus far."

"A stroll in the garden would be in order. But first I need to explain the structure of the EUI Unit because you will be meeting some of these people this week. Paul, you will note the strong similarity to a military unit. EUI Unit receives direction and funding from a small cell in the EU Commission in Brussels headed by Yolina Lambert. Daan is our commanding officer, so to speak, referred to as niner. I am his second in command and referred to as call sign eight. Operationally, we have five Delta units. Delta 1 is surveillance support on foot. Delta 2 is all ground transport support, two- and four-wheeled and small marine craft. Delta 3 is special operations employed to divert or otherwise neutralize a target as circumstances warrant. Delta 4 is both a fixed-wing and rotary aircraft. Finally, Delta 5 is technical services including video and audio surveillance and all computing services."

"One last point," Daan added. "Our team is composed of people connected only to the original EU members. As you can appreciate, some later members such as those from previous Eastern Bock states tend to have divided loyalties. That's just bad for business. If there are no questions, let's go for a walk in the garden."

⌁ ⌁

THE WEEK ENDED AS IT HAD BEGUN with informal briefings and introductions to other EUI Unit members.

"A few times now, I've mentioned there is a fine line between intelligence gathering and operational enforcement," Daan reiterated. "The work you will be doing with us will cross these lines but your mission remains intelligence gathering. Nevertheless, you need to be prepared for any unforeseen consequences. Thus, it will be appropriate to spend some time at the indoor small arms range just to reacquaint you, Paul, and acquaint you, Alexandra with the supplementary tools of the trade. You will spend this afternoon on the range. Matthieu, over to you."

With that introduction, Matthieu handed Paul and Alexandra each a Beretta M9 9mm pistol and demonstrated how to safely strip and assemble the handgun. Alexandra followed his instructions, handling the Beretta with greater speed and precision than either Matthieu or Paul who stared at her in amazement. She returned their gaze with a confident smile and explanation. "My mother taught me how to handle different makes and models of handguns." On the range, she fired perfect targets.

"Your mother also taught you how to shoot?" Matthieu enquired with a curious and amused expression.

"Correct. Either of you care to wager a bet on who gets the

highest score and the greatest number of rounds in the CX in the next serial?"

"Not me," Paul replied immediately and with a humbling bow. "You never cease to amaze me, ma princesse. *Miribilis es* – you are miraculous. And talented with the trigger."

"Matthieu, want to wager?"

With eyes wide open and an equally astonished expression, Matthieu gestured like a sorcerer's apprentice to his mentor: "Not me."

⊣ ⊢

MARIA'S VOICE REVERBERATED IN ALEXANDRA'S MIND LIKE distant cathedral bells sounding clarity in her communiqué. "Run … run! Instead, you took the impossible shot. You saved my life. It was not your fight. But because you are my daughter, you have been drawn into my world of counterintelligence at far too tender an age. Ironically, it is the age when I entered the *Maquis* vortex that defined my future, your future, our future."

Some memories are like arctic wolves, Alexandra reflected. *You can lock them up but you cannot silence their haunting howls.*

⊣ ⊢

"LET'S PACK THE TOYS AWAY AND GO for a walk in the garden," Daan suggested. "The fresh alpine fall air will put what I am about to tell you in perspective. I have some interesting information on your bait books."

"Are you all right, ma princesse?" Paul quietly enquired as they left the range.

"Fine. Why do you ask?"

"You look a little disturbed, distracted, like you had seen a ghost."

Her response was terse. "I'm fine."

Paul returned a brief smile accentuated with a furrowed brow as they strolled into the garden. *Like Ebenezer Scrooge, she too has ghosts from her Christmas Past,* he concluded.

"What's up, Daan?" Paul asked.

"Our tech folks advised that your bait books are on the move. They entered Austria at the Braunau am Inn border crossing, east of Munich. They're currently in a bookbinding shop in Graz."

"Is it by coincidence or simply chance that Adolf Hitler was born in Braunau am Inn?" Alexandra pondered.

"Not sure," Daan replied. "I like your thinking, though. It's worth following up. We do know that this bookbinding shop has shipped many other books to Brazil, especially to Pomerode in southern Brazil. Pomerode could be re-located in Bavaria today and no one would be any the wiser. It has been described as being more German than any other city in Germany. Numerous other forms of freight in addition to written correspondence have been shipped back to Bavaria over the decades. This falls within our mandate, to protect the EU from known or perceived threats. I have received clearance from Yolina to follow up. Your first mission, Paul and Alexandra, is to proceed to Graz and find out what you can about this bookbinding store. Matthieu will accompany you. Delta 5 is already there and will update you on any movement of your bait books. Any questions?"

"None," both Paul and Alexandra replied in unison.

"Just a reminder, our modus operandi is to take our time, observe and cultivate but still be aware of any urgency in addition to our priorities. Enjoy Austria."

"*Festina lente* – make haste slowly," Paul reflected.

"We hope that your vacation with us at the Principality Grande Hotel in Liechtenstein has met your expectations and you will return again," Daan quipped to Alexandra with the politeness of a diplomat and the charm of a courtier.

"You're off the hook for now, Daan," Alexandra chuckled. "And, yes, it was a most enjoyable vacation. We look forward to returning soon."

"A final question, Daan," Paul prompted. "Thank you for introducing Yolina Lambert. Can you provide a brief background?"

"Certainly. She is from Bordeaux. Her parents were turned over to Nazis SS in 1944 by the Vichy government because they were Jewish. Miraculously, they survived the Holocaust and Dachau concentration camp. Suffice it to say, there's no love lost on Yolina's part for either the Third or Fourth Reich, or any threat to the sanctity of the European Union. She worked in French Intelligence, General Directorate for Internal Security before heading up our organization. I can assure you she will have our backs for all threats to the EU, internal or external. Not once has she failed to garner resources for any previous mission. She has been able to do so because, in part, we have always been successful in thwarting all threats. There isn't one member of the European Union who has not benefitted, even the newest members. In the truest sense, we are a team and she is our team leader. You never want to forget that."

"Impressive. Thank you," Paul remarked.

My mother worked under similar conditions and must have received similar support from the Republic of France, Alexandra reflected. Although her jurisdiction was formally defined primarily by the international boundaries with all the countries that bordered France, it also included those nation states whose ethos was to disrupt France's democratic process. The mandate of the EUI Unit was similar. Boundaries had been extended beyond national borders. Yet, mandates remained the same, to neutralize internal and external threats. The focus of French Counterintelligence after the war had not changed substantially. Alexandra had never felt closer to her mother and Sir James than with the European

Union Intelligence Unit, more so because of Maria's connection with Father Luke. Their first mission was to gather intelligence regarding stolen Nazi gold and other artifacts. Their first threat was Russian.

Alexandra would take to heart the sage words her mother had shared and the lessons taught. She sensed she would be drawn away from Collette as Maria had been drawn away from her. In contrast to her relationship with her own mother, she would spend every spare moment with Collette to ensure their relationship would not falter. She had hated what the suitcase at the front door stood for. The pattern would not be repeated.

CHAPTER 35

The bookbinding shop was a pleasurable stroll from their hotel overlooking the Mur River. The old city of Graz surrounding the Schlossberg ramparts offered them ample opportunity to play the part of newlyweds and recent retirees seeking treasures to add to their book collection.

"I hadn't realized just how many antiquarian boutiques there were in Graz. We could retire here and still not have enough time to browse through all the shops," Alexandra commented with the excitement of a child having passed through the gates of Père Noël's workshop at the North Pole. "There are five university campuses here. I could teach part-time."

"You could but that might interfere with our retirement schedule. On the other hand, there is a Harley-Davidson dealership close by that benefits from the European Bike Week *Faaker See* Festival in the summer. We would fit right in. But back to work, madame. There's the *buchbinderei*, the bookbinding store where the bait books have been tracked to."

Alexandra commented, "And a coffee shop just across the square. Let's have a cappuccino and croissant, and just take our time, observe, and cultivate, as Daan directed." Out of habit as a forensic psychologist, she found herself assessing profiles for those who strolled through the square. She took note of their facial features, body language, dress and deportment. Were they *intelligentsia* or *cognoscenti*, tourists or residents, agents of business or agents of surveillance, like Paul and her? Were they coming from or going to liaisons, or neither? Some nondescript patrons of the café seemed lost in books or immersed in newspapers. Many walked with a lack of purpose and gazed with nonchalant casualness. Still others simply stared inquisitively as if memorizing details for novels tentatively conceived in their minds but not yet written. Alexandra continued to gauge them curiously.

After they finished their *petit déjeuner,* Paul whispered, "We've been sitting here for the better part of an hour and no one has entered or left the buchbinderei. Other shops on the square including this coffee shop are relatively busy. It's not that the location is poor. This book-binding shop seems to be doing as much business as Dieter's bookstore in Munich, which was *nichts, rien,* nothing, when we were there."

"I was thinking the same thing. Let's browse other shops around this square. One of us can shop while the other maintains surveillance. We can come back here as it gets closer to lunch and chat with the waiter about business while we dine on the local Styrian cuisine."

"Sounds like a plan. After lunch, we could go into the *Buchhandlung Antiquariat* just around the corner and buy a book in disrepair. I don't see any exterior surveillance cameras around our target buchbinderei. But just in case there are some inside, we can have Matthieu or one of our other colleagues enquire about getting our new purchase re-bound while checking for any interior cameras. We wouldn't want any images of us getting back to Dieter and Katrina if the bookbinder is suspicious enough to have surveillance. Given the fact that our bait books are here strongly suggests there is a relationship."

Paul checked for emails as they paid the waiter. "Interesting. Time for a chat with Daan and Matthieu," he murmured.

"What's up?"

"Jean is asking for my advice on joining the church choir. He says the choir master needs to fill an opening soon so wants a reply by this evening."

⊣ ⊢

"I AGREE WITH YOUR INITIAL ASSESSMENT OF the bookbinding shop,

Alexandra," Matthieu acknowledged. "By itself, it's little more than a montage of anecdotal information. But combined with what we already know about the overseas transactions to and from Brazil and the absence of obvious street business, like Dieter's Munich bookstore, your appraisal warrants a look inside the premises. I'll have one of our team take in your book and enquire about repairing the spine when or if it opens for business. In the interim, continue to play the part of tourists and antiquarians."

"Another matter, Matthieu, possibly related but certainly with significant overtones," Paul announced.

'Significant overtones' piqued Matthieu's interest. "What have you got?"

Paul explained the background to the wedding ring he was wearing including the historical links to the clandestine Runic language, which Jean had revealed over dinner when he and Alexandra had announced their engagement.

"Jean said he would enquire further under the guise of doing research for an article for publication and to be presented at a conference. If he found anything with ominous implications, he would contact me with a code word 'choir.' When I returned his call, he confirmed that the Quer remains an active and elite secret society with tentacles reaching into all the capitals of major nation state players. They are deadlier and more ruthless when dealing with perceived threats than any Sicilian Mafioso. Neither Alexandra nor I know anything more about her father's connections to the Quer except that one of his relatives was apparently a member."

As Paul narrated the details, Matthieu's response became more guarded and cautious. "You never cease to amaze me. The Quer has been on our radar for a long time. Jean's assessment is completely accurate. Deadly is an understatement. We knew of the ring and its importance but have never seen one. May I take a look?"

After showing Matthieu the inscription, he replied, "I need to call Daan and we all need to have a conversation. For now, turn the ring one hundred and eighty degrees on your finger. I'll have Delta 1 monitor your activities until we can decide on our strategy. This revelation is a mammoth breakthrough, and I mean colossal in every sense of the word. The EUI Unit has never been able to make a slightest crack in the armour of the Quer."

※ ※

"OUR TEAM HAS FOLLOWED UP ON JEAN'S research on the Quer. Alexandra's grandfather was indeed a member of the Quer and passed it on to Alexandra's father who was a quieter associate," Daan explained. "Their family tree reaches back to the Gallic period when France was known as Gaul, approximately from the fifth century B.C. to the fifth century A.D. We are researching further. This disclosure and the ring itself could be the most significant breakthrough ever. The only other revelation in modern history of intelligence of equal or greater value would be the discovery of a code that was supposedly developed sometime between the end of the Second World War and the early years of the Cold War. This code could be just a myth. There was a suggestion that the Quer may have developed it and have been using it. That's how they have remained under the radar. But that is just speculation at this juncture. It's on the Russian and Chinese radar screens too, in addition to a few other less-than-honourable players in the intelligence sandbox."

Paul and Alexandra stared at one another as they clasped hands. This reaction did not go unnoticed by Daan and Matthieu.

Daan uttered with hesitation in his voice, "Is there something you haven't mentioned, something else that we need to talk about, Paul? Alexandra? Are you aware of this code? If you are, now is the time to talk. I don't need to remind you how deadly the ramifications would be if it ended up in other hands."

Alexandra quietly described her mother's code and the

connection to Sir James, Major Mike Murphy and the Antiquarian Book Collectors Club. Silence didn't always equate to inner peace. This was one of those occasions when the opposite prevailed.

Daan and Matthieu froze. For what seemed like eternity, Daan blindly stared into the abyss with horror, contemplating what an atomic inferno a trillion times stronger than Fat Boy might be if the code and the Quer were ever to merge in the wrong circumstance, not that there ever would be a right circumstance. The catalysts of such a fusion sat calmly in front of him.

"Oh my God," slipped from Matthieu's lips. "This is as close as I ever want to come to a cardiac arrest," he gasped as he grappled with the implications of this revelation.

"Is there anything else you would like to share?" Daan asked as he regained his composure. "Do you have any idea of the implications of the combination of your ring, Paul, and your code, Alexandra?"

"We do now," Paul conceded. "The dots have just been connected." He had to confess the thought had never crossed his mind.

"And the poisoning of Sir James and Tom," Alexandra added as she placed her hand over her mouth is revulsion. "Oh my God. Are we the link? The catalyst in their deaths?"

"It is unbelievable that the codes sat in Sir James's bookshelf all this time and the ring was in a ribbon box in your apartment, Alexandra," Matthieu exclaimed.

"Order, ladies and gentlemen!" Daan stated with the sternness of a commanding general about to embark on a second D-Day frontal assault. "Matthieu, we need the security team with air support here now, and our A-level surveillance team on immediate standby. If that's acceptable to the two of you, we should secure the code books and all other related documents. Your bank safe deposit box is as secure as it can be at that level, but we need to implement another level above that."

"Fine with us," Alexandra replied as she received a cautious nod from Paul.

"Given the implications," Matthieu suggested, "perhaps we should have our people examine in detail the entire antiquarian collection from Alexandra's mother and Sir James. Both were old-school professionals. I wouldn't be surprised if they built in another layer of redundancy for security."

"I agree," Dann acknowledged as he again transferred his attention to Alexandra and Paul. "You will be living in one of our most secure residences until we have developed a strategy to deal with the Quer. The Fourth Reich still remains a priority and we will adjust our strategy accordingly. I wouldn't be surprised if there is a connection or certainly a strong correlation. I'll need to brief Brussels. I doubt very much that I'll have any problems securing additional resources from Yolina, given the possible consequences of this knowledge."

"What about my son, Jean?" Paul asked. "And Alexandra's daughter, Collette?"

"I'll contact Commandant Parent and arrange security for them both."

"Thanks, Daan," Paul acknowledged with a thin smile. His face reflected the gravity of the ramifications exceeding any circumstances he had faced when serving with the United Nations in the former Republic of Yugoslavia or the war crimes missions.

Alexandra became acutely aware of the extent to which Paul's demeanour had changed. She could not recall one instance during the hunt for Thon when he had exhibited such concern, not even the moment in the warehouse when the gunman held the pistol to her head. This was baptism by fire. The only instance that could cause her more distress would be an imminent threat to the safety of Collette, and Jean.

CHAPTER 36

"Well, brother, haven't seen you for a while." There was impatience and distaste in the voice, rough with resentment.

From the doorway, Jean eyed his brother with caution. His hair was dishevelled, his clothes disarrayed. He smelled like a gutter rat, his complexion pallid. His eyes were as black and vacant as those of a dead fish washed from a polluted sewer outflow. They conveyed a premonition of a looming storm.

Jean replied abruptly as a deep cleft of worry appeared between his eyes. "Last time I heard, you were in Argentina living with our aunt. What are you doing here in Paris?" He purposely kept his expression vacant and for good reason. Yvon would sell his soul to the devil for far less than thirty pieces of silver.

"Aren't you going to introduce me to the cutie?"

"Collette, this is my brother Yvon."

Something touched Collette's consciousness, that miniscule part of the human instinct warning of imminent danger. She immediately became wary. She said nothing but instead stepped back. She wasn't totally innocent, like Eve in the garden before the snake slithered down from the apple tree, nor was she as worldly as her mother.

"So, why are you with him, Collette, when you could be with me?" Yvon blurted sarcastically.

"What do you want, Yvon?" Jean interrupted him before his insulting behaviour erupted into his usual abusive verbal diatribe.

"For starters, you can let me in."

"That's not going to happen, brother."

"At least you can loan me some money. You owe me that much."

"That's not going to happen, either."

"You're still the spoiled brat you always were," Yvon snarled cynically. "Where are Mom and Dad?"

"Mom died this past summer and Dad has moved to Luxembourg."

"So, what happened to her estate? What's Dad's number? Give him a call. Tell him I want what's rightfully mine."

Jean retrieved one of his own business cards from his pocket and wrote down a telephone number. "Here's Dad's cell number. Give him a call yourself. Now leave before I call the police."

As Jean locked the door, Yvon yelled, "You ain't heard the last of me, asshole." Hatred has a taste and texture of its own and Yvon's threat was that personification.

"You told me he was a bad actor," Collette commented as she stared at Jean with a frightened expression.

"He always was a danger to himself and others when he was high on drugs and not much better when he was sober. He's worse now. God only knows what he's on. I need to call Dad and warn him."

"Papa, it's Jean. You'll never guess who tried to barge into my place."

"Who?"

"My long-lost brother, Yvon."

"How long has he been in Paris? What did he want?"

"Not sure how long he's been in town. He wanted money. He's really spaced out on drugs and is uglier in temperament than I have ever seen him. He asked about *Maman*. I told him she was dead. That didn't faze him at all. He just wanted money from her estate. I gave him your cell number, Papa. Hope that that was okay."

"That's fine, Jean. I'll deal with him if he calls. I suppose there was always the chance he was going to come back at some point."

"What was that all about?" Alexandra asked.

"Not particularly good news," Paul answered after a pause. "That was Jean. My oldest son, Yvon, is back in Paris. He wanted money from Jean who described him as being really high on drugs and more abusive than he has ever been. Jean sounded okay but wary."

"Did Jean call the police?"

"No. He will though if he believes there is a danger. Jean gave him my number. I'll deal with Yvon if he calls me."

Alexandra's concern was certainly for Jean but more so for Collette who tended to shy away from loud abusive people. Although exceptionally competent in the art of karate, she preferred not to engage beyond the dojo if she did not have to. She had enrolled in the sport as a form of physical and mental exercise to counter the day-to-day stress in addition to meditation. It also bolstered her self-confidence as she advanced in qualification. As Jean had described her with great admiration, "although slight in stature she was feisty in nature."

CHAPTER 37

"Good morning, Alexandra, where is Paul this morning?" Matthieu enquired.

"He had a dentist's appointment. He should be here by coffee break, although I doubt he will want anything after a root canal."

"Ouch! Not even delicate croissants or soothing cappuccino," Matthieu commiserated as he raised his hand to his jaw.

Alexandra stared down at her phone as an email arrived with "THON" in the subject line. "Excuse me for a moment, Matthieu. My daughter has just coded me an urgent call for help."

"Collette, what's wrong, dear?"

"Please come, Mom. I need you."

"Where are you? What happened?"

"I'm at Jo's. Please come quickly."

"I'm on my way, dear."

"What's going on, Alexandra?" Matthieu asked with concern.

"My daughter is in trouble. I don't have any details. Since the Thon case, I told her that if her life was ever in danger, she was to put THON in the subject line."

"I'll drive you," Matthieu offered. "Just tell me where to go."

As Alexandra and Matthieu entered Jo's home, Collette rushed into her mother's arms. Once calmed by the security of her mother's embrace, Collette related an encounter with Yvon. "He burst into the house when I opened the door. He demanded money and when I didn't give him any, he went crazy. He grabbed me by the throat and started groping me. He tried to force me to the floor and rape me. I fought him off. He was a maniac, Mom, in a psychopathic state, worse than Thon. He ran out the door or hobbled out the door after I kneed him in the groin. I picked up MV and left through the

204

back door and came over to Jo's because it was the safest, closest place. I was afraid of what Jean would do if I called the police, so I didn't. He'd kill Yvon. I know he would. You can't tell Paul either. He'd kill Yvon too. Oh, Mom. I don't know what to do or tell Jean when he sees me with the bruises."

"Let me think," Alexandra calmly responded.

"First, can Collette stay here, Jo?"

"Of course!"

"I'll stay here too. I'm not going to leave you, Collette. This is the story. Jo, you became ill and called Collette. Collette was so frantic about your call that she tripped and fell leaving the house. She called me at work, which she did, and Matthieu drove me over, which he did. That's what we'll tell Jean and Paul. I'll call Paul and explain that Collette and I will be taking shifts over the next twenty-four hours to watch over Jo, so I won't be home. Send Jean an email, Collette, so he won't worry. If he calls, I'll answer your phone and explain that you are caring for Jo and will call him back as soon as possible."

Alexandra told Matthieu in a non-negotiable voice, "You can't tell Paul anything about this. Do I have your word on that?"

"You have my word, Alexandra. You stay here with your daughter and Jo and I'll get back to the office. I'll just tell Daan you had a family emergency and you'll be back at work tomorrow. Based on our previous conversation in Graz, I'll call Commandant Parent and reinforce the need for extra patrols near Jean and Collette's house. All will be taken care of. Rest assured."

"Thank you, Matthieu. You're a good friend."

⇥ ⇤

DELTA 3. MISSION.

⇥ ⇤

JEAN'S WORK PHONE RANG. "DO YOU HAVE a moment if I drop by?" Commandant Parent asked."

"Certainly."

Jean looked up to see his supervisor and Commandant Parent approaching his cubicle.

"Oh dear, not a good sign when you both come. What's up, boss?" Jean asked, not with concern but with expectation.

"Come into my office, Jean. Benoit has some confidential information to share."

"When was the last time you spoke with your brother, Jean?" Commandant Parent asked. His stern posture mirrored a serious tone.

"He came to my house last night demanding money and asking where our parents were. Why?"

"A body was found in the Seine early this morning. Your business card was found in a pocket along with other ID with the name Yvon Bernard. He may be your brother. Can you come to the morgue to see if you can identify him? If it is your brother, I'll call your father. If it isn't him, we won't have to bother him."

Jean looked down at the body on the cold marble slab. In his youth, Yvon had been good-looking. In death his face was contorted. Jean spoke the three words that confirmed the suspicion. "That is Yvon." *Even with bad choices there were worse choices and Yvon had made one too many,* Jean thought. *To say he had the wisdom of a fool would be a gross exaggeration. Fate had finally caught up with him.*

"Thank you, Jean. I'll call your father."

"How did he die?" Jean asked with resignation.

"A drug overdose. Crack cocaine cut with arsenic was the culprit. He had several bags of crack stuffed in his socks. The investigators concluded he was trafficking and sampled too much of his own stash."

"Thank you. I suspected so. When he came over to my place, he was higher than I can ever remember him being. Life caught up with him, and I'm not surprised. Perhaps you can call Dad now and I'll talk with him also. I know he is alone because Alexandra is with Collette, over with a friend who became quite ill yesterday. I'll call Collette as soon as I finish talking with Dad, if that's all right?"

"That would be fine, Jean. And take the rest of today off and whatever additional time you need. There's nothing major in your in-basket."

"Thanks, boss. I very much appreciate your understanding. And thank you, Commandant Parent, for your personal involvement. I know that my father will be most appreciative too."

"It's the team that stands together in such times. Take care, Jean," Benoit assured him.

⊣ ⊢

"DELTA 3, BRAVO ZULU. DROP BY MY office when you have a moment."

⊣ ⊢

"ARE YOU ALL RIGHT, MARCEL?"

"Yeah, I'm okay, Daan. Just need to process. What will I do if he finds out?"

"Only you, Matthieu and I know, and we will take that fact to our graves. Yes, this job has its challenges..." His voice trailed off.

"Challenges!" Marcel uttered. "That's an understatement. I know it was the right decision. Yvon was a bastard who needed to meet his maker sooner rather than later."

Daan added, "In retrospect, Paul wasn't very upset at the news of his death. In fact, I got the feeling he was relieved and has moved on. We have kept Paul busy working on our current mission with Alexandra."

"But it still sucks!" Marcel admitted. "He saved my life in Sarajevo. In return, I killed his son. It's something I'm just going to have to deal with, and I will handle it."

Daan's fatherly gaze and his quiet nod provided reassurance.

"Thanks for asking, boss. I'm good to go," Marcel murmured over his shoulder as he strolled out of the office.

Good to go but best to monitor nonetheless, Daan reflected. *Perhaps it would be better to have Delta 3 work closely with Paul so I can gauge his emotional response.*

Daan had an idea of what Marcel was going through. Early in his own career, he had poisoned the spouse of a childhood friend because she was a double agent. The hit had been authorized but that hadn't made the task any easier. He dutifully but reluctantly followed orders. Like Marcel had just described, he had also experienced sleepless nights and unrelenting flashbacks that lingered for years. Even today, traces of anxiety continued to remind him of his mortality when he thought about his own wife and children. He had been the best man at their wedding. He lured her to a rendezvous where he had mixed the KGB cocktail. The decoy had been easy. They had a history of intimate assignations. Between the silk sheets, she had let slip her bra and her duplicitous life. Adversaries of the Cold War became convenient perpetrators in her death.

"Where is the unemotional Mister Spock when Captain Kirk needs him the most?" Daan muttered.

This aspect of the job was the most distasteful yet sometimes the most necessary. As a junior intelligence officer seeking to expand his knowledge and gain the requisite experience, he had gradually been exposed to less favourable, more secretive elements of espionage and intelligence gathering. His mentor had been a

Second World War veteran who had honed his skills at a time when missions were clear and methodology purposely vague. Adapt and improvise in order to achieve the objective was the mantra. It wasn't just the MI6 double-zero agents who had been given a licence to kill.

CHAPTER 38

"Alexandra, it's Helena. Do you have time to meet?"
"Certainly. I always have time for you. Are you in Paris?"

"I am. I have Tom's antiquarian book collection. He left them to you and Paul in his Will so it would be better if you and Paul came together. I'll need you both to sign for them for the estate records."

"I have a friend who lives in Garches, west of Paris. Can we meet there this evening around 7:00 p.m.?" She provided the address.

"Yes. Look forward to catching up."

"Who are we meeting at Jo's this evening?" Paul asked.

"Helena. Apparently, Tom left his antiquarian book collection to us. She will drop them off."

"Interesting. "What's your *shrew* saying?"

Alexandra gazed from minute details to macro landscapes for any reasons why they should be more cautious than they already were, given the morbid circumstances.

"I know that look, ma princesse. I sense we need to have a chat with Daan before we meet Helena. I'll call him now."

Alexandra nodded. "You read me well."

"Daan. Helena LeDuc, Tom's understudy, just called. Tom left Alexandra and me his antiquarian collection in his Will. Helena wants to meet this evening around 7:00 p.m. to deliver them to us. Alexandra has made arrangements to get together at Jo's place in Garches. Thoughts?"

"Interesting," Daan reflected. "I think she may want to chat. To renew acquaintance. Otherwise the executor for the estate would just deliver them. Mind if I tag along and listen in from another room?"

"Sounds like a plan." Paul confirmed.

⊣ ⊢

PAUL ADJUSTED THE MICROPHONE IN THE FLOWER arrangement in the center of the table. It seemed out of place as all other plants in Jo's house were potted. Perhaps he was being too cautious. He then lowered the volume of the background music. Daan acknowledged the adjustment with a nod.

"I have three boxes of books in the taxi," Helena announced. "Can you give me a hand bringing them in?"

"Of course," Paul replied.

With the bequests stacked in the hallway closet and the door securely fastened, they assembled at the table in the dining room.

"It's good to see you," Helena smiled. "When last we met, just after Tom's death, I said I would keep you informed of any new developments."

"We certainly appreciate the personal delivery service," Alexandra acknowledged. "And it's wonderful to see you too."

"When we first met in Langley, I appreciated your respect for my cultural background, Alexandra. It is for that personal motivation and professional courtesy that I wanted to meet in person. Tom would have wanted me to keep in contact. He thought a great deal of you both."

"We felt the same way about him. His death was a shock," Paul replied. "You are cut from the same cordial cloth." Under different circumstances, he would have been more relaxed. *Would Helena notice the difference? Perhaps, I should say something or would that draw her attention where it was not necessary,* he wondered. "Tom was more than a colleague. He was a good friend. We miss him."

Helena smiled in acknowledgement of Paul's words of sentiment. "Rarely have I met anyone as intuitive as you two. So, I wouldn't be surprised if you realized my relationship with Tom was more than protégé and mentor. I have been with the CIA for a long time, longer than what was initially divulged. I was teamed up with Tom to try to find out who was on to him. We suspected it was the Russians. The FSB defector I told you about confirmed our suspicions. He did not have detailed information but confirmed that an old KGB agent was on Tom's trail and had a personal score to settle. In addition, the KGB has been hunting for stolen Nazi gold, as have others, including the Chinese and Middle East terrorists as of late."

"Thank you for sharing that. It's good to know. But then again, not surprising," Alexandra conceded. "That begs the question. If they found any gold, how would they transport it back to Mother Russia. It is a little bit bulkier than an envelope of diamonds."

"*Das ist wahn* – that is true," Helena replied all the while maintaining eye contact with Alexandra. "The KGB has also been searching for a mysterious code. Not surprisingly, they were aware of your mother and Sir James Pennington." She paused slightly. "They have had strong suspicions that your mother, Sir James and Major Mike were the link somehow, especially Major Mike, whom they believed had perfected it in the latter months of the war while he served with the OSS. At your mother's funeral, they locked on to you, Alexandra, and later on to Paul once you partnered up."

"Is there a connection to Tom's death?" Alexandra enquired, probing for additional details and links to her mother and to herself. The image of the two passengers on the Eurail sitting across the aisle appeared prominent in her mind.

Helena responded without hesitation. "Tom's poisoning was another unrelated yet tangential factor. We concluded that your association with Tom was a coincidence. But from a KGB perspective, where there is smoke, there is fire. I pass this on to you because the old KGB guard are tenacious in not abandoning a scent. The FSB seem less so. I am aware you are working with the European Union Intelligence Unit. You need to be cautious. Unrelated to Tom's death and association specifically, we have reason to believe that the FSB have you under surveillance."

"What's this code all about?" Paul asked. The motivation for his question was two-fold. First, he wanted to keep her attention on Alexandra and himself and not on the flower arrangement. Second, bringing up the code was too close for comfort. Had she mentioned it to test Alexandra's reactions or had she done so out of professional courtesy and personal concern?

"From what I know, it could be myth, a ruse to distract enemy agents," she added. "But when the truth is so precarious, so lethal, myths and ruses are created." She again paused ever so briefly, pursing her lips and shaking her head. "I just don't know."

Her response seemed sincere. "What about the Fourth Reich? What's the Russian take on the neo-Nazis and the gold?" Paul probed.

"The Fourth Reich are good but they aren't that good. They still believe in a Thousand-Year Reich but it's more of a dream, linked to the old Hitler vision. We think the current Fourth Reich leadership sees Hitler as a psychopath, a megalomaniac. There is something else out there pulling their strings. It's like the elusive code – just wariness with no hard facts to back it up. In the final analysis, Communists and Nazis detest each other and that loathing hasn't changed with the evolution of the Fourth Reich."

"Thanks, Helena. We appreciate your concern for our wellbeing," Alexandra replied. "If you are open to it, we'd like to keep in touch, if for no other reason than personal. You're a principled person. We've come to appreciate that such integrity is becoming harder to find as time passes."

"I'd like that. I'm certain Tom is looking down on us and smiling. Now I must be on my way."

"Thanks again for delivering Tom's book collection. You can rest assured we will cherish it."

The thud of the door closing was Daan's signal that he could come out of hiding and share in some coffee.

He looked down the hallway at the closet holding the boxes of books before pouring himself a cup. He put his finger to his lips and beckoned Alexandra and Paul to follow him into the bedroom that had been his listening post.

"Well. That was an interesting conversation," he said in a low voice barely more audible than a whisper but not so loud that his voice could be carried down the hallway. "We only have to look at the fate of Leon Trotsky to realize that the Russians dispatch their assassins as a standard modus operandi. Tom is in good company in this regard. You played along like well-seasoned experts. What are your thoughts? Was Helena being honest or was she fishing for information?"

"I believe a bit of both," Alexandra responded. "She was being open. But as a professional, she was seeking validation."

"And your take, Paul?"

"I bow to the expert on intuition. When we first met in Langley, I believe Helena was touched by Alexandra's respect for her First Nations cultures and it created a bond between them. Helena and Alexandra also had an association with Tom. Accordingly, if Alexandra continues to nourish that relationship with Helena, she could very well be a valued confidante. One point of concern though. When she raised the topic of the code, her attention was solely on Alexandra. I got the feeling Helena was watching for the slightest of reaction from Alexandra."

It was Daan's turn to reflect. After a deep breath, he responded. "First, I agree. Alexandra should continue to cultivate the relationship. Second, she may have been searching for a reaction from Alexandra, although any physiological response could be attributed to the more recent funeral. Let's keep that on the backburner."

"To your first point, I can do that," Alexandra said. "Because Helena believes my respect for her cultures is heartfelt, which it is, I doubt she will suspect my intentions as being confederate. To your other observation, Paul, I too asked myself whether Helena might have been watching for a reaction. The fact that she mentioned the code, caught my attention more. For a supposed secret code, there seems to be too many people aware, suspicious. Perhaps, as Helena alluded to, it is simply a speculation of a ruse to distract attention and consume resources."

"Let's think about that," Daan summarized. "In the interim, I'd like to have our techies scan Tom's book collection, given the fact we now know the old KGB guard killed him. We need to be confident the books are clean. I'd like you both to scan each book to ascertain whether there are any clues Tom may have left, perhaps links to any cases he had been involved in. No doubt the CIA has done the same but we need to be certain. Bugs could be old KGB, more contemporary FSB, or CIA."

"The presence of any CIA devices could provide an indication of Helena's honesty," Alexandra suggested.

"It could if she were aware," Daan suggested. "But like the Russians, the CIA tend not to share all their strategies with all their operatives. If they picked up on the budding relationship between Helena and Alexandra, they would more than likely not divulge their strategy. Espionage and Intelligence agents are a suspicious guild by their very nature."

Alexandra stared past both Daan and Paul, tapping her fingers on her lips as she pondered. Although she had forgiven her mother for squirrelling away the love letters she and Paul had written to each other, Alexandra wondered what other personal family details her mother had not shared. On a personal level, she had not told Philip, Alexandra's father, about her existence. Her mother had been a member of French Counterintelligence, known for its secrecy and deceit. She had confessed in her letter to Alexandra that she had experienced lifelong regret for her actions. And inactions.

Epigenetic research suggests a lifetime of regret alters DNA expresssion. Alexandra was her mother's daughter. Regret and grief had defined her own character right down to the cellular level. She could see the attributes in Collette. Clearly, she had not been candid with André. How much was Paul aware of her less-than-complete honesty? Daan was a lifelong professional operative. Paul had worked with him while serving with the United Nations in the Former Republic of Yugoslavia. She had not. Should she be less trusting of Daan, of Paul? Was her relationship with Paul, both business and intimate, condemned to failure like her marriage to André, because of her own DNA?

"*Medice, cura te ipsum* – physician, heal thyself," her mother's voice resonated in Alexandra's mind. Her mother's voice continued to echo: "You are the psychologist, pull yourself together. André was an absolute jerk. I'm sorry I was not there for you, to dissuade you from marrying him. Paul is your soul mate. You were destined to be together."

After Daan left, Alexandra wrapped her arms tightly around Paul in a long embrace. She said nothing.

"Are you all right?" Paul asked, sensing an aura of doubt.

"Perfectly all right," she replied with a kiss. "Why wouldn't I be? I have you as my partner now and forever."

CHAPTER 39

"Folks, we have the green light from Brussels to proceed," Daan announced. "The Quer is now the highest priority. Given the implications, sufficient resources will be made available. What do we know about other leads?"

"Jean analyzed the numbers Sir James was working on when he died or rather, was murdered. They may have been coded and, if so, he believes they could be associated with a Swiss bank in either Zürich or Geneva. The key Maria left for Alexandra with the ring would more than likely be to a safe deposit box in the same bank because of a series sequence," Paul suggested.

"If Jean is correct and it is a bank account, we'll need to have someone in the bank at a senior level to confirm this, because there is a security firewall in the bank protecting access to some accounts," Matthieu added. "If we ask the wrong person, we may set off alarm bells."

"Alexandra, you said that you have a contact in the Swiss banking system whom you believe is trustworthy."

"That's correct. I contacted him and have tentatively arranged to meet this week if you give the go-ahead."

"Good work. Can you call him and set up a meeting? Bring the numbers and the safety deposit box key. Matthieu, deploy the security team to Geneva. We will leave on the helicopter," Daan directed.

⚔ ⚔

"ONE, TWO, THREE, FOUR, TEST, TEST, TEST."

"Reading you loud and clear, Alexandra," Matthieu responded with a nod. "Your wire is good."

"Excellent. Karl is just arriving."

"Karl, how are you?" Alexandra asked as she held out her hand.

"I am well, Alexandra. How can I help you?"

"I have a favour to ask you."

"I am indebted to you for all the counselling advice you provided to me. What do you have?"

"Can you tell me if you recognize these numbers and this key?"

Karl stared at the numeric series listed on the paper and numbers engraved on the key. The tempo of his breathing increased, his eyes widened and his hands began to shake ever so slightly. He gazed around the café with purpose. "Where did you get these?" He asked in a barely audible whisper.

"You seem anxious, Karl. Have they triggered a concern? When last we spoke about your employment, you expressed similar cautious reactions."

"The number is to a bank account in our branch. The key is to a safe deposit box also in our branch. I can confirm that the account is classified and can only be accessed by the bank manager. It is one of several accounts that have this highest security classification. You need to be very careful with this information. Clients who have these accounts are not nice people. They are very dangerous."

"Can you tell me whose name is associated with this account?"

"I can but, again, I caution you. I would be placing you in danger if I gave you the name because any e-enquiry would trigger a security alarm."

"Is there any way you can by-pass the security system, Karl? I would appreciate your assistance very much." The tone of her voice and the seriousness of her expression emphasized the magnitude of her request.

Karl pursed his lips and drew his hands over his face thoughtfully. "The original manual cards are still in the vault.

They would have all the information associated with the account, including the signature of the account holder."

"Could you photocopy or photograph the card? Could you get it for me, perhaps today?" Alexandra was aware of the stress that Karl was experiencing and his deep desire to fight back against the source of his anxiety. Her request was a potential resolution.

Stroking his chin, he replied with trepidation, "I could. You must appreciate that every square centimetre of the bank is monitored 24/7 by security cameras, including the vault. As the assistant manager, I am responsible for all security systems, including the closed-circuit cameras. Periodically, I run a security check that involves disabling all the monitors and then activating them after a system scan for bugs. I could photocopy the card when the system is down. This procedure is done just after the bank closes and all customers have departed. I could meet you afterwards, if that is possible."

"That would be wonderful, Karl. I cannot thank you enough."

"Doing this for you, Alexandra, would relieve my stress. I've thought of different ways to expose the dirty secrets of the bank for a long while. I won't ask why you want this information but I am confident your motive is admirable. But it's dangerous," he reiterated. Looking at his pocket watch, he confirmed he would be back within the hour.

"Well done, Alexandra," Daan's voice echoed in the earphone as she ran her fingers through her hair. Scanning the other patrons in the café, she gained comfort from subtle eye contact with Paul and Matthieu. She could see Daan's profile as he sat at a window table in a café across the street.

"Anyone noting any trailers or anything suspicious?" Daan asked.

"Negative," Paul replied.

"Nothing from my position," Matthieu confirmed.

"Let's maintain surveillance."

"Delta 1, advise when he is on his way back."

"Roger."

"Delta 4."

"Eye in the sky is in position."

"Roger."

"Maintain surveillance," Daan directed.

Sitting alone, Alexandra could feel the tension mounting as the minutes ticked by. Paul longed to break his position and join her across the café. Matthieu maintained a blank expression with only a twitching foot betraying his apparent calm.

Finally the communications resumed: "He's punctual," Delta 1 confirmed. "He's on the move and it's only been forty-five minutes. It must be the years of adherence to strict banking hours. ETA your location ten minutes."

"Check for trailers," Daan reaffirmed. "Delta 1 maintain close surveillance. We don't want any bumps at this juncture."

"Roger."

"Delta 4."

"I have him. All appears clear. Wait out. Correction. Delta 1, we appear to have a possible trailer. Female, dark hair in a bun, carrying a brown bag under her left arm with her hand concealed in her purse. She is gaining on the target at a rapid rate."

"Seen, Delta 4. Delta 1 bravo and charlie yours."

"Got her, Delta 1. She's just turned into a shoe store."

"Stay with her."

"Roger."

"Delta 4, report."

"All clear. Still clear. He is about to re-establish contact. He is sitting down."

"Roger. We have him in sight."

"How did it go, Karl?" Alexandra asked calmly.

"No problems. Here is the photocopy of the original account card. It is a bit faded but still clear, given its age. The account was opened in March 1870, just before the Germans invaded Alsace and Lorraine and started the Franco-Prussian war. The initial deposit was sizeable as you can see. Today, it is worth hundreds of millions of Swiss francs. That's actually small when compared with some other secret accounts, which are worth billions of Swiss francs. I confirmed that the safe deposit box for your key is still valid. The box is still there. I can confirm that the bank's key hasn't been used since 1924. The last signature on the card dated 31 March 1924 was Jacques Etien Marchand."

"Thank you very much, Karl. How are you feeling?"

"You are more than welcome, Alexandra. I actually haven't felt this good for a long time. My stress level is much lower knowing you have this information and will be doing something positive with it. But remember that these people are not nice so be very cautious."

"Rest assured, Karl, I will be taking action and will be careful."

"Do not hesitate to contact me if I can help you further, Alexandra. I think I'll take my wife out to dinner this evening just to celebrate this day. Though I won't tell her why, of course."

CHAPTER 40

"Maman, please call me," read Collette's text.

"Hello, dear. You texted. What's up?"

An uncomfortable pause followed as Alexandra reached for the amulet that hung round her neck. "Are you there, Collette? Are you all right? What's happened?" Memories of her text for help after Yvon's assault caused her heart to pound in her chest.

Collette choked back the tears. Her voice quivered as she stuttered. "I… I have some bad news, Maman. I don't know how to say it."

Alexandra heard the hurt in the tautness of her voice that was raspier and more delicate than she could remember. "I'm here, dear."

Collette cleared her throat just enough to cough. "I've had a miscarriage, maman. I didn't know that I was pregnant. Jean doesn't know either. I don't know how to tell him or even if I should tell him."

"Where are you?"

"I'm at Jo's. She's here with me. She knows. You talk to her."

Alexandra could hear muffled sobbing.

"Alexandra," Jo's voice echoed. "I'm here with Collette. Understandably, she is very upset but we're doing all right for now."

"Thank God you're with her. I'll be there as soon as I can."

"I think we're all right, Alexandra. The worst is over. I've made arrangements for Collette to stay with me tonight. We told Jean that I had a bit of a relapse and Collette will stay just to make sure I'm okay. Jean seems to understand."

"What happened? Does the doctor know why?"

"The doctor believes the miscarriage occurred a few days ago. It could have been natural or might have been as a result of trauma."

"Was Collette exercising too vigorously?"

"She hasn't been jogging for a few days. She said she just wasn't feeling well. Perhaps fighting a winter flu bug that's going around."

They both paused as they wrestled with the same horrifying possibility.

Alexandra uttered the unspeakable. "Yvon's attack."

"That's a possibility," Jo whispered. "But we can't be sure. We don't have enough facts. It could have been a natural miscarriage. They do happen."

"You're right. We can't jump to conclusions like this. The mere thought of it would drive a wedge into their relationship."

"And your relationship with Paul," Jo responded in a barely audible voice. "Collette is fine with me and I'm confident we can manage so you don't need to come immediately. It might raise suspicions with Jean and Paul if you did. Let's take time to reason things through."

"Do you think Collette connects the miscarriage with…?"

"I don't think so," Jo whispered. "She hasn't even hinted at it. I think she would have. I'll describe the natural causes of miscarriages when we chat. I'll call Jean tomorrow and thank him for allowing Collette to stay with me. We'll keep it on an even keel."

"You're right, Jo. Text me with any change, either good or bad. I owe you big time on this one."

"It's all in the family, Alex." Jo had only addressed her as Alex on occasions that were the most personal.

Alexandra wouldn't keep secrets from Paul. She had committed to that – no secrets in their relationship unlike her disastrous marriage with André. She just wouldn't tell Paul right now, not until all the facts were known. If he pressed the issue or asked if she was all right, she would reassure him with a warm hug and a loving kiss. She had learned how to calm his concerns.

Her immediate challenge would be to control her own emotions so as not to pique Paul's curiosity. He had grown very protective of her well-being from the first time they had worked together on the trip from Luxembourg to Dieppe. His concern for her was in complete contrast to André who had never demonstrated an inkling of interest let alone protection. She was learning how to deal with such knightly chivalry, for the first time in her life.

CHAPTER 41

"**B**ravo Zulu, team," Daan exclaimed as they huddled together in the security of their meeting room. "Alexandra, you were brilliant. This is the first we have become ever so slightly aware of the Quer since it was formed centuries ago. Our next step is to develop a strategy to enter its inner sanctum. Comments, Matthieu? Alexandra? Paul?"

"I reiterate Daan's congratulations, Alexandra. You were cool and in control throughout. You are a natural in this game, a seasoned professional. And, yes, we have cracked the armour," Matthieu added. "Being the first to enter the lair of the Quer will have its challenges as no one has walked this turf before. It's a new game with new rules for how we operate in the future. The future is now. Were there any problems?"

"As Karl and I had previously established a relationship of confidence, it was just another counselling session for me. The key was reducing his stress level. He desperately wanted to take some action against the secrecy of the bank that had become his nemesis. Once I showed him how, he became a willing participant, eager to achieve what he had only dreamt about. So, in response to your question, Daan, where do we go from here? It will be a psychological game of cat and mouse, with potentially deadly consequences for both predator and prey. The Quer has the home game advantage of being higher on the predatory food chain. But predators can become prey."

"Paul, your thoughts?" Daan enquired.

"Brilliant is an understatement, Alexandra. The first time I witnessed your coolness under fire was on the Eurail back to Paris when Thon called you. He was putty in your hands then, as Karl was today."

"We are a team, partner," Alexandra nodded.

Paul paused, worried by her distracted air. His raised eyebrows communicated his unease.

Alexandra returned his expression. But her half-smile mirrored her distraction.

Looking at Daan, Paul paraphrased: "Where do we go from here, Daan? There are two doors to open in order to access the Quer. The first is through the bank account. The second is access to the inner sanctum of the Quer, as you rightly called it. I suspect that will be through the safe deposit box. So, let's start with the bank account."

"I agree with your analysis, Paul," Daan acknowledged. "We need to get someone into the bank and the account. The best person for that job will be you."

"Me? Why not Alexandra?" Paul responded immediately.

"Alexandra is brilliant but you are best suited for this next phase. Let me explain. You have the ring. More importantly, you are a man. The Quer is a patriarchal organization. It always has been from what we know. The last person to sign the bank account card was Jacques Etien Marchand in 1924. He was Alexandra's grandfather. His father, Alexandra's great-grandfather, was Hugo Etien Marchand. We have confirmed he was a prominent member of the Quer. Our research on the Quer revealed that the ring was passed down from father to son. In this case, the ancestry goes back through the Marchand dynasty as long as records have been kept."

"But I'm not a Marchand. Alexandra is."

"Correct. And the fortune rightfully belongs to Alexandra. But she cannot walk into the bank without reams of legal documentation demonstrating her legitimacy to ownership. Even if she had the documentation, it wouldn't get her into the male dominated Quer, which is our primary objective. This is where we divert history enough for Alexandra to access her rightful inheritance, and for the EUI Unit to infiltrate the Quer."

"Divert history?" Paul chuckled. "The victors get to write the history books?"

"Exactly," Daan confirmed. "You and Alexandra are about to get married. Correct?"

"Yes, that's correct. We are looking at next month, in fact."

"Your marriage certificate is being prepared as we speak and it has already taken place. Congratulations!"

"Father Luke will have performed the ceremony," Matthieu said, "if that's all right with you both. The good Lord moves in mysterious ways, and it helps in times like these to have the ear of God's designated authority as a brother in arms, so to speak. You can have a family ceremony later but it should still be very private. A bit of a temporary diversion. Today, the groom is Claude Etien Marchand, heir apparent to a considerable estate."

Alexandra and Paul exchanged looks of amazement. For now, they gazed at their rings and their company of witnesses.

"Our relationship thus far has been a series of cart-before-the-horse events. Why not one more?" Alexandra conceded. "You should be a playwright, Daan."

"Matthieu, please explain what our teams have been up to."

"Thanks, Daan. As we speak, our technical folks at Delta 5 are preparing a new EU passport and other supporting identification for you, Paul, with the name Claude Etien Marchand. We have original letterhead paper from the Ritz Hotel in Paris back in its heyday. Technology will allow us to write in longhand this letter of attestation with Jacques Etien Marchand's signature. Being a wealthy member of the Quer, he would have stayed in Paris at the Ritz Hotel on Place Vendôme. In addition, with the signature of Jacques Etien Marchand on the bank account card that Karl provided, we will have our people prepare a letter from Jacques to the bank manager attesting to the fact that his son is the rightful heir to his estate, the bank account and the safe deposit box. His ultimate authenticity will be the possession of the ring and the key to the safe deposit box."

"Okay," Alexandra said. "According to the records, my father, Philip Marchand, was Jacques's only son and rightful heir. He just didn't access the estate for reasons unknown."

"You are correct, Alexandra. This is where we rewrite history a bit more. Jacques will have had an illegitimate first son named Gabriel Etien Marchand. Amended birth records will show this. Gabriel will be your father, Paul. He will have died in the Algerian revolution in 1961 gallantly defending the Republic of France. Just before his death, he will have asked his dear friend, your actual father, Jean-Paul Bernard, to adopt you as his own."

"Right, but mon père is suffering from acute dementia and doesn't remember anything, so he can't verify any of this."

"Exactly. That is the strength of our story. In reality, Paul, you have Power of Attorney for your father. You recently accessed his personal papers where you discovered your ancestry and the letter from Jacques on the Ritz letterhead. The Quer ring was in the envelope with this letter and the key to the safe deposit box. In addition, the envelope will have the formal adoption records, and your baptismal certificate from L'Église du Sacré Coeur."

Paul glanced at Matthieu, acknowledging fraternal kinship. "Votre frère. Frère Luke. Père Luke."

"*C'est ca.*" Matthieu acknowledged with a warm grin."

His smile was reciprocated as Daan continued to unfurl the final act of the play.

"Paul, you are going to walk into the bank with all this documentation, which you will present to the bank manager. The bank account number will be mentioned in the letter from Jacques along with the safe deposit key. You will wear the ring."

"This is very risky, Daan," Alexandra commented. "So much can go wrong."

"You're correct. It is risky. We will mitigate the risk by having Delta 1 in the bank along with Matthieu and myself. You, Alexandra, will remain outside with the balance of the Delta team because Karl knows you and Paul."

"I don't like it but I'm prepared to go along in a support role," Alexandra consented with reservation.

"We've talked about the need for the white-hatted good guys to wear the black hats just as the bad guys wear white hats to disguise their nefarious activities," Paul replied. "We are a team and you will be with me, as will your mother, Sir James and Major Mike."

The old order of battle had been etched in seventeenth- and eighteenth-century Europe, and centuries before when Gaul was part of the Roman Empire, the Quer had been founded, and Julius Caesar had crossed the Rubicon. Paul understood enough of the cultures of those eras to not only spar in the boxing ring with the bank manager but to emerge triumphant.

"The documentation should be here within forty-eight hours. If the bank manager is associated with the Quer, as we suspect he is, based on Karl's comments, the Quer will be advised of the re-appearance of their long-lost fraternal colleague. In the interim, you need to prepare your script, Paul. Until they arrive, we will spend the time playing the role of the bank manager and challenging you on every possible scenario until you become Claude Etien Marchand, alias Paul Bernard. It will take about two hours for your makeover including your hair dye and haircut and about half an hour for a touch up before you enter the bank."

As the meeting broke up, Matthieu glanced at Alexandra with an inquisitive concerned expression she had come to recognize.

He was checking to ensure she was agreeable. In his disquiet was a suggestion of determination, of laid-back toughness that had been tempered by previous missions. The field of battle tests men of courage. She knew she could rely on such men in a worst-case scenario if there was everything to lose. She had witnessed it in Paul. She had seen it in Sir James. She recognized it in Matthieu. He would be there if the forensic psychologist needed an ear. Or an intervention.

Alexandra subtly nodded back.

"Everything all right?" Paul asked. "I couldn't help notice you were a bit anxious in the briefing. You were rubbing your amulet."

"All okay," Alexandra nodded.

Matthieu monitored the communiqué and her less-than-candid confirmation of her confidence.

Alexandra felt relieved Jo was with Collette, but disappointed she could not be. Her mothering instinct reaffirmed her need to be with her daughter to provide unwavering support as she dealt with the trauma of loss. Her professional and intimate loyalty confirmed her need to be with Paul to provide steadfast support as he was about to embark on a perilous mission that only a warrior tested in battle could anticipate. The familiar pang of abandonment ran through her as she recalled all those times when her mother was not present but her aunt and uncle were.

For now, she needed to compose herself, to disassociate from Collette and concentrate on the mission at hand. She had successfully completed her task in this unfolding drama. She now rehearsed scenarios in her mind and the unscripted role she would have to play if anything went wrong. In the Thon case, she had been captured and faced imminent threat with a gun to her head. Paul had come to her rescue with the Harley cavalry. She needed to play the support role in this mission.

CHAPTER 42

"**T**est, test, test, one, two, three," Paul whispered as he approached the bank.

"Read you loud and clear," Daan replied.

"I would like to speak to the bank manager, please," Claude Etien Marchand announced to the receptionist seated at a desk to the left of the teller stalls.

"Who shall I say is enquiring?" asked the middle-aged woman who sat as prim and proper as a private school matriarch. She wore a perfectly tailored, blue pin-striped suit, which complemented the austere atmosphere of the Swiss bank. Her painted smile was formal.

"I am Claude Etien Marchand."

"Do you have an appointment, Monsieur Marchand?"

"No. Please show the bank manager this letter of introduction."

"Thank you, Monsieur Marchand. Please wait here while I speak to the manager."

Within moments, an elegant figure appeared in traditional banking attire. He looked like a thoroughbred, from his precisely groomed greying mane to his polished leather shoes.

"Monsieur Marchand, my name is Rafael Blosch. I am the bank manager. Please come into my office."

Paul surmised he was speaking to the bank manager of one of the most prestigious banks in Switzerland, a position commanding respect. He was neither Rafael nor M. Blosch. In another lifetime, he could have been Herr Blosch of an international corporation, or Colonel Blosch of the Third Reich or perhaps the Fourth Reich. Today, he was an executive mandarin of his own making. In response, Paul adopted the role of a previous occupation of his own, the colonel and commanding officer of a military battalion.

"Thank you. I appreciate that you probably do not have requests very often to access a very old account." After evaluating Herr Blosch's composure, Paul continued. "I have brought with me several documents attesting to the validity of my request." He confidently took a chair in front of the manager's desk, on which sat a polished mahogany nameplate centered with regimental exactness. It read: *Herr Rafael Blosch, Manager.* The crassness of the decor of this panelled inner sanctum disguised the monstrosity of the betrayal of so many depositors and anonymous deposits. Paul removed the ring from his finger in clear sight of the official now seated in a high-backed leather chair.

"This introductory letter mentions a ring. Here it is. And I present additional documents."

Rafael Blosch appeared momentarily overwhelmed by Paul's authoritative presence and the handful of official documents. The ring commanded his attention above all. He pressed the intercom and asked his executive assistant to come in.

"Please bring me all records of this account and the original account card. You will find them in the reserved file in the vault."

"Yes, Herr Blosch," she replied promptly.

Herr Blosch's demeanour is a ruse. He could be ruthless. Establishing a professional rapport is critical, Paul surmised. He was swimming against the tide. If he was going to be invited into Herr Blosch's world, it would be on his terms as would the extent of the embrace and depth of endorsement.

"Excuse me for a moment, Monsieur Marchand, while I scan through your documents. Can I have my assistant bring you a coffee?"

"No, thank you," Paul replied with resolute promptness. He did not want to suggest any hesitancy in his demeanor.

"This is the account card, Herr Blosch," the assistant advised.

Rafael Blosch nodded in acknowledgement. With careful scrutiny, he compared the information on the account card with the details provided in the introductory letter and other documents. Holding the account card against the letter, he compared the signatures of Jacques Etien Marchand. He then scrutinized with exactness the papers in front of him. He removed a key from the breast pocket of his vest and unlocked the left-hand top drawer and carefully retrieved a small leather box. What transpired next caused Paul's heartbeat to increase in tempo. Rafael Blosch pulled out what appeared to be a duplicate ring and judiciously inspected both. He then returned the second ring to its lined container and placed it back in the drawer. He re-locked the drawer with equal precision. Finally, he replaced the key in the pocket of his vest and patted it gently to confirm its presence.

He raised his eyes and stared at the person sitting in front of his desk for further validation or features of confederacy. "Tell me about yourself, Monsieur Marchand," Herr Blosch asked. The seeds of suspicion had begun to germinate following his meticulous scrutiny.

Paul was prepared with his well-rehearsed reply. Once he had recited his scripts with the expertise of a seasoned actor of the Metropolitan Theatre, Rafael Blosch re-examined the documents and the ring. "Please excuse my careful inspection of all that you have presented to me, Monsieur Marchand. In such matters, as you can appreciate, prudence is necessary. Essential."

"I completely understand. I would do the same if I were in your position."

Herr Blosch summoned his assistant once again and directed her to make two telephone calls.

"I need to verify the authenticity of the ring and the letter of introduction before we proceed further. This process will not take long."

"Please take the time necessary," Paul said with an air of confidence.

Inside the bank, Daan's tension rose when he noticed the bank manager's assistant summon a guard who stationed himself directly outside the manager's office. Additional guards positioned themselves on either side of the front door to the bank. Moments later, Delta 1 adjusted his position. Two professionally dressed men entered the bank and proceeded straight toward Herr Blosch's office.

"Monsieur Marchand, I would like to introduce you to two of my colleagues. Herr Antoine is a renowned jeweller. I would like him to examine your ring. Herr Grasser is an expert in calligraphy. I would like him to examine your letter of introduction. If you would not mind waiting while they complete their analysis."

"Not at all," Paul replied, with a tic of a nod.

Herr Antoine removed the loupe from his pocket and meticulously inspected the image on the ring before looking at length at a worn inscription on the inside. "Seventh of seven," he muttered as he nodded to Herr Blosch with confident confirmation.

Seventh of seven. Sir James had noted the seventh of seven, Paul reflected without expression. Another dot had been connected.

"Thank you, Herr Antoine. I will not keep you further," Rafael Blosch said with a flick of his wrist, a dismissive gesture.

As the first scrutinizer left his office, Herr Grasser looked at Herr Blosch as a subordinate acknowledges a superior, standing at attention as an indication of respect. "It is authentic," he replied.

Herr Blosch nodded. Herr Grasser immediately left the office.

After a contemplative pause, Rafael Blosch, manager of one of the most prestigious banks in Switzerland, responded to Paul's gaze, "How may we assist you with your account, Monsieur Marchand?"

"I would like to transfer the balance of the account into a new account in my name and access the safe deposit box."

"I will personally ensure that the funds are transferred immediately to a new account in your name, Monsieur Marchand. I will have my assistant prepare all the necessary documentation for your signature while you access the safe deposit box. I am confident you will find our bank and our staff very professional."

"I would be honoured to continue the tradition of my family. Now, I would like to access the safe deposit box."

As Paul followed Rafael Blosch out of his office, he took notice of Daan and Matthieu who seemed to express concern. Herr Blosch nodded to his assistant who communicated his order to stand down to the two guards at the front entrance and the sentinel standing outside his office. As they moved away from their temporary posts, Daan and Matthieu communicated the more relaxed posture to Delta 1. They all breathed a sigh of relief. Delta 1 left the bank lobby but remained vigilant by the front door.

Paul emptied the contents of the safe deposit box into his briefcase. They returned to Herr Blosch's office, all under the more relaxed surveillance of the EUI team. Rafael Blosch's assistant was waiting with the documents that would complete the transfer.

"Monsieur Marchand," Herr Blosch asked Paul. "Are you aware of the significance of your ring?"

"Over and above the validation of my identity, I am not."

"Perhaps we might meet for dinner this evening at which time I would be pleased and honoured to explain its significance. You are aware that your family has a long and prominent history. The ring signifies an association with an organization of equal distinction. It would be best to gain a full appreciation of the association. You may wish to establish formal ties with other members of this prestigious organization as there would be mutually beneficial outcomes."

"I would be most interested in exploring the options. I am staying at the Grand Hotel Kempinski Geneva."

"Would 7:00 p.m. be convenient?" Herr Blosch enquired.

"That would be excellent. I'll make reservations at Il Vero restaurant, a quiet table."

"And please call me Rafael. If I may call you Claude. We may be seeing more of each other on personal and business terms, beyond just banking."

"At 7:00 p.m., Rafael," Paul confirmed with a slight bow. Herr Blosch needed, demanded to have his ego stroked but with the caution necessary in the courtship of a viper.

Paul completed a substantial cash withdrawal from his new account to validate the account in the name of Claude Etien Marchand, heir to the estate of the Marchand dynasty.

"Departing now," Daan announced. "Report."

"Delta 1 in position."

"Delta 4 in position."

"Roger, Deltas 1 and 4."

"We have trailers," Delta 4 announced. "Two men in dark suits wearing dark hats and overcoats."

"We have them," Delta 1 acknowledged.

"This is to be expected," Daan announced. "Stay with the protocols. Paul, stop off in the hotel café before going to your room. We will set up monitors in your room and in the Il Vero restaurant in anticipation of this evening's dinner."

"Roger," Paul replied.

"Bravo Zulu, team. Well done, all. And Paul, your performance was flawless, worthy of an Academy Award. As we discussed, we anticipate some probing from the Quer. Accordingly, remain vigilant. You can expect an interrogation from Herr Blosch this evening over dinner. Just stick to the script as planned."

Matthieu reflected on his observations. The balance sheet on his wooden abacus did not seem to balance. "I wonder whether it went too easily," he cautioned. "Herr Blosch was correctly suspicious when first approached. But the validation seemed a little too smooth perhaps, from my perspective. Remain vigilant."

"I'll be with you in heart and soul, mon colonel," Alexandra promised. "Over dinner, if you need time to compose an answer or pose a question, just take a bite of food and an extended sip of wine. Tilt your head and hold it if you would like either Daan or me to suggest a topic. Round one with Herr Rafael Blosch goes to the good guys in the white hats."

"The trailers have followed him into the hotel. One trailer has followed him into the café while the second is now seated in the lobby."

"Roger, Delta 1," Daan confirmed.

"Report, Delta 4."

"All clear. Will remain the eye in the sky for the next hour. Then must land to refuel."

"Roger, Delta 4."

As Paul sipped his cappuccino, he read through the documents from the safe deposit box and examined other items. Speaking just loudly enough to transmit and with his lips obscured by the documents, he commented, "There is a deed to buildings and a reference to adjoining land in what is today the suburbs of Metz. I know this place because it is where I used to live and explore as a kid when we lived in Montigny-lès-Metz. It is where Alexandra and I first met. It looks as though it includes what is today Sainte-Ruffine. This is a considerable tract of land extending to the Moselle River and south-east to Montigny-lès-Metz. Today, it would be worth hundreds of thousands if not millions of Euros, just for the land. Oh, this looks very interesting."

"What looks interesting, Paul?" Daan eagerly enquired.

"These papers are very old and refer to the Quer. It seems there were seven original families who came together to form the Quer. Eureka! Names of all the original members are listed. The seventh was a Hugo Etien Marchand. Herr Blosch's name is not included, but he has a ring. Not sure what to make of that."

"The seventh," Alexandra commented. "The seventh of the seven. That is what Sir James wrote down just before he died. His butler, Walter, mentioned that his final utterance was the letter 'Q'. It wasn't just the letter 'Q' but Quer, and seventh of the seven was the seventh original member to form the Quer, Hugo Etien Marchand. This is further validation."

"Outstanding find, Paul," Matthieu exclaimed. "You can go to your dinner this evening with Herr Rafael Blosch better prepared than we could ever have rehearsed. Probe for his affiliation with the Quer where his name is not listed among the original seven."

"No change in the script," Daan directed. "Just appear uninformed and see how Herr Blosch plays his cards. Let's see what he knows and what he is fishing for, Paul. What else do you have in the trove of papers and artefacts?"

"Another document looks like a Royal Proclamation from King Louis XIII of France and the House of Bourbon dated 13th May 1631 granting other lands to a Philip Etien Joseph Marchand. We will have to follow up on this. I'm not certain what these other items are. They are very old and have symbols like the Runic figures on the ring. I'm going to deposit them in the hotel safe. I think that would be a better strategy because the room safe could be easily accessed by a professional."

"Good plan," Daan acknowledged. "Delta 1, set up additional

surveillance of the lobby and front desk where the hotel safe is located and double-check the surveillance in Paul's room."

"Roger."

"I'm going to go up to my room to powder my nose and get ready for dinner. This should be an interesting evening."

"Room service," a soft voice announced, knocking on Paul's door. "Makeup touch-up time, Monsieur Marchand," the maid said as she entered.

⚞ ⚟

ALEXANDRA CHECKED HER EMAIL. NOTHING. NO NEWS was good news, she reminded herself. She trusted Jo. But it would be a relief to receive at least a cryptic message one way or the other.

Her text to Jo was simple, "All OK?"

Within moments, the confirmation appeared, "All OK."

She looked up and met Matthieu's querying gaze. Her faint smile was relaxed. Her slow deliberate breath reconfirmed her ease.

Matthieu winked back cordially. He would continue to monitor her emotional response to subsequent emails from the unknown sender. Alexandra didn't subscribe to social media platforms nor did she seem to have many close friends. The probability of Jean texting her was infinitely small. He suspected either Collette or Jo had been the author of this latest message. Perhaps both or the subject involved both.

On the one hand, Alexandra felt slightly more relaxed as her anxiety about Collette's condition subsided. Jo would not leave her side. On the other hand, she remained apprehensive about Paul's dinner meeting with Herr Rafael Blosch. Matthieu's words of caution resonated deeply. Had the transfer of funds to the new account in Claude Etien Marchand's name and access to the safe deposit box been too easy? Who would accompany Herr Blosch to the restaurant?

"Daan, I'd be more comfortable with additional surveillance in the restaurant," Alexandra suggested. Her tone was more insistent than social.

"I agree. I'll double the guard. As long as they remain in the restaurant, Paul is safe from any event that would cause a disturbance."

"Thon poisoned his victims. Sir James was poisoned. Tom was poisoned. It wouldn't take much for Herr Blosch to poison Paul or have someone else such as a server administer a poison."

CHAPTER 43

Herr Blosch greeted his new professional acquaintance. "Thank you, Claude, for making the time in your schedule to accept my invitation for dinner this evening. Perhaps my office was not an appropriate venue for us to get to know each other better, to discuss outside interests."

Even in a relaxed social setting, Herr Blosch remained as sharp as his voice. He looked at Paul. He had more questions.

"Have you dined here before, Herr Blosch? What would you recommend?"

"My preference is the Jaeger Schnitzel with spaetzle."

"And a wine to pair?"

"I would recommend a Rhine. A Riesling. And schnapps with coffee."

More German Swiss than French Swiss in cuisine, Paul reflected. "I commend you on your recommendation, Rafael."

"That is settled then." Herr Blosch summoned the server and confirmed the order in exact detail.

Paul observed the rapport between the server and Herr Blosch for any potential employer–employee relationship.

In the interim, Matthieu approached the Maître D'. "I would like to complement you on the excellence of your servers. The young lady who is currently serving the two gentlemen seated in the corner, she is very professional. Has she been an employee long?"

"This is her first evening shift. Her name is Danielle. She comes highly recommended."

"Please pass along my compliments," Matthieu said.

"I will do so and thank you for taking the time to mention this to me," the Maître D' replied.

"Got that," Daan confirmed. "Delta 1 increase your surveillance of the server. Watch her as she handles the water and wine glasses."

"What do you do to fill your days?" Herr Blosch asked.

"My calendar seems to be full most days," Paul said nonchalantly, "so I do not have time for outside activities. I do collect rare books though. I'm what some describe as an antiquarian."

"I have no personal knowledge of old books," Herr Blosch replied, "but I have a few acquaintances who collect them. Perhaps I could introduce you."

"That would be wonderful. And you, Rafael, what do you do when not running the bank?"

"Running the bank and attending meetings is a full-time profession that often overlaps into my evenings. I spend most of my non-work time reading history. I'd classify myself as an amateur historian, mostly early European."

"Married? Family?" Paul followed up.

"My wife passed away many years ago. I have no children. And yourself, Paul?" he countered. The tone of his response was evident, he wanted to ask the questions.

"I am married. My wife travels a great deal as a consultant. She is currently in the United States. But I am intrigued by your reference to the ring. At the end of our meeting this afternoon, you alluded to a history of the ring, a story behind it that I am not aware of. I noticed that you had a similar ring in your desk drawer." The ball was back in Herr Blosch's court.

"You are observant, Claude. Mine is a master ring, like a master key. It's an added layer of security to verify accuracy, like having complete bank account numbers. You will have noted that I also compared the signature of the person who opened the account with the signature in your letter of introduction. Herr Antoine and Herr

Grasser are experts the bank calls upon for this type of validation, especially for accounts with considerable deposits." Herr Blosch hadn't offered any additional information that his dinner guest wasn't already aware of.

"I feel secure knowing that your bank has these added layers of security," Paul acknowledged with a confident smile. "And the history behind the ring? Does the bank issue these rings for special accounts?"

"Yes and no. Your ring was the seventh original, issued a long time ago before there were banks."

"Low tech but very effective," Paul responded as he held Herr Blosch's gaze. "I like it and I'm gaining more confidence in your security systems. When you say a long time ago, how long are you talking about?"

"As you may have noted, your ring is worn with time. There were seven original recipients. All have since died as you might appreciate. They have passed on their rings from father to son. Likewise, the jewellers and other similar artisans have passed on the secrets of their craft to each subsequent generation."

"Much like the early masons of medieval times who passed on the tools of their trade, the compass and square. They eventually evolved into the Freemasons of today."

"That's correct," Rafael replied. "Are you a member of a Masonic Lodge?"

"I'm not but I have known members who have attempted to recruit me. I've just been too busy to explore such options."

"You ask how long? The organization that initially issued the rings, one of which you possess, dates back long before medieval times. The symbol on the rings predates written language. It is actually Runic. In the case of these rings, the symbol is for cattle because if you had cattle then you had commercial value."

"Like a Chamber of Commerce?" Paul suggested.

"A good analogy."

"At that time there were no banks. Today's organization tends to be affiliated more so with banking rather than commerce."

"So, how many affiliates are there today in this ring association?"

"I'm not exactly sure, beyond the original seven. Your ring would be the seventh original," Herr Blosch confirmed guardedly.

"Do these members meet on a monthly basis like members of Masonic Lodges?"

"Again, Paul, I'm not exactly sure. But I could enquire on your behalf and get the information for you, if you would like."

"I'd appreciate that very much. It would help me to gain a better understanding of my ancestry. You can contact me through this hotel until the weekend. I plan to be a tourist here in Geneva and explore the old city. I like browsing through antique shops."

Daan's voice softly resonated in Paul's ear. "For your information, someone has entered your room, Paul, and is conducting a very methodical search. It's not room service! Good decision on your part to store your documents and the artefacts in the hotel safe because this intruder has just opened the safe deposit box in your room. Let's find out if Herr Blosch is aware. Paul, mention to him that you may need to return to your room to retrieve some prescribed anti-acid medication. It's a reaction to tannins in some wines. Let's see his reaction."

As Paul took another sip of wine, he grimaced in discomfort. "Excuse me, Rafael. I sometimes experience acid indigestion from drinking certain wines. I think it's the tannins." With a chuckle, he confided that he had probably drunk too much wine in his youth and it had caught up with him. "I may have to excuse myself momentarily to return to my room to retrieve some anti-acid medication."

The expression on Herr Blosch's face was one of anxiety. He raised his left arm and adjusted his cufflinks before replying, "I often experience such discomfort myself. Like you, I may have consumed too much wine in my youth. I find drinking water often helps. Please try. I also put baking soda in the water. We could ask our server to bring some. I wouldn't want you to suffer and spoil our evening."

"Thank you. I'll try plain water for now."

"Interesting," said Daan. "Moments after he adjusted his cufflink, the intruder in the room scampered out and left the floor through the fire escape. Herr Blosch is running the show. Delta 1, were you able to spot his confederate in the restaurant?"

"Roger. We have him. Another mug shot for the family photo album. Our facial recognition folks are going to be busy."

After schnapps and coffee, Herr Blosch held out his hand. "Thank you for a most pleasant evening, Claude. Getting to know our special clients is one of the more enjoyable parts of my job."

"The pleasure is mutual," Paul replied with a gracious smile.

"I will make a few phone calls and see if we can arrange a meeting with other associates. I believe they may be enjoying some R&R time somewhere close by."

As Paul left the restaurant, Daan's voice filled his earpiece. "Outstanding performance, Paul. You were brilliant. Bravo Zulu to all. Definitely a capstone to the day. Get some well-deserved sleep. Room service will greet you in the morning, Paul."

"*Bonne nuit* – Good night," Alexandra's voice chimed in.

She checked her emails. One brief message was from Jo: "All OK. She is resting."

Matthieu had directed Delta 5 to monitor her emails and identify the source. He had been correct. The text was from Alexandra's friend, Jo. He surmised that Jo was referring to Collette. Whatever the issue had been, it was now resolved. The current mission was safe from emotional distractions. For Paul to be at the top of his game, Alexandra needed to be composed. The Quer mission superseded all else.

CHAPTER 44

Paul's phone rang with a 6:00 a.m. wakeup call. "Thank you," he replied. It was pleasant to hear a real voice rather than an automated recording.

"You are welcome, Monsieur Marchand," the front desk clerk replied. "A gentleman dropped off an envelope for you early this morning. Would you like the concierge to deliver it to your room?"

"No, thank you, I'll pick it up on my way to breakfast."

"Room service," a soft voice announced at his door.

"Be right there," Paul replied.

"Makeup touch up," the maid quietly announced. "It actually looks pretty good. Should take about fifteen minutes."

"Good morning, Monsieur Marchand," Daan's cheerful voice danced from his earphone.

"Communications are good," Paul replied.

"All teams report."

All teams responded with strong communication signals.

"I have an envelope waiting for me at the front desk. Going down to breakfast shortly."

"We have an intelligence update," Daan advised. "The Quer have controlling tentacles in some of the Swiss banks where stolen Nazi monies and treasures are deposited. Thus, they are strategically situated to control the decisions of the Fourth Reich. Our Herr Rafael Blosch is related to a high-ranking official who was appointed by Adolf Hitler to the Reichsbank. It appears he was skimming off money and depositing it in a personal account in a Zürich bank. After the Allies bombed the Reichsbank in February 1945, he moved additional gold via rail to his personal bank. Our Herr Rafael Blosch is the current and sole account holder. We can confirm that some of these funds were used to finance the recent attacks on the synagogues in the U.S. as Karl alluded to when he first spoke with Alexandra. Additional funds are financing current Middle East terrorist activities, some of which we suspect have EU targets. It's not about money for the Quer. These attacks are just diversionary tactics. Their real motivation is to take down Western economies, to make the 1929 stock market crash seem like child's play. We have the authority to neutralize this threat by whatever means before it metastases further."

"Thanks for this update," Paul murmured as he went down to breakfast. After ordering coffee, he opened the envelope. "Interesting. Herr Blosch has arranged a meeting with a few associates. A private yacht will pull up to the CGN boat cruise wharf today at 3:00 p.m. Herr Blosch will pick me up at the hotel at precisely 2:45 p.m. The yacht will depart immediately after all are on board. It will not wait for stragglers." Herr Blosch's written communiqué was as abrupt and meticulous as his verbal communication.

"Roger. That doesn't give us much time, team," Daan announced. "O Group briefing, my location immediately."

⚐ ⚑

"I'M SORRY, SIR. THIS IS A PRIVATE yacht. You may not come aboard."

"This will give me and my colleagues permission to board."

The captain looked down at a pistol jammed against his diaphragm. "This is piracy," he exclaimed.

"Do exactly as I say and no one will get hurt, especially not your wife and infant daughter. If you need proof, look at this monitor."

The captain gasped as he saw a live video of his wife, hands bound, with a gun pointed at her head. "Do as they say or they will kill me and Sarah," his wife pleaded. The audio mute icon appeared on the screen as his wife continued to speak.

"If you want them to live, captain, keep your hands on the controls at all times and follow your cruise plans exactly. Your crew is being relieved of their duties as we speak. If you want them to live also, you need to do exactly as I say. Understood?"

The captain nodded repeatedly as beads of perspiration ran down his forehead and the palms of his hands slipped on the wheel. The yacht pulled away from the jetty.

It was 2:45 p.m. exactly when a car pulled up in front of the hotel. "My apologies for the short notice, Claude. This was the only time the associates could be together. I will be joining you," Herr Blosch explained.

"It is no problem, Rafael. I can be a tourist another time."

"To the wharf quickly," Herr Blosch barked at the driver.

As they approached the wharf, Paul looked at his watch. It was 2:57 p.m. "Right on time if that is the yacht."

"It is," Herr Blosch replied. "And there are the other associates arriving at the wharf. Stop the car here, driver. Claude, walk quickly to the wharf and board swiftly. It will only tie up for a moment."

As Paul and Herr Blosch followed the others onto the wharf and up the gangplank, a speedboat pulled along the starboard side of the yacht and a final guest started to climb up a rope ladder that had been lowered for him.

The guests entered the lavish boardroom. There, men wearing black balaclavas greeted them with pistols pointed at their heads. A single command rang out, "On the deck, gentlemen, now!" Each guest was grabbed and forced to the lush, carpeted floor where their hands were tied behind their backs and their ankles bound.

Paul glared at Herr Blosch in shock. "What the hell?"

"Say nothing," Rafael replied under his breath. "Don't worry. We have friends in high places, including the police department. We'll be out of here in no time."

Paul looked up and saw a man, his face covered in a balaclava, gagging others on the floor with tape over their mouths, and draping black hoods over their heads. "I don't think these are police because police don't put hoods over the heads of prisoners," Paul whispered to Rafael who stared back. The expression of horror on his face said it all.

The final guest looked between the rungs of the rope ladder through a porthole at men bound with hoods over their heads. He immediately jumped back into the speedboat and yelled, "Get out of here! Go! Go! Go!"

"Delta 4, we have a runner in a speedboat heading north past the *Jet d'Eau* and into open water."

"Roger. Have him in my sights. That boat is built for speed. Dropping down to get some better family photos."

"Stay on him, Delta 4. Can you disable the boat with a well-aimed projectile? We don't want the occupants harmed if at all possible."

"Roger. Am locked on to the starboard engine. One away... Engine disabled. He is turning to port toward Parc Barton. Am in pursuit. He just struck the shore. The boat is on fire. I have one on foot running toward rue de Lausanne. Can't tell if it's the passenger or the driver. I've lost him in the crowd."

"Delta 2, are you able to engage?"

"ETA one minute."

"Delta 4, maintain your surveillance until Delta 2 is on scene."

"Roger."

"Delta 1, report."

"All on board the yacht are secure. Transporting cargo to the jetty."

"Delta 2, report."

"On scene. The crowd is gathering to view the burning boat. Negative."

"Delta 4, report."

"Negative. Local police have arrived."

"Roger. Delta 2 and Delta 4, remain on scene and report any change in status."

※ ※

"MONSIEUR MARCHAND, I HOPE YOU ENJOYED OUR scenic tourist tour of wonderful Lake Geneva. We will be providing you with customer satisfaction questionnaires. Please complete them and hand them to your driver. We always strive to improve our client satisfaction."

"Customer satisfaction questionnaires? You jest!" Paul exclaimed. "You owe me a paid vacation to my hotel of choice in Liechtenstein, Daan. I'm getting too old for these gymnastics."

"Alexandra will be here shortly to aid in your recovery if that is of any solace. I am pleased to see that your makeup didn't smudge. It's expensive stuff and our budget is already overblown."

"Give me a status report on the operation, Daan," Paul requested.

"One escaped into a waiting speedboat. Delta 4 was in pursuit when it crashed into the shore. One person escaped. We're not sure if it was the target or the boat driver. The remainder of the targets are en route to a warmer climate for interviews. It will be twenty-four hours before they arrive, shower, and change into their fluorescent green resort coveralls with matching ankle bracelets."

"You accomplished what no one has been able to do so since the Quer was created," Matthieu congratulated Paul. "Their secrecy has been broken. We have enough information to halt their activities. Outstanding job. I can understand why Dr. Paul Bernard received the distinction of the Commandeur de la Légion d'Honneur for heroics. Let me shake your hand."

"You'll have to wait in line, Matthieu. Let me congratulate

him first with the biggest hug he may ever receive," Alexandra announced as she wrapped her arms around him.

"*Doucement, ma princesse* – gently. The body took a few dents from the boat cruise. Cognac would certainly be in order."

"And a lot of TLC," Alexandra seductively whispered into his ear.

"Let's pack up and redeploy to Paris," Daan directed. "We will debrief first thing tomorrow morning."

Alexandra's email to Jo was succinct. "On my way." Her immediate priority was Collette. She would have her in her arms before sunset.

Matthieu gave her a reassuring smile.

⊨ ⊨

THE THREE AND A HALF HOUR EURAIL back to Paris allowed the passengers time to decompress. First- and second-class coaches arrived at La Gare du Nord simultaneously but first class, with wider reclining seats provided added comfort for those with physical and mental bruises.

"Talk to me, ma princesse. You seem very tense, even more so than when Thon was closing in."

"I was extremely worried for you. This was our first mission with the EUI Unit and life and death stakes, and with you in the crosshairs. I had complete confidence in you and your battle-tested Gallic warrior ability. But the possibility still crossed my mind – what if? I wasn't there beside you. I felt vulnerable and anxious."

Paul kept his gaze on her. He tried to read what was in her voice and her eyes. He commiserated with the description of her emotions. He was acutely aware of the potential lethal consequences had he missed a line as the drama played out live. Life in his lab amid samples germinating in petri dishes was undeniably simpler and more mundane. Still, he felt something else simmering beneath the surface. He reached over and took her hand for confirmation. There it was. The delicate tapping of her fingers. He had witnessed this metronome cadence when she was unsettled. He would not press for a full disclosure for now.

"Je t'aime," she whispered to him, and to herself as an affirmation of her love for him and her unwavering devotion to their relationship, which would be tested at a future time. With André, there had been too many unspoken details and untold avowals. She would not allow that wedge to be driven between her and Paul. But now was not the time.

"Je t'aime, aussi, ma princesse," he responded as he held her hand and tenderly caressed her fingers. He was one with her.

She was one with him and with Collette, separate but inseparable. She would not leave either feeling abandoned as she had been. Love would not be at a distance with occasional business trips interspersed with phone calls. She and Paul were indivisible business and intimate partners. She needed to reconcile her insecurity. How she missed those tender moments when her mother brushed her hair and held her in her arms. She experienced fulfillment from Paul's closeness but yearned for connection with Collette. She would have this conversation with Paul, but in the future.

Once on the platform of the Gare du Nord, Alexandra told Daan she needed a brief visit with Collette. Matthieu nodded at Daan who directed a Delta 2 Unit to accompany her.

"I'll tag along," Matthieu quietly suggested. Daan read Matthieu's tone and knew that he would brief him at an appropriate time.

"I'll meet you at the safe house," Alexandra whispered to Paul. "I just want to check in with Collette. I shouldn't be much more than an hour or so. Delta 2 and Matthieu will be with me so I'll be all right."

"I'll soak my aching bones in a hot bath until you return."

Within two hours, Alexandra was pouring the cognac, complemented by a personal massage.

"Is Collette okay?"

"She's great. I just needed to see her, more for my comfort. After my mother returned from her business trips, I always looked forward to a quiet one-on-one time. I just needed to reconnect with Collette in the same way. Jo sends her love."

Jo sends her love. *Strange*, Paul reflected. *Was Collette at Jo's or vice versa?* He texted Jean. "Am back in Paris. All good, Jean?"

"All good, Dad. Collette spent the night with Jo who had a bit of a relapse. She just let me know she would be home this evening."

"Good to hear," Paul replied as if he were aware of the situation. Alexandra hadn't mentioned anything. *Perhaps she didn't want to distract me in the midst of the Quer mission.*

CHAPTER 45

"Good morning, ladies and gentlemen," Daan welcomed the teams. "Bravo Zulu, all the way round. With the exception of the last guest who escaped our net, the core of the Quer is all but disassembled. We have the identity of the inner circle members in addition to other associates. The captain of the yacht is cooperating fully in return for personal security for himself and his family. That's a bonus. Our other guests will be landing shortly in a warmer climate where they will be provided with their private accommodation. Interviews will get underway immediately. As information is received, I will update you all. The documentation each of the guests was carrying has confirmed much of what we already knew and suspected. Brussels is ecstatic about the mission's success."

Matthieu added, "The bank has been advised that its manager has had to take an extended leave of absence for medical reasons. The assistant bank manager has been promoted to the position of acting manager."

"When can I remove the makeup?" Paul asked.

"We now know that Herr Blosch is a high-ranking member of the Fourth Reich in addition to being the bank manager. Accordingly, we must assume he passed the information along to his superiors that the seventh member of the Quer had come forward. Karl confirmed there are cameras in the bank and in Herr Blosch's office. We must also assume that Herr Blosch provided the video images to his superiors. We have confirmed that the Fourth Reich is the enforcement arm of the Quer. So, they may be looking for Claude Etien Marchand. Just after you left the bank, Paul, Matthieu suggested that Herr Blosch's acceptance of your credentials may have gone too smoothly. So, we must remain on high alert. In response to your question Paul, you need to keep your disguise a while longer. Matthieu, please carry on."

"If Monsieur Marchand is seen in public, the Fourth Reich may contact him. If they do, we will certainly take every advantage of having a private chat with them. We will carefully plan your public appearances, Paul, under the surveillance of all the Delta force. Keep your wire and GPS on at all times."

"Paul is bait?" Alexandra asked.

"Like the bait books. That's correct," Daan interjected. "You will stay in the safe house where you were before, the address you gave Herr Blosch for Claude Etien Marchand. The Fourth Reich will be aware of this if Herr Blosch passed along your identity. We must assume this."

"That should make our job of maintaining surveillance all the easier," Matthieu added. "Room service with your favourite maid has already been arranged. Look at it this way, Paul. How many people do you know who have a private live-in hairstylist and beautician?"

"We believe the Fourth Reich will step up their efforts to contact Monsieur Marchand when they discover Herr Blosch has disappeared off their radar," Daan added.

Paul glanced at Daan and Matthieu. "And I thought my biggest decision as a recent retiree would be whether to play a round of golf or not."

"And Monsieur Claude Etien Marchand and his new bride haven't had the opportunity to enjoy their honeymoon. The ink on the marriage certificate hasn't even dried," Alexandra laughed. "I'll join you in the vacation suite later, husband. I need to pick up a few things first."

"Delta 2 will take you back to the safe house now, Monsieur Marchand. If there are no other questions, our debriefing is adjourned. Again, Bravo Zulu to all," Daan concluded. "Oh, one last related point," Daan added. "None of the books that Tom left for you in his Will had any tracking devices. They are all clear. I still want you to check for any connections to cases Tom had been working on. When you have time, of course, given your relaxed retirement schedule."

Paul looked quizzically at Daan. "Retirement schedule? What's that?"

As their car entered the Pont de l'Alma tunnel en route to the safe house, the thought crossed Paul's mind. *This is not what I had imagined retirement life to be, surrounded by bodyguards and chase cars.* His musing was abruptly interrupted as traffic came to an unexpected halt deep in the tunnel. Delta 2 stepped out and stood on the edge of the running board to get a better view of the situation. Immediately, a shot rang out and he tumbled to the ground. A second shot shattered the windshield at the same time as Paul was yanked out and flung into the trunk of another vehicle that had stopped in the adjacent lane. It then accelerated through the tunnel with Paul in the trunk.

"He's been abducted," Delta 2 echo yelled from the back-up vehicle. "Delta 2, alpha and charlie are down."

"I lost the signal when they entered the tunnel," Delta 4 advised. "I've just picked up a much weaker signal leaving the tunnel. It is going north, zigzagging through back streets."

"Stay on him, Delta 4," Daan directed. "An ambulance is on the way, Delta 2, echo. Remain on scene. All other units, converge on Delta 4's general direction."

"I can barely hear his voice, niner. He's saying he is in the trunk," Delta 4 updated. "They've just turned east on the boulevard Ney."

"Roger, Delta 4. I am in direct communication with Commandant Parent. Police backup is converging on your coordinates."

"The vehicle has just turned north on the N1," Delta 4 updated.
"Signal is still weak. They are zigzagging, going in the direction of the Parc des Automobiles Hotchkiss."

"Roger, Delta 4. Stay with them."

"Signal is still weak and his voice remains muffled, niner."

"They appear to have stopped. They have taken him out of the trunk and into a building. Signal is strong. I just heard him say the old Hotchkiss factory is unsafe and shouldn't be entered."

"Roger, Delta 4. Police ERT is closing in on your location."

"His signal is getting weaker. They must be taking him deep underground."

"Roger, Delta 4. I have advised Commandant Parent."

Paul bounced off the walls as he was dragged through corridors and downstairs into a basement chamber. A steel door was unlocked. He found himself facing a desk with a Nazi flag covering the back wall.

"What is this room?" Paul demanded of his abductors.

"I'll ask the questions, Monsieur Marchand, if that is your real name. Now who are you?"

"You know my name. I'm Claude Etien Marchand. You need to release me. I have some very influential associates."

"And where is Herr Blosch?"

"Who?"

A fist came from nowhere and smashed into his chest. He was then pulled out of his chair and slammed against a concrete wall. The impact dazed him as his head bounced forward. Fuzzy images of Muslim mortars raining down on their own children in Bosnia and the little girl lying face down in the ditch with red blood staining her blue dress spun through his mind amongst other scenes at war crimes. The Élysée Palace and his award ceremony for the Commandeur de la Légion d'Honneur flashed by. He knew that only willpower and discipline could keep him conscious and alive. Yet, muffled voices reverberated.

"These are not nice people.... You need to be careful.... Welcome to the New World Order.... The Pope isn't always right..... Those that guard and those that bless share in time life's timelessness.... You have been pre-destined to take up the standard to fight against the forces of evil, and you will be successful together...."

Then the fog broke with Alexandra's distant shout, "Come to me, *mon colonel*!" Fuelled by determination, his eyes re-focused on the Nazi flag.

"We have ways of making you talk, Monsieur Marchand. Now this can go easy for you or it can go hard," the man behind the desk said calmly as he held up a syringe. A stream of liquid shot out as he squeezed the plunger ever so slightly.

A series of stun grenades exploded. Amid the dust and confusion, a second explosion threw Paul and his captor to the ground.

"Bring him fast," the voice from behind the desk rang out. This time it was far from calm but still direct. As they clambered through a hole in the wall that had been created by the second explosion, Paul recognized the sign for a Metro stop. As his hearing returned, he could make out voices yelling. They were members of the ERT team.

The light almost blinded him as he was dragged up the staircase from the Metro station. As they emerged, he was thrown into the back seat of a black Mercedes C-Class.

"At least you people have good taste in transportation," he laughed. "Are we going to a game at the Stade de France next?" he asked. "This is the way I usually come via the Metro."

"Shut up!" He was hit again in the solar plexus with a massive fist.

Paul groaned and gasped for breath. His eyes struggled to refocus.

"I have a strong signal," Delta 4 barked. "They are back on the N1 heading northeast."

"Roger, Delta 4."

"He's wearing a wire," an unknown voice exclaimed.

"Well, pull it off and throw it out the window."

"Damn," Delta 4 exclaimed. "They found his tracking device. They've pulled it off him and have thrown it away."

"Do you still have a visual, Delta 4?"

"Roger, niner. But traffic is heavy and the vehicle is blending in."

"Just follow them, Delta 4. Commandant Parent has requested traffic back up but there are numerous black Mercedes sedans on the N1. He'll do his best. Keep updating on your location, Delta 4."

"I think I know where they may be going," Alexandra came on the air. "It's the forest in Compiègne. I'll tell you later why I believe that."

"I'll advise Commandant Parent," Daan confirmed.

"I'm on the D1017 running parallel to the A1," Delta 3 joined in. "I can cut across the N31 and be there before they arrive. Niner, advise Commandant Parent to let his traffic cops know not to stop a dark-blue BMW Z4."

"Roger, Delta 3. Done. You may be all we have."

"I owe the colonel this one from Sarajevo," Marcel declared. "I'm now on the N31."

"They have just exited the N1 and are going northeast on the D200," Delta 4 advised. "This will take them into Compiègne if they stay on this route. I'll be close, Delta 3. You may have a few more minutes because there is road construction around the turn-off to Jaux. That will slow them down."

Commandant Parent confirmed that a traffic unit was going

west on N31. "You should all be converging about the same time. I've reminded him, no lights or sirens as they get closer. We don't want to spook them."

"I've exited the N31 and going toward the Compiègne woods," Delta 3 updated.

"They're slowed by the construction," Delta 4 confirmed. "You are ahead of them Delta 3 but not by much."

"I'm stopped at the site now."

"You qualify as an honorary Delta 4 pilot with a no-wing aircraft. Bravo Zulu," Daan chuckled.

Delta 3 checked the magazine in his Beretta M9, locked it back in position, cocked the weapon and sank low in the seat. Within moments, a black Mercedes C-Class slid into the parking lot and skidded to a halt adjacent to the woods. The driver got out with his handgun drawn and quickly opened the back door whereupon a second man dragged Paul from the back seat. Delta 3 rushed forward with his pistol in the aim position.

"Drop the gun, drop the gun!" he yelled.

The armed driver turned and took aim. Delta 3 fired two shots and the driver fell to the ground. As he continued to rush the black Mercedes, he moved his aim to the man holding Paul.

"Let him go and drop to the ground." The man held Paul as a shield in front of him as he pointed his gun at Paul's head. Paul dropped to his knees as if fainting. Delta 3 fired two more shots at the man now grappling in vain to hold on to Paul. As the bullets tore through his chest, this second captor tumbled to the ground, joining his compatriot.

Paul heard two additional shots ring out. Delta 3 holstered his pistol as he ran up to Paul. Blood was pouring from Paul's mouth onto his already blood-stained shirt. He was semi-conscious.

"Colonel, it's me, Marcel. Talk to me, Colonel. We have to get out of here fast."

Delta 4 hovered above. "Police are about three minutes away." Marcel steadied his former commanding officer as they stumbled back to his car. The sound of the two-tone sirens increased in intensity.

"Two minutes away," Delta 4's voice echoed in Marcel's ear with renewed urgency.

Delta 4 looked down like a hawk as Delta 3 sped away from the scene.

"Niner, they are on their way back. Advise Commandant Parent that the traffic unit is close to the scene. Tell him that two occupants have been shot and are lying on the ground beside the black Mercedes. A third has run into the woods."

"Roger, Delta 4. Bravo Zulu!"

Paul fell into a semi-conscious state as Marcel drove back to Paris within the speed limit so as not to attract attention. He was vaguely aware that Marcel was updating Daan on their whereabouts and his condition. With each left turn, he cringed in pain as he was wedged against the door. With each right turn, he cringed in pain as he was held in place by the restraining seat belt. He laboured for breath as his chest muscles compressed in response to the sharp pain emanating from his lungs. If not fractured by the blows of his captor's fist, he was certain that some ribs had been cracked. The images of Alexandra in the photos he had taken of her with Sophia at the warehouse in Versailles and the memories of their intimate moments kept him in the moment.

His last fuzzy memory before he lost consciousness was Marcel explaining, "We're here, Colonel."

CHAPTER 46

Paul gazed at a gorgeous mirage through blurry eyes as his headache pounded in protest at the bright light. "You are a most welcome sight for very sore eyes, ma princesse," he uttered in a tone of endearment as he reached for her hand. "*Decorus es* – you are beautiful."

"I'd kiss and hug you but that will have to wait because there aren't too many places on your body that don't have cuts, bruises or serious dents. You are going to have to take better care of yourself if you want me to stay with you as a sleuthing business partner."

"I'd laugh but it hurts too much," Paul replied with a laboured gasp.

"Good morning, Paul," Daan saluted him light-heartedly. "Are you ready for a well-deserved vacation at your hotel of choice in Liechtenstein?"

"Sorry for being late for work this morning, boss, but I had a rough night. It won't happen again."

"Forgiven, but just this once," Daan chuckled.

"Can you give me an update? My memory is a bit foggy."

"Let me read you the headlines from this morning's newspaper. "Two people were shot and killed in Compiègne. One has been identified as Claude Etien Marchand. The identity of the second has not been confirmed. Police are looking for a third man who has been classified as a person of interest in these shootings. This incident is believed to be linked to the fatal shootings of two others in the Pont de l'Alma tunnel. Police are not releasing names pending notification of the next of kin and further investigation."

Paul did not reply immediately but just blankly stared up as his chest sank. After taking a slow shallow breath, he responded to the news. "They were great comrades. They gave their lives to protect me."

"And to defend our principles," Daan added. "A team could not ask for more loyalty."

After a solemn pause, Paul looked at Alexandra with a renewed sense of purpose. "You kept me alive after I had been knocked semi-conscious. I could feel you even though you were not physically touching me."

"I was calling to you with more emotion than I have ever mustered." She leaned down and ever so gently kissed her teenage puppy love.

"So, Claude Etien Marchand is dead?" Paul noted.

"That is correct. And Dr. Paul Bernard has returned."

"Where is my hair stylist and beautician?"

"As soon as you are up to it, we will ask for room service."

"I'm up to it now. Call her in. I need to get back to my training routine for the Palermo marathon. I've only got a couple of weeks."

"Ah, maybe you are pushing it, mon colonel." Appreciating his resolute expression, Alexandra corrected herself. "Okay, let me call Collette so she can jog with you. I may even tag along."

"I leave you in capable hands, Paul," Daan joked as he took the hint and bade his colleagues adieu. "But before I leave, I need to ask you, Alexandra, how you knew that Paul was being taken to Compiègne."

"Nazis like ceremony if nothing else. Compiègne is where Hitler took General Foch's surrender in June 1940. The other hallowed place for warriors of the Third and Fourth Reich is Versailles where the Peace Treaty was signed on 28th June 1919. Actually, the warehouse just outside Versailles because artefacts from that momentous day are stored there. That's where Thon took me."

Daan paused for a moment, tilted his head and gazed at

Alexandra. "You are exceptional. Remind me to consult with you more often."

⊰ ⊱

THE OBITUARY ANNOUNCED THAT THE MEMORIAL SERVICE for Claude Etien Marchand would be private. The remains would be cremated and the ashes scattered in the Moselle River in the Province of Alsace. In lieu of flowers, donations should be sent to L'Église du Sacré Coeur. Only family and close associates attended the private reception.

"Madame Marchand, how are you? I don't know if you remember me. I am Dr. Paul Bernard. I knew your husband briefly. I sincerely hope all estate matters are proceeding quickly. I know from personal experience just how bureaucratic and frustrating they can be sometimes."

"Dr. Bernard, how thoughtful of you to attend this memorial service. My late husband's Will appointed me as executor and sole beneficiary. I was recently informed that all estate matters should be completed shortly. The new bank manager in Geneva expedited the transfer of all funds to my personal account without question."

"I sincerely hope you are able to move on with your life, Madame Marchand. Please do not hesitate to contact me if I can assist you in any way."

"You SOB," Alexandra mumbled under her breath as she gently jabbed Paul in the ribs with her elbow.

"Oh, *doucement* – gently, ma princesse. The cracked ribs are still very tender."

"And I thought I could trust you to stay out of trouble. I'm never letting you out of my sight again."

"Is that any way for a grieving widow to talk? Now you are officially a widow, I suppose we should get married officially."

"If that is a marriage proposal, then I should accept. I do."

⊀ ⊳

THE MEMORIAL SERVICE FOR THE TWO COLLEAGUES killed in the tunnel was more sombre. No obituary was released. As with the funeral for Monsieur Marchand, the service was limited to family members and close colleagues. At the private reception, glasses were raised to fallen comrades.

"Double tap at Compiègne," Paul whispered to Marcel.

Marcel held his gaze. "To the New World Order, mon colonel. There is a moral rationale for neutralizing Fourth Reich Nazis as there was for killing Third Reich Nazis."

Paul and Marcel raised their glasses a second time. "To the Muslim children in the courtyard and to the little girl with the blood-stained light blue dress laying in the ditch with her little arms tied behind her back with barbed wire that had ripped into her wrists," Paul acknowledged.

"D'accord, mon colonel. Salut," Marcel acknowledged with a solemn voice.

⊀ ⊳

"UPDATE ON OUR DEBRIEFING OF THE MISSION, ladies and gentlemen," Daan announced to the assembled team members. "Five points on the agenda. First, the bait books that were tracked to the bookbinding shop in Graz are en route to Pomerode, Brazil. Our colleagues in that community will be following up once they arrive. Second, we are awaiting feedback on the results of the preliminary interview with our Quer guests. At this early stage, Herr Blosch seems to be the weakest link, but time will tell. Third, the acting bank manager in Geneva has been confirmed as manager. He reports that funding to the Fourth Reich from the Quer accounts is nearly terminated. However, transfers from other accounts have increased. The newly appointed bank manager will monitor closely and advise. Next, the Fourth Reich appears to have suspended their search for Claude Etien Marchand. Finally, we have no word on the identity of the fugitive from the speedboat that crashed into the shore. The body of the person in the boat had been burned beyond recognition. Accordingly, we must assume that the fugitive who escaped is one of the seven members of the Quer. We have authority from Brussels to make his capture our primary objective. More to follow on this subsequent mission. Matthieu, please update us on stolen Nazi gold and other related deposits in Swiss banks."

"Thanks, Daan. Two points from me. First, there are additional revenues from pre-war and war deposits in Swiss banks. You are aware that in 1998, Swiss banks finally paid out millions of dollars to some but not all survivors of the holocaust. These banks still have not acknowledged Jewish deposits made before 1939. The probability of there being additional validation with subsequent financial transactions to victims is infinitely small. Accordingly, we are suspending our traditional avenues of investigation into stolen Nazi gold and other treasures held in banks in favour of different options. Instead, we will monitor the flow of funds and neutralize the recipients before they can use their Judas monies. We are confident that such strategies will slow the flow to terrorists and other nefarious players."

"Other stolen monies?" Alexandra prompted.

"Indeed. That is my second point. From the underground room in the old Hotchkiss factory in Saint-Denis where Paul had been briefly held, we recovered tens of thousands of dollars in bearer bonds among other stolen property including some gold bars that Reichsmarschall Göring and his compatriots had hidden. I say some because we believe that there are more elsewhere. The Fourth Reich had been using them to fund some of their activities locally."

"You say that the EUI Unit is suspending traditional avenues of investigation directly into stolen Nazi gold and other treasures in Swiss banks. What do you consider traditional?" Paul asked.

"Am I sensing you have a proposition that might be beyond the arrow slits of traditional ramparts?" Matthieu reflected curiously.

"In Greek and Roman mythology, Hydra was a multi-headed serpent. Its lair was purported to be in the depths of Lake Lerna. Hercules killed the monster with a sword and fire by decapitating all the heads. Hydra was invincible only if it kept at least one head from which others could regenerate. Let us presume that the Quer is the multi-headed Hydra, in this case with seven heads representing the seven original families. We know that the Quer has been directing Fourth Reich activities, including the recent attacks on the synagogues in the U.S. We are not sure of the identity of the person who escaped from the burning boat. So, we must conclude that he is the sole surviving Hydra head of the Quer. I submit that we need to find a modern-day mongoose with Herculean strengths before Hydra re-grows additional heads."

"I like your analogy," Matthieu said. "We haven't given up on the stolen treasure, especially on the recovery of the bonds and Nazi paraphernalia from your temporary detention room in the basement of the old Hotchkiss factory in Saint-Denis. Daan, comments?"

After a moment of reflection, Daan complimented his former colleague and newest member of the team. "You haven't lost your talent for the art of stratagem, Paul. You are a fountain of wisdom." He glanced over at Matthieu. "Set up a meeting. I want everyone to attend. In the interim, I would like you, Paul, to flesh out your thoughts." Scanning the room, he directed them all to identify a potential Herculean mongoose.

"Any other points?" Daan enquired.

"Not so much a question as an observation," Paul offered. "All those paintings and other artefacts in the room where I was temporarily held reminded me of the final scene of the 1964 Hollywood movie, *The Train*, starring Burt Lancaster. In that final scene, the stolen French art was strewn beside the berms alongside a disabled train. I wonder what else has been stolen and remains hidden. Is it ironic that some of the scenes from that movie had been filmed along tracks opposite the house in Moulin-lès-Metz where Capitaine Dominique Roland and Rudolf Heydrich had been murdered, and Francine wounded? Is that too much of a coincidence? Serendipitous? Is the Thousand-Year Reich more than a myth? Was it the ultimate strategic vision of the Quer from its inception?"

CHAPTER 47

Alexandra and Paul sat without words, holding hands while being serenaded by the crackle of burning logs in the gargantuan stone fireplace of their favourite Liechtenstein hotel. The shadows of the flames danced lazily around the room like otters playing gracefully in the ebbing tide.

Alexandra turned her head and drew him into focus. "With the inheritance from the Marchand estate, we could purchase this spa and hotel with just the interest. In fact, we could buy every other hotel in Liechtenstein and barely put a dent in the account. So, why are we here just recuperating as guests?"

Paul remained entranced by the flames while he continued to stroke her palm. He ruminated over her proposition. "Good question, ma princesse. We could have lived comfortably just on our pensions. We could have lived much more comfortably with Sir James's bequests. But it was never about the money. It was, instead, about picking up the unfinished quest that your mother, Sir James and Major Mike passed on to us. Something changed for me after we met at your mother's funeral."

It was Alexandra's turn to ponder in the golden firelight. "So, I ask again, why are we here just on vacation? Is it because we are who we are? Could we be completely happy just contemplating whether to play a round of golf or not?"

Paul gazed into her eyes and smiled.

"It was initially about my mother. Finishing what she had started. Putting an end to Thon's murderous rampage. Then avenging Sir James's poisoning. Perhaps avenging is an inappropriate word. Redressing a misdeed might explain my motivation more clearly. And then there is Tom's death. My mother's work is not complete and the old KGB and its successor the FSB remain a menacing reality. But should it be our responsibility, our standard to carry?" Alexandra allowed the crackling fire to fill the space before reflecting. "You have mentioned Sarajevo a few times."

With that observation, Paul released her hand momentarily. "Images of those Muslim children being killed by their own people and the little girl in the blood-stained light blue dress resting face down in the ditch will remain part of who I am. I entered the black abyss of my own soul. I experienced the insanity and the hell of war. But I have returned a stronger person. The children no longer haunt me as much. Instead, I am reminded of the words of Ralph Waldo Emerson in his poem *Success*: 'to know even one life has breathed easier because you have lived.' Perhaps that is behind my desire to carry on."

"So, can we find a balance?" Alexandra wondered out loud. "To carry on with the tenacity of warriors and also to sit by a fire together holding hands in the tranquillity of intimacy? We still have to complete our inaugural retirement ride to find out about Kurt Welter. But that will have to wait until spring."

Paul grinned. "Let's propose that to Daan. We work the cases with the greatest potential to ensure that even one life will breathe easier."

"And to know that those despicable individuals who market carnage and suffering breathe much harder or preferably not breathe at all," Alexandra quietly murmured as she snuggled closer.

CHAPTER 48

"**H**err Blosch, I did not see your family name among the original seven in the Quer register. May I conclude that you are not a real member but just a wannabe?"

Herr Rafael Blosch sat expressionless on the edge of the wooden plank that had become his bed, perspiration beading on his forehead. The simplicity of the spartan furnishings were incongruous compared with those that had defined his lifestyle barely a month before in Geneva. His face revealed his emotion, both cornered and weary.

"Your colleagues from the yacht are also guests at this desert springs resort. As you may have noticed, unfortunately, there aren't any springs, nor air conditioning in your suite. But it is located in the middle of a desert. Just stinking heat, snakes, spiders and other creepy creatures, some of which have crawled up from the dank, stained foul hole in the floor of your executive suite accompanied by less than fragrant odours."

Herr Blosch continued to stare unresponsively into the abyss in his cramped desolate accommodation. His dry mouth and parched cracking lips settled into a contemptuous sneer.

"Now you can spend your remaining days in your one-piece fluorescent green vacation outfit with matching ankle bracelets. We try to be fashion conscious. Or you can co-operate. What's it to be? We have forever to await your reply. Solitary confinement can weigh heavily on your mind. Eventually, you won't be able to remember the fresh air and mountain vistas of the Swiss Alps or your Bavarian birthplace."

"What do you want?" Herr Blosch asked.

"Now that's more like it. Would you like a drink of fresh ice-cold water to wet your parched lips?"

Herr Blosch held his host's eyes for a brief moment before looking away and returning to his self-imposed stare. He was aware that much can be concealed in the stealth of silence. Herr Blosch also knew that this ruse was all about transcending the strategy through the austere Prussian discipline he had been taught by graduates of the Teutonic Wewelsburg castle.

"Well, perhaps later, Herr Blosch. I sense you would like to contemplate your surroundings and the glass of fresh ice-cold water a little longer."

CHAPTER 49

"Mom, Paul, we received your cryptic email saying you had some family news that would involve us both. Is it what I think it is?" Collette quizzed them with an expectant beaming smile.

"That all depends on what you think it is, ma chère fille."

"When and where, and who's invited?" Collette prompted with a girlish giggle.

"First things first, daughter," Alexandra replied, glancing over at Paul who looked at Collette, then Jean, before finally gazing at his puppy love.

"As you are aware, Sir James Pennington, an old friend and colleague of Maria's, has died. He left his sizeable estate to Alexandra and me. We thought we would take advantage of this windfall. Would you like to join us on a vacation to the Aegean, island hopping? We would start in Palermo where I would run a half marathon. From there, we would travel to Santorini and then go wherever we wanted." Paul reassured Jean, "I had a brief chat with Commandant Parent who felt you could be spared for a few weeks, if you wanted."

"An all-expenses-paid vacation to the Aegean in December? With Collette. Twist my arm, Papa!" He glanced over at Collette. "Might I assume that you wish to accompany me?" he added.

"I took the liberty of asking Jo if she could dog-sit MV. She was happy to," Alexandra added. "Collette, are you on board?"

"Will we have to chaperon our parents?" she grinned.

"No, my love, because before we depart, we will go to Luxembourg where Father Luke will marry us in a very quiet and private ceremony. And I emphasize exclusively secretive and discreet. Not even Jo is to know. In the fullness of time, you may come to realize the extent and gravity of this dictate."

Alexandra gave Collette one of her stern stares. Jean picked up on the seriousness of the silent communiqué between mother and daughter. The translation was abundantly clear. The gravity was confirmed when he became aware of his father's penetrating eyes on him.

"Life with Maman is life with Maman," Collette compliantly murmured. "And Jo is not to know. That places it at the zenith of seriousness and urgency."

"Life with Papa is life with Papa," Jean echoed.

In Collette's congratulatory embrace, Alexandra whispered, "Is everything fine?"

"I'm okay, Maman," she whispered

Alexandra gave her a long hug. *Perhaps all is not completely okay with ma fille*, she surmised.

⚭ ⚭

IN THE WAITING LOUNGE OF THE LUXEMBOURG airport, Collette took advantage of the semi-privacy to whisper to Jean, "That was about as low-key a wedding as I could ever have imagined."

"I sincerely hope our wedding will be celebrated with more merriment," Jean whispered back as he relished in the intimacy of their closeness.

Collette snuggled closer and wrapped her arm around his waist. "I'm confident we can organize a far more festive wedding."

The amorous exchange did not go unnoticed by the newlyweds who exchanged reassuring smiles.

"Our flight departs shortly," Paul announced. "Palermo and Zeus await us."

"As does Hera, the goddess of marriage," Alexandra murmured as she touched her wedding ring. Paul's wedding band was standard conservative. The Quer ring had been locked in the safe deposit box in a very secure location known only to the newlyweds and the senior executives of the European Union Intelligence Unit.

"I'm picking up on your uneasiness, ma princesse. You're rubbing your amulet. Talk to me."

Her shrew was beckoning her to remain vigilant. She felt the honeymoon and holiday still needed personal wariness despite the protective surveillance of Matthieu, Marcel and a select few of the Delta team who also sat in the waiting lounge.

"Just reflecting on Daan's briefing that Francine communicated through her handler: we may be contacted by an old colleague of hers, an Armenian Turk. I don't feel an ominous threat as at the Thon level, but heightened situational awareness is in order. Perhaps most worrying is the warning that the old KGB focus, ever present with my mother, has been transferred to me, to us, to Collette and Jean. Somehow the old Cold War Russian agents had moles who were convinced that Maria was the source of the super code that was connected to her search for stolen Nazi gold."

"Доверяй, но проверяй," Paul commented astutely.

"The old Russian proverb, trust but verify," Alexandra translated.

"C'est vrai, madame. I don't know if I am more bothered or intrigued by the fact that your mother had tracked Nazi stolen art to the St. Denis region of Paris."

"Regardless, it's now apparent that the former KGB was following my mother, for how long we don't know. They may well be on our trail as we speak. The image of the distant couple on the Eurail remains front in my mind."

Paul paused in acknowledgement before clarifying earlier conversations. "Daan's sources conclude that Reichsmarschall Göring had secreted contraband away somewhere in St. Denis. That is where I was taken. It's too much of a coincidence. I think the significance goes beyond just stolen art and other valuable property, including the bearer bonds. I feel a strong connection to the Quer and Herr Rafael Blosch."

"And that raises the stakes exponentially," Alexandra validated.

"Although I was dazed when I was in the basement of the Hotchkiss factory, I got the distinct impression the Quer were associated if not directly connected to the St. Denis locale. It's been gnawing at me," Paul confessed.

"Maybe we need to go back to the factory in St. Denis and follow up. You can take me to where you were when you experienced the strongest sensations."

"Let's run it by Daan."

⊣ ⊢

"RUN... RUN!" MARIA YELLED AT ALEXANDRA. "YOU took the impossible shot. You saved my life." Her mother's words resonated in her mind.

⊣ ⊢

THE FIRING OF THE STARTER PISTOL SIGNALLED all runners to begin the marathon. Normally, Paul would have immediately manoeuvred to the front third of the pack as a positioning strategy. But today, his intent was to run the race for his puppy love, not at an aggressive competitive pace but more steadily. In addition, he was reminded that he was still recovering from the physical abuse his body had taken in the Geneva raid and, more recently, in the Paris St. Denis abduction. He had a wager with Delta 1 and Delta 3 who were shadowing him just a few steps behind that he would be able to complete the race with a lower cardio rate. Although older than his escorts, he had the experience of the long-distance runner.

"Dr. Bernard, Francine sends her compliments."

Paul looked for the source of the message. "Excuse me," he replied nonchalantly.

"Francine Myette sends her compliments."

"And you are?" Paul enquired without breaking his stride.

"I am an old colleague of Francine's. Perhaps not old. But we once worked together."

"And your name is?"

"Just refer to me as the Armenian Turk for now."

"And where did you first meet?"

"Francine and I share the same alma mater, the University of Rostov in southern Russia close to the Ukraine. We attended many classes together."

"Where is Francine now?" Paul enquired.

"She apologizes that she could not be here in person. After an extended vacation in England she travelled to Canada, to Victoria on the Pacific coast. We audited a few classes together at the University of Victoria."

These descriptors were the code that confirmed the authenticity of the Armenian Turk.

"Thank you for passing along Francine's greetings," Paul replied quietly as he raised both arms over his head as if stretching. It was the pre-arranged signal to Deltas 1 and 3 that contact had been established and validated. "I sincerely hope Francine is recovering from her injuries and loss of family. I would be pleased to continue this conversation over a cappuccino."

"That could be arranged. Perhaps in Santorini," the Armenian Turk proposed. "Please call me Rakici."

"Raki is a traditional Turkish drink that one shares with friends," Paul responded. "And if I am not mistaken, ci is a suffix that normally means someone who sells. Or in the case of Rakici, someone who drinks Raki as a social habit."

"You know your Turkish culture, Paul. Francine mentioned you are well travelled and aware of Mediterranean traditions. Just call me Rakici for now. It's safer."

"Thank you for your introduction, Rakici," Paul replied.

"As a final note, Francine very much appreciated the kindness that you and Alexandra extended to Dominique. Accordingly, she cautions you both to be wary of the old Russian guard. The President of Russia has many loyal colleagues from his days with the KGB, and he has a long and unforgiving memory."

"Thank you for this caveat."

"You can contact me through the concierge at the Santorini Palace Hotel. *Gorusmek uzere* – until we meet again," Rakici, the Armenian Turk, uttered under his breath as he quickened his pace and left Paul to complete the race in his own time.

Paul had met Francine only briefly at the culmination of the Thon case. Alexandra had felt uneasy in her presence. He now felt more comfortable with her apparent partner, the Armenian Turk. Paul had suggested to Daan that they needed to find a modern-day mongoose with Herculean strength before Hydra could re-grow additional heads.

As he observed Rakici veer off the marathon route and disappear into the crowd, he felt confident he and Alexandra could work with Francine and Rakici. They seemed like an offbeat couple who were once on opposite sides of the Cold War. Now, together as a tag team, they might be odd friends rather than formidable foes – Francine from the communist East, Paul and Alexandra from the democratic West. In contrast, the Armenian side of Rakici was politically neither East nor West. The Turkish side was politically both East and West. The rapport spelled a possibility for détente diplomacy.

Images of Sarajevo came to mind, not as haunting thoughts of unfortunate casualties but as curious consequences. He had befriended a Russian major who was also serving as a United

Nations peacekeeper. In 1988, this Russian had been on the Berlin Wall pointing his gun at Paul because his politicians had ordered him to do so as a foe, as had Paul's politicians. Five years later they were friends, fellow blue beret peacekeepers, because their respective politicians had ordered them to be so. Ironically, the Russian major did not consider himself Russian. He was a Ukrainian conscripted into the Russian army. He hated the Russians with a passion for what they had done to his countrymen in the years leading up to the Second World War and following the Nazi surrender. He yearned for the day when Ukraine would throw off the oppressive Russian yoke. Thus, Paul surmised it was feasible that Rakici and Francine could work together with him and Alexandra. Today was the first day of a New World Order with new and promising rules.

www.ingramcontent.com/pod-product-compliance
Lightning Source LLC
Chambersburg PA
CBHW060546180626
46817CB00002B/748